THE VEGETARIAN TIGERS OF PARADISE

THE VEGETARIAN TIGERS OF PARADISE

by

Crystal Jeans

HONNO MODERN FICTION

First published by Honno Press

'Ailsa Craig', Heol y Cawl, Dinas Powys, Wales, CF64 4AH

1 2 3 4 5 6 7 8 9 10

ISBN 978-1-909983-44-1 paperback
ISBN 978-1-909983-45-8 ebook

Published with the financial support of the Welsh Books Council.

Cover design: Sue Race
Text design: Elaine Sharples
Printed in Wales at Gomer Press, Llandysul, Ceredigion, SA44 4JL

For Dani and Ellie, my clowns gone odd

Acknowledgements

Thanks to Catherine Merriman, Rob Middlehurst, Christopher Meredith, Tony Curtis, Maria Donovan, Philip Gross and Tiffany Murray for all the help and encouragement, you're all exceptional people. Thanks to all my fellow MPhilers, you beautiful bunch of lushes, who had to read the damn thing probably three times over: Melissa 'Bob' Ledwidge, Bert Pastore, Clover Peake, Amy Mason, Cheryl Parry, Dion Storr and Leon Qualls and Phil, and special thanks to Lloyd Markham, my tried and trusted feedback guy.

Thanks to Caroline Oakley and Gwen Davies for liking my writing enough to publish it.

Thank you, family and friends, all of you, but especially Mum, for inspiring me, supporting me and allowing me to parasitically feed off our shared experiences in the name of literature. And thanks to Pauline and Rod Gunn for, among other things, giving me those child-free Tuesdays for writing.

Contents

Birds for Breakfast

Mum usually stays in bed until three o'clock in the afternoon. She lies there under her duvet like a dead walrus. The thick brown curtains will be closed, gulping up all the daylight and turning the room into a cave. Sometimes me and Veronica will sneak in and circle the bed on tiptoes, our breath stopped, eyes twitching back and forth between each other's faces and the lump in the bed. It's a game. If she makes a noise or moves, we get down on our bellies and crawl out like soldiers, whispering for back-up and enforcements.

Once up, she'll call Dad. She'll make him go down the shop for a Jumbo Mars Bar. He has nothing better to do because he's Jobless. He'll take us with him and sometimes we get to choose something for ourselves, a Chomp or a Fudge or a packet of 10p crisps. When we get home, Mum will be dressed. She doesn't have many outfits, just a few massive tent-dresses made for fat women with patterns like wallpaper.

Mum will eat her Mars Bar in front of the TV, her legs spread wide like a bloke-man because her thighs are so massive she can't bring them together. The times Dad can't afford to get us a treat, we sit on the floor, cross-legged, and watch her eat, our zombie eyes slowly following the bar as it moves from lap to mouth and back again. Most of the time she leaves a bit at the end for us and we eat it in tiny rat nibbles.

She'll get around to chores when most mums are watching *Coronation Street*. Our furniture is brown and old and gross and the walls are painted crappy colours, like peach or mint, but it's not messy and never dirty. She lets us draw all over any white door in the house with marker pens, but only the kind that can be wiped off. We'll do red mermaids and blue houses and yellow suns. She'll tell us how good they are and then clean them all off ready for the next pictures. When no one's looking I'll draw men with massive muscles and long willies then quickly drag my sleeve through them.

By the time Mum's ready to start relaxing it'll be mine and Veronica's bedtime. Mum will get a book out. Stephen King, Clive Barker, James Herbert. Books with covers that frighten me. Dripping, melty monster faces. Sometimes she'll get her watercolours out and do some paintings of Marilyn Monroe or Grace Jones or one of our pit bulls. Other times she'll put a film on, something she's recorded off the telly recently or a rental from the video van that comes round our street every Thursday. Usually a horror: *A Nightmare on Elm Street, Hellraiser, Child's Play*. Veronica always begs Mum to let her stay up and watch because she *lurves* horror films and sits as close to the TV as possible, her demented eyes fixed on every blood splatter. The times Mum gives in to Veronica I'll be too scared to go to bed by myself, so I watch the film with them, covering my eyes with a scratchy cushion when the scary bits come up. But mostly she says no, making a number 11 come up between her eyebrows. We go to bed, Veronica sticking out her bottom lip in a sulk, and Mum stays up till the early hours watching films and eating Mini Eggs or Peanut M&Ms if it's after the government have given us our money, a bowl of raw cake mix if it isn't.

Next day, same again.

There must be times when this routine gets boring. So it's just as well she has us.

I'm sat on the carpet cross-legged, leaning as far forward as possible. Veronica is sat next to me, her cold knee just touching mine. We're at the bit in *Ruthless People* where Bette Midler's character, Barbara, realises she's lost weight and she's about to try on the colourful dress with the huge square shoulders – the one Sandy designed.

I don't know how to thank you – I've been to ten different fat farms in the last – I don't know how many years, says Barbara, flapping her arms about so her bangles jingle-chink.

I always feel a bit nervous at this point because Barbara and Sandy are about to make friends, and so far, Barbara has been nothing but mean to Sandy. It's like when Tom and Jerry stop fighting so they can gang up on Spike the Bulldog. It puts me on edge.

I'll be right back! shrieks Sandy, running up the stairs.

And then, cutting through the film like a rusty saw:

'Hey, kiddies! Guess who?'

Me and Veronica whip our heads around and stare at each other. Her already bulbous eyes are bulging out so much she looks like a pale, blue-eyed frog. I turn round, look at my mum. She's upright in the chair, her book laid page down on her belly-desk.

'Where'd that come from?' she says, brow crinkled, the 11 up.

'I don't—'

'Iiiittt'ss *Freddy*!' That same voice – horrible and shredded – coming out of the walls or the air. 'It's Freddy and I'm comin'-a getcha!' Then a nasty, raspy laugh that keeps going and going.

My stomach turns into a prawn. Freddy Krueger.

The laughter stops. We are all frozen as can be, waiting for more.

Barbara: *So Sam told you I was his partner? No way, he was just passing the buck.* In the corner of my vision I see Barbara flick her big red hair.

Then: 'One, two, Freddy's comin' for yoouu.' – A creepy baby-child's voice – 'Three, four, better lock your dooor – '

'Muuum!' I'm up, off the floor. I jump into Mum's lap, knocking her book off, and bury my face in her warm neck.

'Five, six, grab a crucifix. Seven, eight, gonna stay up late...'

'Where's he *comin'* from?' says Veronica.

'Nine, ten—'

'I don't know,' says Mum and I can feel her words vibrate through her throat. 'If he's coming for you, I'll, I'll – I don't know – I'll do my best to protect you, but—'

'Mum,' I cry, 'I'm *scared.*'

The laughter's back, bubbling out of Freddy's melted lips. I pull my face from my mum's soft blubbery neck, leaving snot, and turn to look at Veronica. She's running round the room, skinny legs a blue-white blur, looking under cushions, peering behind the TV.

'Vron, you're not going to find Freddy Krueger hiding under a pillow,' says Mum. 'If he's anywhere he'll be outside, trying to – trying to get in.' Her eyes flick to the window, to the black night outside.

I stick my face back in Mum's neck.

'But it sounds like it's comin' from in *here,*' says Veronica, and her voice floats around because she's on the move.

Freddy's laughter is like when my Spectrum loads up, the awful jagged electrical screaming, like a calculator being murdered.

And then it's louder and clearer. Like when you bring your head up out of the bathwater.

He's here. Freddy's here.

My prawned-up stomach and floppy body tell me to stay still, stay buried, but I have to look, I have to see Freddy. I peep over my shoulder, ready for that stringy, burnt up face ...... but there's no sign of him. Instead Veronica's there with a face that doesn't know the answer, holding Mum's grey ghetto blaster in the air.

The laughter stops again. I can see the tape reel spinning around inside the deck. Freddy un-phlegms his throat, then goes on. 'You scared yet, kiddies? I'll be there any—'

Veronica presses a button and the voice stops. She looks at the thing for a while, her brain going tick tick.

4

Danny Devito: *My wife – I gotta get her back.*

Veronica looks at Mum. Her white-blonde eyebrows come down like a drawbridge.

Mum starts to shake. I turn back to face her and our noses almost touch. Her face is bright pink, her mouth scrunched up. Her fat is jiggling under me. She looks like she's about to explode. Then her mouth opens and the laughter bursts out, and it's her own laughter this time, not Freddy's.

'Mum!' I shout, smacking her on the shoulder. 'It was you!'

She puts her face in her hands and laughs till she cries.

Mum isn't like Emma Frost's mum, Linda, who spends most of her time in the kitchen frying chips, smoking fags and gossiping. She isn't like Pauline the Mormon, ten doors down, who cleans her house all day and makes you take your shoes off in the hallway. She's not like any other mother in Paradise Place, but if I had to compare her to one, it would be Suki Fisk who lives in number thirteen. Suki Fisk is a hippy who drinks Stonehouse cider all day and falls over a lot. My mum doesn't do any of those things, but she's too poor to buy nice things and most of the other mums in our street aren't her friend. And that's why she's like Stonehouse Suki.

Sometimes, when I imagine the inside of Mum's head – her mind – I see a dark cave like in the *Alien* films, with green mist and hangy-down icicles like rotten werewolf teeth, and the slow drip drip of water plinking into puddles, then the echoes – *drip, drip…drip drip…*

This one time, me and Veronica raced all the way home from school because it was Scott and Charlene's wedding on *Neighbours* and we were dying to see it – we'd spent all night whispering about it in our beds, what Charlene would wear, if they would kiss with tongues or sex each other.

We legged it home, got through the door, ten pit bull puppies yapping around our ankles, and ran into the living room. Mum was sitting on the sofa, one leg up on the cushion. *Woman's Own* in one hand. She was humming the Wedding March. When she saw us she stopped, sat up straight, put her magazine on the armrest and looked at us all serious. 'Girls,' she said, 'come here. I've got something to tell you.'

We approached.

'I think you should sit down.' Her eyes all sad like sick kittens.

We sat on the floor, cross-legged. Tilted our heads up.

'It's bad news.' She shook her head. 'I wish I wasn't the one telling you.' She did a nose-sigh. There was confetti in my stomach.

'I'll just say it.' She closed her miserable eyes, opened them, raised a hand in the air. 'I'll just come out and say it. Veronica. Christina. I watched *Neighbours*. The lunchtime showing. You're not going to like this.'

A big silence like an empty church.

'Scott and Charlene don't get married. OK? There's no wedding. Scott shoots Charlene. He gets a gun and he shoots her in the face.'

My mouth dropped open like a Pez dispenser. Me and Veronica looked at each other, our faces mirror images of blue-eyed despair.

Most of the time Mum will use horror films to frighten us. Like when she said that Freddy Krueger sometimes hides in the drains, and if we're not careful he'll creep his knife-fingers up through the toilet water while we're weeing and drag us down to the sewers. So we pee hosepipe-fast, feeling the shivery air under our fannies, and as soon as the hosepipe slows down we leap off, dripping on the seat, which we blame on Dad.

Freddy Krueger is so much in my brain that I even dream about him. This one time, I dreamt that him and Snow White were doing sex to each other in a mole tunnel underground. Another time, Freddy was there on a beach drinking a Malibu, and he goes, 'Mmm, Malibu in the sun, mon,' like a Jamaican, and then suddenly he screams with a banshee mouth and his face melts and the dream has turned from silly to terrifying.

When I was four, Mum dressed me up as Freddy for the school fancy dress contest. Red jumper with dark green stripes painted on, a hat, and a glove Mum made all herself with foil and cardboard and leather. I didn't win anything. The teachers pretended I wasn't there, like an old lady fart. A cowboy won first prize. On the way home we stopped in the chemist for Dad's psoriasis shampoo, and I hid behind Mum and scraped my finger-knives slowly along the top of the counter, over the Fisherman's Friends and Tunes, and the chemist lady looked at me and did a little Mary Poppins laugh, and I wondered why she wasn't scared. I was Freddy Krueger. She should grab her crucifix.

Outside, Mum said it was because I was two feet tall and I had gorgeous blonde curls poking out from my hat. I turned my face evil and poked her giant thigh with my finger-blade and said, 'I'll kill you slow!' And she said, 'OK, pooey, but do me a favour and wait till after *Brookside*.'

Freddy has a cousin, Robert, who isn't in the films because he's shy. He lives in a flat in Splott. Mum says Robert is a bit nicer to children but still a monster with eyeballs that drip like little candles and a tongue made of old scissors. She says that in the day he wears dark glasses and a big hat and works as a tax collector, and in the night he helps his cousin kill people in their dreams...and sometimes in real life. When Robert's around, he tries to stop Freddy killing small children. He says things like, 'Calm down, Cuz, the little bastard ain't worth it.' And Freddy says, 'But I wanna kill it, lemme kill it.' So Robert says, 'How about you just chop the tongue off and we can have it in a sandwich later?'

It's good to know we have someone on our side.

A winter's night. Outside, gale force winds screech and whistle. *The Company of Wolves*. Mum doesn't really want us watching this because it isn't just a horror: 'It has naughty bits in it.'

'What kind of naughty bits?' I ask.

'Well. It's just a bit sexy.'

Veronica smirks.

Mum puts the tape in. 'When I tell you to cover your eyes, you cover your eyes, OK? With your hands.'

We agree. The thing about hands is gaps can be created by spreading the fingers, but Mum doesn't seem to know about this.

'Especially you, Christina,' she adds, looking at me.

'Don't *call* me that.'

She rolls her eyes. 'I'm sorry. *George*.'

I make everyone call me George because, even though I'm not a boy, I will be one day.

We watch the film. At points Mum tells us to cover our eyes. When she speaks to the both of us it means a rude bit is coming up. We put our hands over our eyes and peek through the gaps. The rude bits aren't very rude. There's this bit when a man takes his clothes off, but you can't see his willy because it's covered in shadow. Then his wife says, 'Come out of the shadows, my love,' but the spoilsport camera moves up so you don't get to see anything. I keep thinking it's going to get rude because of the music and the way everyone looks at each other with their eyes made of sex-smoke. But no.

Then there are times when Mum speaks only to me. 'Cover your eyes, Crissy – sorry – *George*.' This means a scary bit is coming. I slap my hand over my face and squish my eyes shut. But my fingers spread and I peek through the gaps. I know it'll cost me – for weeks, maybe months, I'll be sneaking into Veronica's bed in the middle of the night, just like last time with *Gremlins*. But I look anyway. I have to.

These are the scary bits in *The Company of Wolves*:

At the beginning a girl gets chased through a dark, misty forest by a gang of wolves with eyes red as traffic lights.

The old grandmother, played by that lady from *Murder, She Wrote*, gets her head slapped off.

8

A man turns into a wolf. He starts ripping his own skin off in big rubbery shreds and underneath is all slimy pink muscle. Then he changes shape, parts of his body growing hairy lumps, a raw, steaming wolf nose sprouting out of his face.

By the end of the film I'm curled up next to Mum, hugging a cushion. It's so dark outside. And the wind is howling. It sounds both angry and afraid.

I ask Mum when Dad's coming home.

'I thought he'd be home by now,' she says.

'Ju fink he's OK?' I ask.

'I hope so.' But she looks worried. 'You know he's walking home through the woods, don't you?'

Veronica gasps. 'At night-time?'

Mum nods. 'It's a shortcut.' She shakes her head. 'I hope he'll be OK.'

I imagine him being chased by ten red-eyed wolves. Stumbling past trees that slap him in the face with their claw-hand branches. I can see the little puffs of air coming out of his mouth as he runs. The whites of his eyes big and shining. Then I see the moon coming out from behind a cloud and now my dad's tearing his skin off and it's coming away like melted cheese.

'Mum, I'm scared,' I say.

'So am I,' says Veronica, huddling into my back.

And Veronica doesn't scare easily.

'Maybe he'll be all right,' says Mum. 'Maybe the wolves won't get him.'

And now she's turned my thoughts into words and I'm really scared.

'Muuum!'

She swats the air, shakes the frown off. 'Oh, let's not worry about it. Let's watch another film, distract ourselves. Yeah?'

Indiana Jones: Temple of Doom. I make Mum turn the volume up to drown out the sound of the wind howling. I never get bored of this film. I like the bit with the monkey brains and the pregnant snake. What I don't like is when Mola Ram tries to tear Indy's heart out with his hand. It's not scary in the Freddy Krueger way – I never have to sleep in Veronica's bed after watching it – but it makes my own heart beat so fast I worry it'll burn out, like our old video player after Veronica stuffed Jaffa Cakes into it.

Indiana and Mola Ram are hanging off the broken bridge. The crocodiles are snapping in the water down below.

'Mum! Wake up!' It's Veronica. She's shaking Mum's shoulders. 'Wake up.'

Mum reluctantly opens her eyes. 'What?'

'Don't go to sleep.'

'I wasn't. I was resting my eyes.'

'You were goin' to sleep.'

'I wasn't. Just resting my eyes. Watch the film.' Her eyes close.

Veronica leans over and prises open one of Mum's eyes with her finger and thumb. 'Don't go to sleep.'

'Oh for God's sake.' Mum heaves herself out of the chair. 'I'm going for a wee.' She waddles out of the room, her leather sandals slapping the carpet. We hear her go into the toilet and lock the door.

By the end of the film, Mum still hasn't come back.

'Ju think she's doin' a poo?' I ask Veronica.

'Maybe.'

'Ju think Dad's OK?'

The credits have stopped rolling. I can hear the wind again. I try not to think of the slimy pink muscles underneath my dad's face.

Mum comes back. She stumbles in slowly with her arms out, like she's blind. Her eyes are all wrong and weird. She's not blinking. She finds her chair with her hands, knocks over a book, says 'Ooh shit,' and sits down. We quickly surround her. 'What's wrong wiv yer eyes?'

'Nothing.'

And now I'm closer I can see: her eyes are closed, and drawn on the lids, in glittery blue eyeshadow and black eyeliner, are pretend eyes.

Does she think we're stupid or something?

'Mum!' We tug on her sleeves. 'Those aren't your eyes.'

She smiles. 'What d'you mean? Course they're my eyes.'

'No they're not. You've drawn 'em on.'

'Don't be silly.'

'You're not going to sleep, Mum,' says Veronica.

'How could I sleep with my eyes open? Really?'

I reach out to touch the wrinkly skin of her eyelid with my finger. She yanks her head back.

'Ouch! Don't poke me in the eye, Vron!'

'It wasn't Vron,' I say. 'It was me. And look' – I shove my finger in front of her unseeing face – 'there's make-up on my finger. Stop lyin'.'

Mum goes quiet. We've got her. She exhales loudly from her nose then her eyes flick open. 'Why can't you let me sleep?'

I nuzzle my head under her flabby arm. 'I'm scared.'

'When's Dad comin' home?' says Veronica.

'Soon, Vron.'

The TV screen is grey and fuzzy and the room is full of shadows. The wind is still going. Whistling, shrieking, grumbling. I keep looking at the curtains, the thin black gap between them. I keep thinking of the wolves outside, trying to get in. Will my dad get through them? Or will he be one of them?

Mum sits upright and starts saying something in a low mumbly voice.

'Mmm shhhvvaa, mm mm shhvva.'

Her eyes are wide open and staring. Only her mouth moves. The words coming out of it get louder and clearer.

'Om num shavay, om num shavay, om num shavay.'

It's the chant from *Temple of Doom*. The boy with the turban says it before Mola Ram rips his heart out of his chest.

'Om num shavay, om num shavay, om num shavay.'

'Mum,' I whine. 'What you doin'?

She stops. Eyes still staring. Her hand turns into a stiff claw. Turns over. Dead spider. Starts rising, rising toward her boobs. In a loud voice: 'Kali ma. Kali maaa. Kali ma, shakti day.' Her eyeballs roll in their glittery sockets. The hand goes on rising like it's possessed.

'Muum!' I grab her wrist and pull it back. But her arm, or the evil spirit in it, is too strong. The clawed hand keeps reaching. She is going to rip her own heart out.

'Kali maaa! Kali maaaaaaaa! Kali ma, shakti day.'

Now Veronica's hanging on to the arm too, and though there's terror in her eyes she's laughing in that crazy way that leads to wet knickers. Because this is a joke. Mum is playing a joke on us.

Then why am I so scared? Why, when Mum's hand reaches her breast and starts to twist like a pastry cutter, do I start crying hot tears and yanking on her arm?

'Oh, George, it's OK.' She scoops me up in her arms and she's Mum again. She squeezes me against her chest. Where her heart is. Protected by boob and bone. 'I was only acting. Did I scare you?'

I nod, my face screwed up, and wipe the snot off my chin with the back of my hand.

'I knew she was only playin',' says Veronica, smiling proudly.

I want to tell her that I knew too, I knew all along, but I can't get my words out.

Then I hear the front door opening and the wind screeching into the hallway and my tears stop dead.

Five minutes from our house is Blackweir, a small area near the dirty, swirly River Taff. Blackweir is partly fenced-in bits for horses from the nearby riding school for rich girls and muddy playing fields where all the men go to play rugby or football every Saturday. But mostly it's woods.

In the middle of the woods, near Blackweir Bridge, is a cottage. The Lock-keeper's Cottage. It's an olden days cottage, white with black wooden strips criss-crossing it, and a roof made out of moss.

It's where Freddy lives.

I've been bad. All day I've pushed her and pushed her and pushed her. I haven't been listening, I haven't stopped, I haven't taken no for an answer. And this is the last straw.

Today I found out I shouldn't say 'twat'.

Today I called Veronica a twat. And she told.

'You do not. Say. That. Word,' says Mum, putting down her iron and looking at me with her 11 up.

'Why? What's wrong with "twat"?'

'You just don't say it, George. Just don't say it.'

'*Why?* What does it mean?'

'I told you. You just don't say it.' She turns the shirt over, smooths it down and picks up the iron.

'But what does it *meeeaan*?'

'It's rude.'

'You probably don't even know what "twat" means, do you?'

She takes her eyes off the ironing for a second, looks at me. 'Oh, I do.' Smears the iron over the sleeve of dad's denim shirt. 'And I told you – you don't say that word.'

'What? You mean "twat"?'

Iron goes down, eyebrows go up. 'What did I say, Christina?'

I stick out my chin. 'You said I shouldn't say *"twat".*'

There's a moment of silence. A silence like a clean, cut throat the second before the blood belches out. And then she's coming for me, face snarled. And I'm running.

'Christina! Don't you make me chase you!'

Cuz you can't, you fat cow, I think, laughter fizzing out as I run into the hallway.

'Christina, you get here now!'

'Don't call me that!' I shout over my shoulder. And because I'm

13

full of sugar and fizzy laughter I add a loud 'Twaaaat!' that echoes off the crap wallpaper.

I open the front door and sprint toward the car. I risk a look over my shoulder and see her thundering down the hall, mad as King Kong. I reach the bonnet of the car. She comes out the front door, sees me, runs right at me. When she gets close to the bonnet I run round to the other side, giggling hard. So she comes again, and I run back to the bonnet. She can't catch me. No way.

She stops and glares at me over the roof of Dad's Ford Escort. 'I'm going to give you such a hiding,' she says.

I know she means it but I just can't help myself. I jump up and down, waving my arms around. 'Twat! Twat! Twaaaat!' I yell.

Mum glances nervously over her shoulder to see if any of the neighbours are out.

'Twat! Twit-twat, twit-twat, twit-twat! Twaaaaaahhhht!' This last twat I sing out in a high voice, my eyes closed, a hand over my heart like what Jason Donovan does. I break down laughing. A bit of wee comes out.

And then I feel the hand grab my top at the shoulder and close into a fist. More wee comes out.

Through her teeth: 'In the house, now.'

She drags me in and slams the door behind us. She's still got me by my jumper. She twists me away from her and brings her palm to my bum with a thwack. Then she does it again. And again. And again. Six or seven in total.

She pulls me to the bottom of the stairs and lets go of my top. 'Get upstairs, out of my sight.'

I won't look at her. I won't look.

'Up to your room and stay there.'

I run up the stairs, my throat and the insides of my nose all tight. Won't look. Won't cry.

I get to my room. I don't cry. My face scrunches up like I'm about to, but I stop at the last second. Instead I stamp up and down on the floor as hard as possible, screech so loud it burns my throat. Jump, stamp, kick the door, screeaam. I know she'll hear it downstairs.

I hear her thundering up the stairs. I can feel the floor shaking a little. I stop, look at the door and wait. Soon it flies open and she's standing there with her brown curly hair big and crazy and eyes like blue fire.

'That is *it*,' she says, slow and clear. 'You've pushed and you've pushed. I don't have a choice, Christina.' She closes her eyes for a long moment. The rage drops away like a veil. She shakes her head, sadly. 'You're going to live with Freddy Krueger.'

I stare at her.

'I hoped it wouldn't come to this,' she says, her face a mixture of disappointment and regret.

I cross my arms. 'Well, I'd rather live with Freddy than *you*.'

This hits her like a brick to the jaw. 'Would you? Well. You think about that when he's making you shoot birds for your breakfast every morning.' She backs out of the room and closes the door.

Three hours later. It's been arranged. I overheard her on the phone ten minutes ago. 'Mister Krueger? Sorry to bother you, I hope this isn't an inconvenient time to call, this is Catherine Jones of Paradise Place – yes, number four, that's right. Why thank you, Mister Krueger – oh, really? OK – *Thank* you, Freddy. And please, call me Cath. Well, the thing is, I was wondering if you need any children at the moment…um…female, small, around four stone, blue eyes, blonde hair…Well, you can always shave it off….Yes, she's had all her jabs…Oh, I'm sure she'll be quiet as a mouse. Really? Oh, Freddy, that's wonderful! Is eight tonight OK? Brilliant. I can't thank you enough, Mister Krueger – *Freddy*, beg your pardon. Thank you. Bye…bye.'

Now Mum's on the couch with her sewing tin out. 'He said not to pack much, just a few things.'

Tugger is sniffing my foot. I get on the floor and stroke her between the ears. 'Will I be able to see Tugger again?'

Mum shakes her head.

I wrap my arms around Tugger's neck. 'Why not?'

'You won't be able to see any of us again. Sorry. This is what you want, remember.'

'But what if I don't like it? Will I be able to run away?'

'No, Georgey. He'll know. He knows everything.'

Mum's cutting up an old tablecloth. Baby blue squares on a white background. Her scissors make lovely snip, snip sounds.

'Ju think he'll hurt me?'

'Only if you're naughty.' She puts the scissors on her thigh, holds the fabric up, examines it. 'Why don't you go and pack? You don't have long.'

'What should I take?'

'Your toothbrush. And some clean knickers.'

'Can I take my Action Man?'

'No. He won't allow that.'

'What about my cuddy blanky?'

'No. You can't take that either.'

I go quiet, playing with Tugger's velvety ear. Tears spill down my cheeks. Mum puts her hand on my shoulder. 'Look,' she says. 'Why don't you take your Action Man with you and hide it under your bed? Maybe he won't find it.'

I nod, wipe my tears away.

'Now go get your things. Don't worry about clothes – he'll have you wearing bin bags and old sacks most likely.'

'Bin bags?'

She nods. 'This is what you wanted, remember.'

Dad's taking me. Mum told him the situation when he came home. He looks miserable – his blue eyes aren't as bright as usual and his lipless Rodney Trotter mouth is a straight unsmiling line. Who will he play football with now?

Mum uses the old tablecloth to make me a knapsack for my things. She wraps it into a bundle, ties it onto a stick and gives it to me. 'Put it over your shoulder – that's right.' She looks me up and down. I'm wearing my Teenage Mutant Hero Turtles jumper that Nana knitted for me, a grubby pair of leggings, baggy at the knee, and scuffed, white daps with Velcro straps. She looks like she's going to cry.

'Are you going to say goodbye to everyone then?' she says.

I nod.

'Go on then.'

So I give Veronica a hug and tell her I'll miss her, even though she started this whole thing by being a twat. Even though she looks like Macaulay Culkin with a wonky fringe. Then I hug the pit bulls, Rutger, Slug and Tugger, and let them lick my face.

'You'll be good, won't you?' says Mum, at the doorway.

I nod.

She bends down with a wheeze and gives me a hug. 'I'm sorry it came to this, but there we go,' she says. 'I will miss you, though I doubt you'll miss me.'

I look down at my feet and mumble something.

'What's that?'

'I *will* miss you.'

She smiles at me. Ruffles my hair.

'Mum?'

'Yes?'

'Will I really have to shoot birds for my breakfast?'

'Yes.'

'What ones?'

'Um. Sparrows and robins. And budgies.'

'Why can't I have Frosties?'

'Freddy doesn't like Frosties. He shoots a bird every morning at daybreak. He told me.'

'How does he use a gun? He's got knives for fingers.'

'All these questions! You'll find out for yourself.' She turns me around on the doorstep and pats my bum. 'Off you go. Be good.'

Dad takes my hand and we head off down the driveway. He

hobbles because he broke his leg falling off a ladder a few months ago and it still hasn't healed properly. I turn back at the end of the driveway, wave sadly and bravely.

'You can have my dolls, Vron,' I say, and her smile is so wide I can see the gaps in her teeth.

I look at my mum one last time and blink away the tears. Hoist the knapsack onto my other shoulder and head off.

'Don't make him angry!' calls Mum.

The lights are on in Freddy's house. I can see the top of a bookcase. The soft glow spills out, lighting up the edge of the tall black tree next to the cottage. There's a Fiesta parked outside the colour of blood. How does he drive with his blade fingers? Maybe he has a chauffeur? Maybe he'll make me his chauffeur? Maybe that's why he's willing to take me in?

I'm going to be shooting guns and driving cars. Things aren't all bad. And Freddy might even be nice. He might be nothing like how he is in the films. He might be like a daddy.

I look up at my own dad. His face is pale in the blackness. A breeze flaps his hair, giving him a silly fringe. He nods his head toward the cottage. 'You better go and knock the door then.'

'Will you come and get me if I don't like it?'

He scratches his big pointy chin, raises his eyebrows. 'Uh……
yeah. OK.' He bends down, kisses my cheek. 'Be good then.'

And he turns and runs. Except he can't run, because of the leg, and sort of gallops like a spasticated pony. I look at the cottage and see movement in one of the windows. Freddy. Freddy Krueger, who pulled out that boy's veins with one blade-finger and turned him into a puppet; who sucked lovely Johnny Depp into his bed and spat him out all over the ceiling; who turned himself into a sexy blonde woman and snogged that man and then bit his tongue and pulled it out all long and thin like stretched Hubba Bubba.

I run after my hob-legged father. I tuck the bundley stick under my arm and grab onto his wrist tight. 'I don't wanna live with Freddy!' I glance back at the house expecting to see his silhouette coming toward me, one arm stretched out, his metal claws scraping the walls of the cottage. 'I don't wanna live with Freddy!'

Dad's laughing. He lifts me up in his arms. 'Then you'll 'ave to 'pologise to your mother.'

'But I didn't do nothin'.'

I glance at the crouching shadows and quickly bury my face into his neck. I won't look. I won't look.

The Vegetarian Tigers of Paradise

When I was five Mum and Dad decided to become Jehovah's Witnesses. A nice young couple in churchy clothes had knocked on our door one afternoon and Mum and Dad had liked the things they said – love, paradise, eternal life. They came round our house a week later for a Bible talk, and that was it – we were Jojos.

Dad took it all serious – he stopped putting bad chemicals in his body and gave up smoking. Every night he would come into my and Veronica's bedroom, sit on the edge of the bed and read out a chapter from *My Book of Bible Stories*, pointing out the illustrations with an enormous finger. And then we would pray together. Sometimes Mum would join us for the prayer, closing her eyes and saying amen at the end, but it was Dad who actually spoke the prayer because he was A Man. Mum instead would tell us about Moses and Abraham and Jezebel (my favourite) while peeling parsnips in the kitchen. She carried on watching horror films, even though they weren't allowed, but otherwise she was a good Jojo, like Dad.

Mum was still the fat woman in the long yucky-green mac who dragged her pit bulls everywhere with her. Dad was still the quiet man with pale, staring, one-blink-a-minute eyes and a past made out of words like 'heroin' and 'Amsterdam' and 'hooligan'. Me, I was still a tomboy, always climbing trees and playing football, but I wasn't George anymore – I was a girl and I would always be a girl and there was no willy for me, that was that. We were a family with two little blonde girls and a car and parents not divorced, but that didn't seem to matter. We were the gypsiest family of all with our wild messy garden and third-hand furniture, and along with Stonehouse Suki at number thirteen, and the man who had done sex with his daughter at number twenty-two, the least popular.

But we had God now.

The front door opens. A tall man with white-blond army hair stands there, looking down at me.

'Good morning,' I say in the voice I've been practising.

The man nods a hello, his face crumpling into a smile. He leans against the door jamb and waits for me to explain myself.

'Today I am going from door-to-door to spread the word of Jehovah –'

He flinches at this last word as if I've accidentally spat a bit of soggy crisp into his eye. I go on.

' – and to tell you about paradise on earth. Can I have two minutes of your time, please?'

'Go on then,' he says.

'Fank you,' I say. I shift my weight and squeeze the rolled-up script in my sweaty hand. 'In today's society there is – there is hunger and famine and killing. All the time. But one day there will be Armageddon and Jesus will come and – um, he will come and –' I unroll the script and take a peek. My sweat has turned the letters to spider's legs, but I can read the words. 'Jesus will come and wage war on Satan and he will win and then there will be Judgement Day. And after that, there will be, um, there will be –' I take another look at the damp paper in my hand. 'There will be *paradise*. Paradise on earth.'

I look up at the man. He's still smiling. He thinks I'm cute, standing there in the old-fashioned dress my mother forced on me this morning, the plaits that hang over my shoulders like yellow turds. But there is sadness in his smile. He feels sorry for

21

me. It's a Saturday in June. Other kids are out playing football and climbing trees or watching *The Chart Show* in their pyjamas.

'But only some people will get to live in paradise,' I say.

'And who's that?' he says.

'Jehovah's Witnesses,' I say.

'Ah, I see.' He scratches the corner of his mouth with his little finger. 'And what's paradise like?'

I think about the pictures of paradise in my book of bible stories. 'It's like the Garden of Eden 'cept the people wear clothes. Like, T-shirts and stuff. And the people are all different colours. And lions and tigers roll around with lambs. And everyone smiles.'

He covers his mouth with his hand and laughs silently. 'So all the lions and tigers are vegetarian?'

I don't know what 'vegetarian' means. 'Yes,' I say.

'So what about Catholics and Protestants and Muslims and all the other people? They're all going to hell?'

I shake my head. 'No. We don't believe in heaven or hell. They'll just die and stay dead.'

He frowns. 'Well I'm a Catholic. So I'm just going to stay dead?'

He looks at me. I look at him. Then my feet. Then I remember the brochures. I go in my bag and bring out *The Watchtower* and *Awake*. I hold them out. 'Would you be interested in buying these? They will tell you all about how to get into paradise.'

He takes them, lazily flipping through *The Watchtower*, mouth drawn down at the sides. 'How much?' he asks.

My heart beats a little faster. 'A pound each,' I say, 'which is a pretty good deal if you consider the everlasting life it might give you.' I smile wide. This last bit I thought up all by myself.

He looks at me again. He has a kind face. It's a shame he's Catholic.

He rolls the brochures up and lightly taps them against his thigh. 'Go on then,' he says. 'Since you spoke so nicely.'

He goes away and comes back with two pound coins. He drops them into my sweaty palm, smiles, winks, and closes the door before I can say thank you.

I run to the end of the garden path, snatch open the gate, run out. Tim's there.

'How'd you get on?' he says.

I hold out the two pound coins flat on my palm.

'Well done!' He pats my shoulder. 'Let's try a few more, shall we?'

The only good thing about flogging *The Watchtower* and *Awake* on a beautiful Saturday morning is that I get to keep the money. Which means sweets and crisps and *Beano*.

I start walking alongside Tim, who I love love love. He's young with a light, fluffy moustache and blue eyes. He's the gentlest, kindest man I know and Veronica and me often argue about who'll get to marry him. It doesn't matter that he's already engaged to the cold, never-smiling Babette, a squat half-cast woman who walks like a pigeon. There's a good chance Tim will realise the mistake he's making and come to his senses before the wedding day. Babette might even die.

'You want me to do the next one?' asks Tim. 'Or shall we do it together?'

'Together.'

Across the road I see Veronica coming out of a front garden with Babette in her long, blue button-down mac. They walk far apart from each other. I see my dad too, a few houses down from them, standing at an open doorway with Bill Perch. He's standing with his hands clasped behind his bum. Bill is doing all the talking.

'I wonder if Vron's sold any yet?' I say as Tim holds a gate open for me.

'It's not a competition,' he says, his voice like baby bird feathers.

'Yeah it is.'

He laughs and follows me through the gate. We stop at the

23

front door. It's white and the sun is bouncing off it so we have to squint. I stand on tiptoes and press the buzzer. We wait. Finally the door opens and a kid a bit younger than me is standing there. He's wearing *Captain Planet* pyjamas and there's snot crusted on his upper lip. He gawps at me like I'm something from a different galaxy, which I might as well be in my stupid frilly dress. Then his eyes move up to Tim.

'Yeah?' he says, and his mouth stays open.

'Is your mum or dad in?' asks Tim.

The kid turns his head and shouts, 'Muuuuuuum!' He turns back to us and carries on staring, mouth still open.

I'm jealous of his pyjamas.

His mum comes to the door. Pink and brown stripy dressing gown, bleached perm, a triangle of floppy toast in one hand. She stares at us, eyes hard.

'Yeah?'

Tim clears his throat. 'Morning. I wonder if me and my friend could have a minute of your –'

'You Gee-ovah's?'

'Um. Yes.' He laughs nervously. 'I guess you could say—'

'Not intrested.'

She slams the door shut.

Tim smiles with his lips curled in. 'Okey dokey.'

Sunday morning. Nine o'clock. Me and Veronica don't make a sound. We're cross-legged on our beanbags a couple of inches away from the TV. *Thundercats*. The volume is turned down so low we strain our brains to hear.

We must not wake Mum and Dad.

Sunday mornings there's a meeting at the Kingdom Hall. This is how a typical meeting will go:

We go there dressed in our Sunday best. All women and girls must wear dresses or skirts. All men and boys must wear suits. Everyone must be clean and smart. Dad only has one suit. It's a strange, messy grey and if you look real close you can see, in between the grey, tiny stripes in primary colours and it's like looking at a TV screen close up. Mum wears her tent dresses. They're all she has. Me and Veronica are forced into the vilest, oldest, stupidest dresses that not even a gyppo would be seen dead in, and on the short walk up we nervously watch out for kids from our school.

We enter the Hall and find seats. The Hall is nothing like a Church. It has lime green carpets, bright lighting, grey plastic seats, and fake flowers everywhere. It is clean and new and there are no murals of Jesus bleeding out of his hands and feet like in Nana's church. 'Sterile,' Mum said once, and this made no sense to me because I thought sterile is when dogs can't have babies anymore, and what's that got to do with the Kingdom Hall?

An elder – always A Man – starts the meeting by asking us to stand. He says a prayer, we say Amen and then we all sing a hymn. Then another man comes to the podium and starts his talk. Tim is the only person in the whole congregation who makes his talks interesting to both children and grown-ups. The rest just read out a script full of verses and quotations boring enough to send Jehovah Himself to sleep. When something from the Bible is mentioned the congregation has to look up the quote. The whole meeting all you can hear is pages being turned all at once, people fidgeting, coughing, clearing their throats, babies crying and the endless drone of the elder going on like a mouldy scroll down a staircase.

We stand for another hymn. Then there's another man – usually an elder – with another talk. Another hymn. Another discussion, one last hymn, a closing prayer. Amen.

It lasts two hours.

It's flippin' boring.

When we were very young, me and Veronica were allowed to sit on Dad's lap and go to sleep. When we got too big for this we were moved to our own seats and ordered to stay awake but we were allowed to eat sweets – always Softmints – and do drawing and colouring. Now I was eight and Veronica nine we were expected to sit quietly and follow the talks. No talking, no eating. Look up all scriptures. Be *intrested*.

If we don't behave ourselves there's always The Smacking Room.

There is a meeting every Thursday evening at half-seven at night. We attend without fail.

During autumn and winter the Sunday meeting starts at half-one in the afternoon. We attend without fail.

During spring and summer, for no good reason, the Sunday meeting starts at ten in the morning.

Twenty-past nine. We hear noise upstairs. We freeze. Look at each other. Then up toward the ceiling. Movement. A door opening. The fast, scattered footsteps of paws on the staircase. The dogs, thank God, just the dogs. They explode into the room and run up to us, wagging like crazy. Veronica jumps up off her beanbag and lets them out the back garden, shushing wildly with a finger on her lip. I lie back and relax, lifting my legs in the air and turning them into scissors. Veronica comes back to her beanbag.

'Hole in yer jamas is gettin' bigger,' she whispers.

My Roger Rabbit pyjamas have a hole in the crotch the size of a fifty-pence piece.

'Can almost see yer fanny.'

I squeeze my legs together. 'Shut up.'

We go back to the TV. *Muppet Babies* now, my favourite. Veronica keeps fidgeting around on her beanbag and the rustling drowns out Miss Piggy's song. I punch her in the shoulder. 'I'm tryin' a listen!' I hiss. I move even closer to the TV. I can see the pixels. Red, blue, yellow. Like dad's suit. I poke out my tongue, lick the grimy screen and watch how the spit makes the pixels brighter. Veronica pushes my head to the side.

'Yer 'ead's in the way!'

'Then stop makin' so much shittin' noise.'

'*Ommmm.* I'm tellin' Mum you swore.'

I spin around and kick her arm. 'I'll tell her about the Barbies then.'

Last year I caught Veronica making her Barbie and my Ken do sex. She was rubbing them together and saying, 'Oh, Barbie, you are so sexy,' in a French accent.

She glares at me. I glare back. She pulls a mong face, hands spazzed up under her chin, and turns back to the TV.

Nine-thirty. Too late now. Time it takes to get dressed and walk over, we'd probably miss half the meeting. But best to be safe.

We wait. *Muppet Babies* finishes. We turn the channel over and start on *Pink Panther*. I scrunch up a Wotsit and sprinkle it in Veronica's hair when she isn't looking.

Ten o'clock. Veronica runs to the door and screams up the stairs, 'Muuuum, Daaaad, we've missed the meeting!' The dogs come in from the garden and get excited with us, whipping our legs with their thin tails.

Veronica gets *Karate Kid* from the video shelf and we sit down to watch it.

The ten o'clock meetings are my *fucking* favourite.

I'm five, Veronica's six. It's class assembly. We're in the infant's library, just the two of us. I look through the keyhole. I can see the top of someone's head. They're all out there, the whole of the infant school. Sat on their bottoms cross-legged. Mrs Andrews the headmistress is at the front talking to them. Something about the dinner lady being poorly......our thoughts being with her. Then Mrs Wedlake plays a few notes on the piano and everyone starts singing 'He's Got the Whole World in His Hands'.

I've never sung 'He's Got the Whole World in His Hands' in my life.

I go sit on a small blue chair at the small red table. Veronica's there looking at *I Knew an Old Lady Who Swallowed a Fly*. 'Crissy,' she whispers.

'Wha?'

'I need a wee.'

'You'll 'ave to wait, Vron.'

She squirms, her face full of suffering. 'But I need to *gooo*.'

There's no toilet here. She can't go out and disturb the assembly. Everyone will look. All fifty or so faces will turn to watch the Jehovah shuffle through the Hall. She knows this.

I carry on reading. Then I hear a trickling. Veronica's squatting over the wooden floor. A puddle the colour of apple juice spreads out. We both watch it grow bigger. Soon it's touching her powder-blue daps. She stops, pulls her knickers up. Looks at me miserably, bottom lip trembling, then bursts into silent, chest-banging sobs.

And without even thinking, I know what to do. There's a heavy rug in the middle of the room. I grab a corner and drag it over to the wee, letting it drop on top. I wait a minute while Veronica stands and watches, her crying stuck on pause. Then I drag the rug back to where it was. The wee is gone, all soaked up. And you can't see a wet patch on the rug because it's covered in colourful pictures of rainbows.

Veronica looks at me like I'm Jehovah. 'Wow,' she whispers. 'That's really clever.'

The muscles in my cheeks are hurting I'm trying so hard not to grin.

'Fanks,' she says.

We sit back down at the table and start reading. Except I can't focus because I'm too busy thinking about how clever I am.

Mrs Wedlake starts on the piano again and 'All Things Bright and Beautiful' tumbles out of the mouths of fifty children.

I'll never sing 'All Things Bright and Beautiful' in my life.

It's my birthday. Grandad takes me and Veronica to Victoria Park in his new burgundy Ford Escort. Burgundy, he tells us, is a posh word for dark red. He jingles the new keys on his finger and whistles something happy and olden-times. Victoria Park has an outside swimming pool which is a square hole cut out of scratchy concrete and filled with chemical water and wee and bits of dead leaves and crisp packets. It's always busy. Grandad puts armbands on us and we splash in whatever free space can be found between all the other splashers. Afterwards he towels us down and we sit on the grass and have a picnic. He says it can be our little birthday party.

We love Grandad. He tickles us and cuddles us and smiles at everything we say with his mouth going sideways in what Mum calls an Elvis Sneer, which Veronica has inherited.

Here are some things about Grandad:

His name is Walter Roger Jones, but he likes to be called Rog.

Before he married Nana he lived in India for three years working as a nurse.

He was also in the Merchant Navy, and he had a pet monkey called Mavis aboard the ship with him.

Nana was already engaged to another man when Grandad started chasing her. He hounded her non-stop until she agreed to break it off with the other man and marry him instead. Nana says it was her Bedroom Eyes that did it, though she says Bedwoom Eyes because she can't always say her r's proper.

He is a Proud Protestant. 'Proddy and proud to the end!' he tells people. This is why Nana didn't want to marry him at first. She is a Proud Catholic.

He is dumb-silly in-love with Nana and lets her Wear The Trousers, even though he is A Man.

He is an accountant.

Mum says he is a nice person and a good father-in-law except he is so tight with money he hangs his teabags on the line to dry so he can use them again, and he collects all the leftover toenails of soap and squeezes them all together to make a secondhand soap. Also, when Mum was pregnant with Veronica and had to move in with Nana and Grandad for a short while, Grandad said she wasn't allowed to bring her pet rats. But she snuck them in, and when

Grandad found out he went up to her attic room and took the rat cage and drove it all the way to Caerphilly and let the rats run into the wild. 'Straight into the jaws of death,' Mum later told us. 'Suprised he didn't just kill them himself to save on petrol.'

When the daylight stops being so light, Grandad drives me and Veronica home and kisses us goodbye. We tell Mum about the swimming and the birthday party and her 11 comes up. 'A birthday party?' she says. 'You know we're not supposed to have parties,' she says.

When Dad comes home later Mum has a word with him. There are words like 'pagan' and 'Jehovah' and 'spies,' and Dad scratches his chin and stares at the wall.

'Do you want that Glengerry arsehole disfellowshipping us all?'

Dad shakes his head.

'Well…that's what'll happen if the girls have birthday parties.'

'It was only a little one. There wasn't even cake.'

'Still a party.'

Later that night, around eleven, Grandad is coming home from his local social club. He is tipsy but not drunk. He never gets drunk. While crossing Whitchurch Road a man on a motorcycle runs Grandad over. The man is called Harry Windsor. He is drunk. He rides into Grandad and knocks him into the windshield of a car coming the other way. Grandad bounces onto the road and the car drives over his head and then stops. On his head. There are two witnesses. They are the men who own the motorbike shop over the road. One is skinny and ratty and always dressed in dirty denim and big black boots and the other is fat and bald and always dressed in black leather waistcoats. They are boyfriend and boyfriend. Which is gross. They run over and lift the car off Grandad's head and phone for an ambulance. Nana is in Cornwall with her sisters. When she finds out she pays a taxi to drive her the four hours from Cornwall to Cardiff.

In the morning a policeman comes to our door and tells Dad.

He goes sweaty-white and his skinny mouth is full of mumbles and the ghosts of mumbles. When he visits Grandad in hospital he doesn't recognise him. Grandad's head is swollen two times bigger than normal. It's the size of a massive freak-grown watermelon. He has tubes coming out of his big swollen-up watermelon face and there are tyre tracks and bandages and pink spots on the bandages.

Grandad goes into a coma and stays like that for a month. Just before he dies, Nana has a priest come in and convert him into a Catholic.

Proud and Proddy until the end.

Julie comes round every Wednesday night for Bible teaching. She sits in the room with Veronica and me and teaches us about Jesus and the other stuff in a lovely teacher's voice. Mum and Dad usually stay in the kitchen with the dogs, but sometimes they pop in, offering Julie cups of tea. She has it milky with no sugar. She is already sweet enough.

Julie is the most beautiful woman in the world, even more beautiful than Kylie. She has big curly brown hair and perfect cheekbones. She looks like the woman in *Beetlejuice*, the one who becomes a ghost. She is also the nicest woman in the world, and sometimes I imagine her married to Tim. Her and Tim, the perfectest, most good-looking couple, never mind that Babette monster who is probably ungrateful for the wonderful man she has and doesn't deserve him. I like to imagine Tim and Julie at their wedding. Tim with his handsome moustache and kind blue smiling twinkles. Julie wears a white dress and she looks like the woman from *Beetlejuice* in that scary scene at the end, except a fat man doesn't do spells on her to make her go super-old and wrinkled-up dry till her jaw drops off like tapped cigarette ash.

I like to imagine Tim and Julie kissing.

Tonight I am sat on the floor cross-legged in my Roger Rabbit pyjamas with the *Children's Book of Bible Stories* on my lap and

Veronica is next to me in a Roland Rat nightie. Julie is explaining about metaphors. She's sat all neat and pretty on the couch with one leg crossed over the over and a Bible on her lap. Her legs are perfect.

'It's like when Job says, "By the skin of my teeth".' 'A person doesn't have skin on their teeth, do they?'

Veronica stares at her book with her gob open and her eyes stupid and dreaming.

'I have skin on *my* teeth,' I say. 'Plaque!'

Julie laughs for a long time and my belly feels like chocolate because I made her do a proper grown-up laugh and not a pretend one for children.

'OK,' she says. 'Good point. But we're not *supposed* to have skin on our teeth. It's a metaphor. It's also a—'

Mum opens the door and comes in. 'Cup of coffee, Julie?'

Julie smiles like a humble film star visiting a starving African village for charity and says yes please.

'Everything going OK?' says Mum.

There's a blob of cake mix on her chin.

Julie smile-nods.

Mum looks at me and Veronica with expectant, are-you-learning-new-things? eyes. It's quiet for a bit. I'm staring at Julie's perfect face.

'Julie?' I say, and she looks at me. 'How did you get those cheekbones?'

Silence.

'Cuz they're the lushest cheekbones I've ever seen.'

Julie looks at Mum and Mum looks at her, and something passes between their eyes like invisible angel lasers and I feel a squirmy worm-shame and I don't know why.

Julie clears her throat and smiles. 'Um. Thanks, Christina. Well, I guess Jehovah made me this way.'

Mum spreads her arms out. 'And he made me *this* way? It's good to know Jehovah has a sense of humour!'

And we all laugh, and the worm-shame crawls away.

'Oh, you're great as you are, Catherine,' says Julie.

'All creatures great and small, eh?' says Mum, and then she goes back to her cake mix.

I lie back and lift my body up and cycle my legs like I saw a woman in a leotard do on morning television once. 'Look what I can do.'

'Oh! Very good, Christina.'

I scissor my legs in the air, sidewards and frontwards. 'And this! Look, Julie!'

I keep scissoring. Julie doesn't say anything. I do one more scissor, the most widest and scissoriest of all, and then I drop my legs and sit back up to face Julie, smiling. She's staring down at her Bible, flicking through the pages.

'Christina,' whispers Veronica, eyes horror-happy. 'That hole in yer pyjamas has gotten *massive*.'

I look at Julie. She still has her face stuffed in the Bible and her divine cheekbones are sizzled pink.

Shame squirms in my belly again and my cheeks catch up to her sizzle.

'We could see your fanny, Cris!' says Veronica in a voice made of glory and nervous-joy, as if she just saw the edge of Jehovah's massive sandal poking through the clouds.

I swivel on my bum and kick her in the thigh, hard.

The Hall. I'm stood on Dad's shoe, holding on to his leg. I step from shoe to shoe like crossing stones in a river. He isn't paying any attention: he's standing in a small circle talking to Alain, Norman and Joseph. Except he isn't talking so much as watching them talk.

Dad's shy. He isn't like the other men. They are confident and professional and they talk like politicians, smiling and cutting the air with their clean hands. Dad just stands there grinning, his creased-up eyes moving from person to person. I feel sorry for him. Especially when he tries to speak and his words come out like a whispery dog fart and no one hears.

One time Dad, being A Man, had to present a talk to the whole congregation. The week leading up to the talk he couldn't eat or sleep properly. He just sat in his chair going over his notes, his face cheesy. The day before the talk he took me to the cemetery to visit his father's grave and he smoked a cigarette and told me not to tell Mum.

The talk went OK. He was like a robot with a gun pointed at his robot head, but no one expected anything more.

Now Dad and Alain Dupont have broken off to talk about football. I like Alain. He's a wild French man with an Action Man body and a thick black moustache and eyes that are ALIVE. Once, he almost got disfellowshipped, and no one knows why, but Dad reckons it was over 'a sneaky joint', whatever that is. He looks after his wife, Karen, a wheelchair-stuck woman with shrivelled legs who used to be beautiful but now looks like a wasted, wilted flower version of Audrey from *Coronation Street*. Sometimes just looking at her makes me want to cry because she's so nice. But I'm sure Jehovah knows what He's doing.

'Did you see Grobbelaar's save in the Sunderland game?' says Alain.

My Dad's eyes light up like a little boy in a gun shop. 'Yeah! When 'e punched it away.' He demonstrates with one meaty fist.

Alain smiles. 'He has style, no?'

Dad nods and grins like an idiot.

Norman Glengerry leans in, smiling unsurely. 'What's that?'

'Grobbelaar's save last Wednesday,' says Alain. He kisses his fingertips.

'Pardon?' says Norman.

'Football,' says Alain.

'Ah. Football. Not my thing I'm afraid.'

'Your wife must be very happy,' says Alain.

Norman smiles and nods, his eyes closing. He looks exactly like

Kenneth Williams from the *Carry-On* films except he's short and blond. His nostrils are the size of brazil nuts. In a few years time he will be arrested for showing his willy to frightened little girls my age down Blackweir. And disfellowshipped, of course.

'I just caught the end of that game,' says Joseph, a pointy-headed black man with a perfect English accent. 'And I saw a re-run of the save later. It was good, very good. But he's no Schmeichel.'

Alain gasps. 'I might have to kill you for saying that.'

They all laugh. Even Norman Glengerry who doesn't understand the joke. I look up at him, my eyes fixed on his cave-black nostrils. I wonder how much stuff you could fit up one of them. He notices me looking and gives me a smile so smarmy I freeze and stare, my mouth open.

His smile disappears. He blinks slowly. 'Why don't you go and play with the other children?' he says.

I look up at my dad but he's just nodding and grinning and trying to fit in. I jump off his shoes and go and find Veronica. There are children everywhere. Little people in grown-up clothes leaping off the plastic chairs, playing catch. I pass by a group of blond boys who I don't like because they never let me play with them. One is standing on a chair, shouting, 'I'm on cree, I'm on cree!' while the others zip around like water fleas. I pull a face at the oldest one but he doesn't see. Two Saturdays ago our congregation went to the rec grounds at Roath for a sporty funday. The blond boys wouldn't let me play football with them, until Tim told them what Jehovah thinks of such spitefulness, and within five minutes I scored with a Pelé, and they all acted like it was nothing and said it was a fluke, but I could see wows coming out of their nasty boy eyes.

I see Veronica. She waves and skips toward me. A big beige hand grabs her elbow and she jolts to a stop.

Babette.

She glares down at Veronica, her jaw like a fist. 'No runnin' in

35

the Kingdom 'all,' she says, in a strong Cardiff accent. 'You *walk*.'
When she says this last word I can see the big gap in her front teeth.
She goes on glaring, her hand clamped on Veronica's squirming
arm. Then she lets go and walks away, toes pointed inward, legs
stiff and wide as if she's recently done a massive, painful poo.

Veronica's white eyebrows are fighting to get to the centre of
her face. 'Did you see that?' she says.

I nod.

'She didn't say nothin' to any of the other kids.'

'I know. She's a flippin' *bitch*.' This last word whispered.

'Let's go and tell Mum.'

We go and look for her. I follow Veronica. As we pass into the
foyer my thumb gets stuck between the heavy, lime-green double
doors. They close almost completely on the joint. I scream so loud
every Jehovah in the hall stops and looks. I yank it out from
between the doors and the screams turn to cries. My mum is there
in seconds. She looks at the thumb. It's swollen and there's a
vicious red dent in it.

'That needs some ice,' says Joan Lemon, a small, neat old
woman who both my parents like ('One of the nice ones.'), and
who, in twenty years' time, will live in a care home in Llandaff
and spend most of her days crying like a little girl and the only
thing she'll eat is custard creams and everyone will call her Moany
Joany.

'I think we'll have to get her home,' Mum says.

'Get her home and give her some sweeties,' says Joan.

I sink my face into my mother's stomach and grin wildly.

Dad is called and we regretfully make our way to the exit just
as Norman Glengerry smarms up to the podium to begin the
meeting. Veronica smiles. On the way out I see a woman dragging
her blond son into The Smacking Room. I smirk into Mum's hip.

On the way home Mum stops in the little off-licence known
throughout Gabalfa as the Paki Shop, a phrase me and Veronica aren't
allowed to use because only mean, ignorant people say things like

36

that, according to Mum, except we *do* use it, behind her back, because we're different enough from the other kids as it is. She buys me some Softmints and a box of Ribena. Veronica tells her about Babette. Mum gets angry and tells Dad that they've got it in for our effing family, the Witnesses, and all because we're poor. 'Very Christian of them,' she adds, shaking her head and frowning. My dad just shrugs.

We pass the dark, manky house on North Road which has three long knife-scratches in the wall and as usual I say, 'Mum, did Freddy *really* do that?' and as usual, she says, 'Yes, it's his mark, it means he's going to kill who ever lives there,' and I go quiet.

'Dad?' I say as we reach the top of Maerdy Road.

'Wha'?'

'Is Schmeichal really better than Grobbelaar?'

Dad snorts. 'Nuh!'

I walk with my thumb held out in front of me. The cold night air is making it throb.

'Mum?' I say.

'Yes, Kissy?'

'Why are Norman Glengerry's nostrils so big?'

'So he can smell everyone's shit,' she says.

'You shouldn't swear in front of the kids,' says Dad.

'So he can smell everyone's bowel movements,' she says.

'Dose children are not goin' widout presents at Christmas!'

I hear something heavy being slammed down on the kitchen surface.

'It's not down to me, Mum. It's Cath.'

'Oh, yer useless! What koind of mother is she?' says my nana. 'You can't 'ave kids goin' widout presents at Christmas!'

'Well in the Bible it says—'

'Oh shuddup, Neil. Yer father must be turnin' in his grave.'

Something else is slammed. The sound that rings out is close to where me and Veronica are eavesdropping. We move away from the kitchen door and run out into the garden.

My nana is Irish as well as Catholic, and this, according to my mum, is the worst kind of Catholic.

To Nana, not letting kids celebrate Christ's birthday is child abuse. All this Jehovah's Witness business – Mum and Dad might as well beat us black and blue every day and make us go to school naked, that's how damaging it is.

We've dressed up in Nana's clothes and we're playing a game called Minnie the Minx which has nothing to do with Minnie the Minx. Veronica's dragging her stiletto heels across the patio floor. She's got one of Nana's leather handbags over her shoulder. I'm wearing green eyeshadow on my cheeks and hot pink lipstick on my eyelids. Nana comes out. She's angry. She stands there and looks at us, shaking her head.

'That bloody mother of yours,' she says. 'Christened Catholic, you were. Now look atchoo – goin' widout Christmas.'

I do a handstand against the wall. When I come back down, Nana is still shaking her head.

'Nana?' says Veronica.

'What?'

'Why do people eat turkey for Christmas?'

'Because it's *noice*!'

Dad's gone out. Me and Veronica are watching *Mickey's Christmas Carol* with Mum, who is eating a bowl of raw cake mix. We try to dip our fingers in but she snatches it away and says it's not for kids because there's raw eggs in it, risky raw eggs, but really she just wants it all for herself. The lights are off. The dogs are asleep. No decorations, no tree, no mistletoe.

At ten we hear the sound of Dad's car coming up the drive. The dogs bark and me and Veronica run to the front door. Dad climbs out of the car, goes in the boot and lifts out two black binbags bulging with stuff.

'Wha's that?' I say.

'Ho ho ho,' he says.

'What *is* it?' says Veronica.

'Ho ho *ho*,' he says.

Mum stands in the doorway, almost filling it, her arms crossed over her boobs. She has this look on her face which is annoyed and happy at the same time.

Dad comes in, holding the bags up in the air out of our reach. The dogs are going nuts. Dad suddenly stops, turns around and lets out a trumpet-like fart in Rutger's astonished face.

'Happy Christmas, Scumboy!' he says to him before dumping the black bags on the floor.

'From your nana,' he says to us.

'Don't tell the Jehovah's Witnesses about this,' says Mum, picking up her bowl of cake mix.

'And don't tell your nana you opened them on Christmas Eve,' says Dad.

We dive in. The bags are full of presents. Roller skates, candle-making kit, socks and knickers, felt pens, pyjamas (blue for me, pink for Veronica), Disney videos, dolls (Barbie for Veronica, Ken for me).

I spend Christmas morning roller skating round a square of concrete in the garden in a duffel coat and bobble hat, my chapped smile frozen on. The presents make me happy. If Jehovah has a problem with this then He can't be very nice, can He?

Instead of a traditional turkey dinner, dad makes moussaka with salad. It's so tasty it makes turkey look like a giant dried-out turd. We are also allowed Lambrusco, just a little, and we spend the afternoon rolling around on the floor exaggerated-drunk while half-watching Christmas films on TV and playing with our dolls.

Our Christmas, I reckon, is better than everybody else's.

The day Mum and Dad decide to leave the Faith it's raining hard. Me and Veronica are playing on the Nintendo when Dad knocks on the bedroom door.

'Your mother wants a word,' he says, face all serious.

Me and Veronica look at each other. We follow him downstairs. My stomach goes all slimy-cold. At ten I'm too old to get the slipper but she'll find a way to make me suffer.

'What ju reckon it is?' I whisper to Veronica.

'*I* don't know.'

Mum's sat on the couch, one beefy leg up on the cushions.

'Sit down,' she says, so we do. Dad stands by the door, his hands clasped over his crotch like someone's about to aim a free kick at him.

Mum picks up the remote control from the floor and turns down the volume all the way. The sound of rain spattering the window fills the room.

'It's like this,' says Mum. 'We're leaving the Witnesses.'

We stare at her.

'Wha'?' I say.

'The Hall. We're not going anymore.'

Veronica clenches her hand into a fist and hisses out an aggressive 'Yesss!'

Mum smiles. 'I thought you'd be happy, Vron.' She turns to me. 'What about you?'

Well. I have mixed feelings. I've recently started to pay attention to all this Jehovah stuff. I believe. That's what six years of it will do.

On the other hand I'm moving up to High School this year and now I don't have to put up with the bullying Veronica's had.

'I dunno really. Um. I dunno. Why we leavin'?'

Mum looks at Dad, who is picking his nose and not paying attention, and rolls her eyes. She turns back to me. 'You know we've been disillusioned for a while?'

I nod. Our attendance at the meetings has got bad. We haven't been door-to-door in a while. Mum feels that the Witnesses, especially the elders, are a bunch of holier-than-thou hypocrites and that they look down on our family. Earlier in the year,

Bernice, Babette's sister, had organised a picnic in the park for the children. Frisbee, football, hide-and-seek, lots of food.

Me and Veronica had not been invited.

Bernice, who was nicer than Babette but who shared the same blood, had claimed it was an innocent mistake. She gave me and Veronica a packet of Rolos to share and apologised, a mortified hand on her heart. Mum liked Bernice but she didn't buy it. That night she raged around the house, slamming cupboard doors and muttering swear words before sinking into a dark sulk in front of *A Nightmare on Elm Street*.

Dad thought Mum was being paranoid and that she was expecting too much from the Witnesses – they were only people, they were not perfect; only Jesus was perfect, and God. And Pink Floyd. And sure, it was shocking that Glengerry had turned out to be a serial flasher, like, but you couldn't tar them all with the same brush. Still, he had lost interest himself.

'This is wicked,' says Veronica.

I don't know what to say. The possibilities are starting to fly at me. Halloween, birthdays, Easter, free Sundays, free Thursday evenings. No more *The Watchtower* and *Awake*, no more flippin' dresses.

No more fucking shitting bastard dresses.

'I like the religion itself, the teachings,' says Mum. 'But the people – well, they've done their best to exclude us and make us feel this big –' She holds her thumb and forefinger an inch apart. 'And all that blood transfusion crap...' Mum spits out air, disgusted. 'As *if*. If one of you two were in hospital, sick, and you needed blood, ju think I'd let you die just because of a few words in the Bible?' She shakes her head. 'Ridiculous.'

Mum looks at us both, studying our faces. 'So... OK?'

'OK,' I say.

'Yep,' says Veronica.

Mum aims the remote control at the TV and turns up the volume. 'Meeting over. Amen.'

I Can Smell the Earth

I'm walking down a freshly-painted corridor toward the main lounge. That's what they call it here – a lounge. At home it's a living room. But no one here is really living, that's what I think. The sharp paint fumes mingle with the smell of old people – biscuits, talcum powder and vegetable farts. My great-gran follows behind, her walking stick thudding against the carpet. Veronica and Mum are at her side.

Great-gran is wearing an Easter bonnet. Spirals of pink and yellow crepe paper drape her NHS glasses. A tiny yellow chick sitting in a broken egg bobs around on top.

'Now, don't yew touch that wall, Christina,' she says to me.

'My name's not Christina,' I say.

'Fine. Don't touch the wall, *George*. The paint's wet.'

I turn and look her in the eye. Raise my hand up to the wall.

She gives me a look of warning. '*George*,' she says.

I plant my hand on the sticky wall.

My great-gran snatches a twiggy set of fingers to her chest and gasps theatrically. 'Wicked! She's got the devil in her!' She turns to my mum. 'Catherine – that girl's got the *devil* in her!'

This is my earliest memory of Gwendolyn, my great-grandmother.

My mum was born Catherine Winters on October the twenty-ninth, 1964 under the sign of Scorpio. Six weeks later, her father, Oscar, died of a bad heart. Her mother, Moira, had a nervous

42

breakdown and went to live in Whitchurch mental hospital for a rest. She had her brain zapped with electricity, so it couldn't have been that restful.

This is what I know about Oscar:

He was an English teacher.

He had a poem published in a book once.

His mother was born a Summers, his father a Winters.

He smoked, smoked, smoked, all the time smoked.

He had short, wavy dark hair, intelligent eyes, and a little tufty moustache cornering a small, sarky mouth.

His favourite writer was Edgar Allen Poe.

Moira got her brain fixed in the mental hospital, but not her heart. She came back to the family home, Oscar-less, and went on with being a mum and a widow. She decided she would love no other man as long as she lived.

Here's a thing or two about Moira:

She was a maths teacher.

She looked like a dark-haired, big-hipped version of Susan Sarandon. Same bulby, pretty eyes. Veronica has them also, but hers are light light blue, more Culkin than Sarandon.

She was lazy. She drove her car to the corner shop. She would spend all her free time at the coffee table in the smoked-up kitchen, gossiping with her mother, Gwendolyn, in Welsh so the children couldn't understand.

She had all her teeth taken out at twenty-one and replaced with dentures. She said it was the best thing she'd ever done and recommended it.

She was kind and gentle but didn't take any nonsense.

The only thing she ever cooked was chips. Chips and fish fingers. Chips and sausages. Chips and pie. Chips every day.

She had two pet corgis and a Siamese cat.

She smoked, smoked, smoked, all the time smoked.

Mum was brought up in Lakeside, a nice posh area in Cardiff, by Roath Park lake, which is my favourite place in the world – all dark ripply water and row boats, pedaloes, swans, ducks, geese, even a small lighthouse at one end of the lake. She lived with her older brother, Henry, who was tall and thin and all Oscar in the face. They had some family near Swansea – dragon aunties and kind old uncles and some nicer aunties in horn-rimmed glasses and a few cousins with mean, freckled faces who sang 'Hey Fatty Bum Bum' when the grown-ups weren't around. But these were now-and-again relatives. Christmas and summertime relatives.

Gwendolyn lived nearby and was an Everyday Relative.

Here's a list for Gwendolyn:

She was known as a witch in her hometown of Pontardawe. People came to her for herbal remedies. Mum says she once found a box full of strange instruments – syringes, tubes, a bulbed thing, a bedpan – under her gran's bed. It was for sucking babies the size of baked beans out of the mum early on, if the mum didn't want it or couldn't afford it. Gwendolyn did it in secret to help out the mums. In the old black and white days, mums weren't given free money by the social like what we have. I wonder what she did with the baked beans. Flush them down the toilet?

She married her uncle.

During the Second World War she was the lieutenant in a bomb factory. She saw some of her friends blown up to bloody bits halfway through making a new bomb. Thumbs and fingers all over the conveyer belt.

She thought black people were savages. 'Look at him, ooh, what a savage,' she'd say in a horrible-loud voice if she ever saw one.

She had a bonk-eye – one on stick, the other on twist. Like a chameleon.

She was able to cross one long leg over the other and then tuck it behind her ankle so that her legs looked wrapped together like a Celtic band.

She had a catchphrase, 'I can smell the earth!' which she'd say all melodramatic like a Shakespeare actor whenever she got upset.

She had a wicked sense of humour.

She was sharp and liked to tell it how it is.

She was nobody's fool.

Mum reckons I'm very much like her.

Mum wasn't so close to Gwendolyn, who preferred Henry, the brother. Henry had lost his father – become Oscar-less – when he was seven, whereas Mum had never known him. Henry was full of allergies and had bad asthma. He was a poorly little boy. Also, the day his dad's heart burnt out and he fell over in the hallway and died, Henry had to step over him, little legs creeping around the dead still dad, to get out of the way for the doctor and out of the house, and his dad's arms had twitched and touched his bare ankles, and this *might have damaged him*. Gwendolyn saw a sad and angry little boy with runny eyes and an asthma pump stuck in his gob eternally and she tried to make things better. She spoiled him, Mum reckons. Sided with him always.

Moira made sure to give Mum enough attention. Apart from all the chips, Moira was a good mother and they were close. When Mum wasn't at the lake, rescuing hurt ducks and learning about wildlife and running away screaming from shadow-hiding men who flashed their willies, men like Norman Glengerry, she was at her mother's side in the kitchen, helping with crosswords and eating bara brith while Gwendolyn prattled on in Welsh and the corgis slept under the table.

Henry didn't always like Mum. She was hyperactive and greedy. Always on the go, busy busy, always sneaking food into her mouth, running around chewing and guzzling, all flabby energy. And she came into the world when their father was leaving it – a rubbish association. Henry would look at his plump little sister and feel his Oscar-lessness grow to a thunderstorm. Sometimes he beat her up. And Gwendolyn would always be looming, a

45

cross-eyed statue, to tell her that she deserved it, and that's what you get when you steal people's chocolates and talk back.

When Mum was fourteen and Henry twenty-one, Moira started getting headaches. She went to the doctor. Brain tumour. Six months to live. But the doctors didn't like to use the 'c' word in those days, so they lied.

You'll be fine, Moira. You'll get better.

Give it time, Moira.

Her headaches got worse, she had crazy moods, up and down, she had blackouts and lost chunks of memory. Her family looked on with sad, guilt-sparkly eyes. She was admitted to hospital. When Mum went to visit she couldn't find her. It was like Dad looking for his dad after the road accident. She walked up and down the ward, scanning the beds. Where was she? Finally, a shaved-bald woman with purple eye bags called her over. When Mum got to the bed she realised it was Moira. She burst into tears, sudden slammed door tears. Moira sat there with wet eyes.

'I know I'm dying, Catherine,' she said. 'I know it.'

And Catherine just cried.

Gwendolyn decided to take Moira out of hospital. She would die in her and Oscar's marital home by the side of the lake. Not some ugly ward filled with chemical smells and sickly moans. They set her up in the living room. Mum and Gwendolyn bathed her, changed her, kept her company. Henry let his hurt be eaten up by anger.

Moira would switch between crazy confusion and normal Moira-ness. One day she was Moira for longer than usual. Calm and present. She listened to *Tony Hancock's Half Hour* on the radio with her family and later watched the sun sink out the large bay window.

The next day she died. Forty-five years-old.

Mum went to the funeral with a black eye.

Mum felt very alone. Moira-less. So when she met Neil Jones, a quiet man with shocking light-blue eyes, even more light-blue than hers, and a skinny-lipped mouth hidden under a moustache, she saw him as a rescuing knight. A knight in corduroy flares. Dad. He used to be a Cardiff City football hooligan and a criminal and a drug-addict. He had squirted yucky brown stuff into his veins for a year, and sniffed powders up his nose. And there were tiny squares of paper too, which he'd put on his tongue and they'd dissolve like sugar and make his brain go like the *Yellow Submarine*. All the drugs had murdered his thinking and his blinking. He stared a lot.

Mum thought he was wonderful.

They snuck into Roath Park at night and Dad would climb the lighthouse and write his name in big black writing while Mum watched from a rowing boat like a hungry damsel. They used to do all their sex in a Wendy House in the park. Dad wasn't very interested in Mum. He wasn't romantic. Although this one time, he laid down his jacket on a damp bench so Mum could sit down and she said, 'Oh, you're a right Walter Raleigh!' And he said, 'How ju know? Who told you?' and glared at her, because his secret real name was Walter, and Mum responded to this by laughing in his face.

And maybe this put him off romance.

Mum got pregnant at sixteen with Veronica and Dad was bullied into marrying her by his mother, my Nana, who is a Trouser Wearer with everyone. The wedding was in a Catholic church. Dad wore a grey suit too short in the leg, and Mum wore a pink two-piece suit with a pink hat like some plump American woman who sells Avon. When the priest said, 'Will you, Catherine Winters, take Walter Neil Jones to be your lawful, wedded wife,' Mum did a laugh like the bark of a lonely scared Jack Russell, and Dad's blue robot eyes stared straight ahead. Her laugh disappeared into the dusty-dim church corners and someone coughed, and she said, 'I do.'

In the wedding photos my dad looks terrified and unhappy.

Moira's house at Lakeside was sold, and the money split between her overgrown orphans. Mum and Dad bought a flat on Flora Street, in Cathays, which they soon sold so that they could move to Senghenydd, a miserable town in the valleys full of brown yucky stuff. The money ran out super-fast. Mum blames Dad for this and says he twisted her inheritance money out of her to spend on get-rich-quick druggy schemes, but he reckons she was just as bad for shitting money away. After I was born they moved into a hostel filled with vicious pregnant teenage girls who wanted to beat up Mum because she had a man and they didn't.

As for Henry, he spent his inheritance living it up and recording an album with his rock band, the Ghosties.

Here are some other things about Henry:

He is very funny. Mum reckons that when he was younger he could walk into a crappy party and within five minutes he would have everyone laughing like mad, and the party would turn into a cool party.

He loves chess, and won the British championship once.

He plays guitar and the organ and bass.

When younger he looked a bit like David Bowie but with curly hair. All the girls went nuts over him.

He has his father's intelligent eyes and sarky mouth.

He has Mum's 11s between his brows.

He loves Indian food more than any other food. Sends Christmas cards to his favourite takeaways every year.

He did Kung Fu for a while, and even though he only got to a yellow belt, he once had a fight with a gang of drunken men outside his favourite Indian takeaway because they were being mean about Pakis. And though he didn't win, he managed to fight them off, so he didn't lose either.

He is lazy like his mother.

He's good with computers.

He's selfish.

I'm probably a bit like him.

Mum and Gwendolyn got friendlier with each other. It was like their bad blood turned into a bad scab, and over the years the scab got drier and bits started to flake off. Gwendolyn went to live at Ty-Glas Residential, an old people's home in Llanishen and Mum visited once a week with her family – me, Veronica, Dad.

When I was a baby I had this illness called reflux, where I couldn't keep any food down and I puked and cried all day and night, and it was a chronic case said the doctors. I almost choked to death a few times. Blue-faced and gargling on sour milky sick in my crib with Mum and Dad looking down with eyes terror-filled before going into action mode and unblocking me. I spent the first six months of life screaming. I was ugly and red and spotty with a warbley mouth that never stopped crying crying crying. Mum used to lock herself in the bathroom to get away from me. The only person who could get me to shut up was Veronica. I'd lie on her lap and stop crying for a few minutes.

When Mum and Dad took me to visit Great-gran, she would hear me coming when we were half a street away, like an air raid siren, and even the oldest, crumbliest, deafest ladies with their squealing hearing aids would lift their heads off their bibs in the communal lounge and say, 'Ah, I hear your family coming, Gwendolyn, how … *nice* for you.' It would get louder as we went up the lift, like someone's finger stuck on the volume button. And when we arrived, Great-nana would look at Mum's tired fat face and say, 'Catherine, that girl is *scrrreaming* the devil out of her,' with her Rs rolling like custard off a knife. 'She is scrrreaming the devil *out* of her, Catherine, all of it, so when she is older she will be *lovely!*'

I don't think I got it all out.

Veronica was the opposite. Quiet. She couldn't speak at all. When she wanted something, like a biscuit or a Lego block, she'd

49

point at it and go, 'Mmmm mmm,' like a dumb gerbil. She got to four years old and still couldn't speak. 'Yew want that child looked at by a specialist, Catherine,' Gwendolyn said. 'It's not normal.' So Mum called in a speech therapist who knew how to unlock voice boxes, and soon Veronica was speaking the Queen's English posh as anything, just like she was taught, and now instead of pointing and mmmm-ing, she'd say, 'May I have a biscuit please?' and Great-nana would dip her head with eyes half-closed behind her giant specs and say, 'Why of course, Your Highness!' and grizzly Welsh witch laughter would splurt out and fill the little-old-lady bedroom.

Mum made friends with Henry too. He had learnt to Be Nice. That Hitting Girls is Wrong. Or maybe he wasn't so angry now? He would come over our new council house in Paradise Place for nights in with Mum, Dad and some friends, and they'd all eat muddy mushrooms raw out of an Asda carrier bag and spend the night giggling like crazy, pupils like black pennies.

Mum became 'Little Sis'.

When Henry's first marriage went kablooey, he moved into a giant tent in our back garden. I liked having him around. I'd go out to the tent and follow him about like a small mongrel. He taught me to play chess. He bought me a child-sized guitar, a proper one made from wood, and tried to teach me to play that too, but Mum sat on it one day and it got crushed. I paid back his kindness by walking on his back every day to get the clicks out. I'd sit and watch as he smoked his rollies and drank his coffee, and cleared his sinuses every few minutes with a gross honking sound, and if I cried out at a thick brown garden spider hanging in the corner of the tent, he would give the spider a personality and a name and tell me that spiders were very important because they killed flies, and flies were shit.

Best of all, Henry never forgot that my name was George, not stupid, wrong-sounding *Christina*. I was going to grow up to be a real boy one day and I was going to marry a pretty woman and she would wear dresses and I would wear trousers.

'Yes,' Uncle Henry would agree. 'And you're going to grow a willy. It'll start out small but it'll grow. Cross my heart. It'll happen.'

Great-nana's room at Ty-Glas House…

'Crissy, don't you think it's time you started using cups?' says Mum. 'Hmm? You're not a baby anymore.' Mum looks down at me, her brows raised.

I frown and tighten my grip on the orange baby beaker.

'Oh, leave her alone, Catherine,' says Gwendolyn. 'If she's not ready, she's not ready.' She turns to me and smiles. 'Yew do what yew like, Christina.'

Frown stays.

Gwendolyn brings a hand to her spidery mouth. 'Oops – I mean George. I do apologise, bachgen bach.' She shakes her head, smiling. 'Georgie Porgie, pudding and pie, kissed the girls and made them cry. When the boys came out to play, Georgie Porgie ran away.' She stretches her colourless lips into a grin, showing her large tea-stained false teeth. I smile back, shyly, but it's not a real smile. I don't like that song. It makes me feel like a dirty monster. Like Freddy Krueger.

I sit on the floor and watch Veronica do her jigsaw. A London Bus, 200 pieces. Mum and Gwendolyn start talking about Dad. The word 'useless' comes up. Mum goes quiet, her hands clasped together on top of her hillock of a stomach. Gwendolyn leans forward, legs crossed twice, her eyes swimming behind the chunky lens of her spectacles. 'What kind of husband just buggers off to Amsterdam for six weeks, Catherine? What kind of *father*?'

Mum shakes her head sadly. 'I know. But he's promised he won't do it again.' A pause. Pursed lips. 'Because he knows I'd cut his balls off.'

'I should bloody well think so. Duw, duw, duw. These girls need a father, Catherine, not some twp drug user. They need a—'

'Well what about Henry?'

Gwendolyn leans back. 'What about him?'

'He's no better. Amount of drugs *he's* taken.'

'But he doesn't have children to support.'

'He has a wife.'

'Oh shush, that doesn't—'

'I'm just saying, Gran, Henry is no angel. When was the last time he visited you?'

Now it's Gwendolyn's turn to go quiet.

'Go on. When was the last time the golden one got off his lazy arse and came to see you?'

'His car is off the road.'

'And you believe that?'

'Cau dy geg, Catherine, cau dy—'

'You *actually* believe that?'

'If that's what he—'

'He doesn't give a shit about—'

'Bloody hell!' Gwendolyn raises her hands in the air, shoulder-height, like a preacher in pain. 'I can *smell* the earth!'

'Oh, shut up, Gran. I'm just saying. They're as bad as each other.'

Gwendolyn raises her wiry black eyebrows, lids lowered. She pats her cloud-white hair and her mouth turns into a squiggly line. She and Mum stare at separate spots on the wall. Gwendolyn manages to stare at two spots at the same time.

I was six. I remember after the funeral, holding my dad's hand and looking up at his face, noticing how sad he looked. He was thinking about his father, whose poor watermelon tyre track head had been laid to rest on the other side of the cemetery just two months before.

I remember getting into the car after Great-gran's service. Squeezed between Veronica and Mum on the back seat. Mum's black-swaddled flab like a rolled up duvet against my arm. Nana

Eileen, Last Remaining Grandparent, at the front, her wrinkly-silky eyelids painted coral blue. Dad slumping in behind the wheel and starting the ignition. Eileen straining her neck to face my wet-eyed mum and launching into a monologue about her new curtains and conservatory. Mum glaring at her. And this moment going down in family history as The Time That Stupid, Thoughtless, Bloody Woman Started Talking About Her Fucking Curtains Five Minutes After The Funeral.

I remember driving around the Gabalfa roundabout, looking out the window, thinking about my great-gran and having a silent little cry. I remember the song that was playing on the car radio: 'This Time I Know it's For Real' by Donna Summer. And now every time I hear that song, I think of death and roundabouts.

I remember the day before the funeral. Me and Veronica waiting outside a cream-coloured building. Mum inside looking at her grandmother's dead body. We were too young, me and Veronica. Too young for death. And besides, Great-gran had gangrene. I didn't know exactly what gangrene was, but I imagined it as a nasty-smelling moss that grew on the skin as fast as a blush. Zombie skin. I wanted nothing to do with zombie skin. I was happy outside, kicking gravel at Veronica or pushing her into the tall hedges by the car park.

Soon Mum came out. She was holding a small brown envelope. The whites of her eyeballs were pink and you could see the tiny jagged veins like red forks of lightning. She stopped and looked back at the building she'd just left. She opened the envelope and pulled out a curl of white hair. She held it to her nose, closed her eyes and started crying, silently. And she stayed like that for a long time.

I'm sitting on Gwendolyn's bed. She is sharing the two-seater with Mum. Mum's bum takes up one and a half seats, leaving Great-gran squeezed into just half. But that's OK – she's skinny, tall and skinny.

53

They're talking in angry voices, but I don't think they're angry with each other. I'm not listening – listening to grown-ups talk is as boring as watching the news.

Great-gran gave me a packet of Space Raiders and some sherbet earlier, and I mixed them together to see what would happen. *Stupid*. So now I'm picking out each crisp and trying to wipe the sherbet off with my cardigan sleeve, and I'm sad because it's not working and I've ruined my crisps. Veronica is munching on hers with dead eyes, like her brain's switched off, and when I ask her to share, she frowns and shuffles around on her bum so her back is facing me.

'How long's it been, now?' says Mum.

Gwendolyn breathes out a mouthful of air through her frilly lips. Shakes her head. 'I don't know. Months? He only comes to me when he wants something. Oh yes – when he wants something he can't come quick enough. Yew can be shewer of *that*.'

Mum makes a humph noise. 'I know all about that,' she says. 'He only bothers with us when things are going bad with Jane.'

They're silent for a while. Then Gwendolyn turns to Mum.

'Catherine. I was wrong. I was wrong—'

'Oh, come on now, Gran, it's all—'

'Always running after that boy like a fool.'

Gwendolyn looks at her knees awkwardly and places a scrawny, brown-splodged hand over Mum's plump one. Pats it.

Mum's eyes get wet. She sniffs and nods. They take their hands away and look at separate spots on the wall. Gwendolyn's eyes manage to look at two spots at the same time.

Voice Box

About once a year the house is filled with puppies. They start off in a large newspaper-floored cardboard box, squirming around all blind like worms, squeezing out small greeny-black spirals of poo and then falling in them. Me and Veronica watch for hours, our big heads peeking from over the cardboard wall, like blonde gods.

Soon Mum and Dad give them names. The last lot went like this: Dixie, Babushka, Baldrick, Splodge, Fat Tulip, Hendrix, Merthyr Boy and Bruno. When they get older, me and Veronica are allowed to play with them, as long as the mother is OK with this. The mother is usually Tugger, a tan and white pied (cow-patterned) with boobs so hangy and stretched, they look like icing bags. Tugger is a brilliant mum, unlike Miffy, the English Bull we used to have, who ate all her puppies a few hours after they came out. Tugger doesn't get jealous or angry. She wags and smiles as soon as you look at her, even with ten babies sucking the life out of her. Dad says if Tugger was human she'd be a hippy like Suki Fisk, but without the cider problem.

Soon the puppies are old enough to run around the house and garden. Me and Veronica make-believe whole worlds for them using gardening tools, rubbish and our toys. The puppies run around in a big mess, chasing the cat, play-fighting, sniffing things, and we grab them at random and throw them through the gates (two planks of wood) of Christina and Veronica's Crazy Fun World (formally known as George and Veronica's Crazy Fun

World, but Veronica reckons I need to move on now that I'm seven), where they can try the rollercoaster (a rollerskate up an apple tree), the dodgems (a rollerskate and Barbie's Beach Buggy crashing into each other), or even dirty dancing lessons taught by Patrick Swayze himself (naked Action Man). Our favourite is the ghost train, which is pushing a puppy in a rollerskate through some shade while Veronica does a witch's cackle and I say, "Welcome to prime time, bitch!", like Freddy Krueger.

It's the saddest thing when they're all sold. But sometimes Mum and Dad decide to keep the best ones, which is why we have Rutger and Slug.

Rutger is handsome, stupid and charming. All black except for a white nose. It's hard not to fall in love with Rutger. He is like his mother – soft and loving. Sometimes he does funny things, like walking into lamp posts or eating a whole block of lard and puking it up all over Dad's shoes, and once he got stuck in the cat flap and pulled it out of the door, wearing it around his waist like a tutu. If he was a person he'd be James Bond with brain damage.

Slug is hard. Small, black and bullet-sleek. Dog fighting is evil, so we just enter her in contests of strength. Last year she came in first place – she pulled seven people in a trailer across a large hall. If Slug was a person she'd be Ripley from *Alien*.

Our dogs *could* be dangerous, Mum says – if they wanted they could rip out a person's throat in two seconds. But they weren't raised that way.

Six sprouts left. Rutger is sat in front of me watching my plate, two long, fat strings of drool hanging from the sides of his mouth.

Dramatic drumbeat – the *EastEnders* omnibus is finished. Mum gets up to take her plate to the kitchen. I quickly grab my sprouts and hold them out to Rutger. He snatches at them without sniffing and swallows without chewing. I wipe the drool and gravy on the carpet. Across the room, Veronica picks up her burnt-black roasties. 'Oy, Rutger,' she whispers. He bolts over to her and eats them.

Dad is watching from the couch, scratching his balls. He tosses Rutger the parson's nose and winks at us.

Mum comes back in the room. *The News* is starting. I hear the word 'pit bull'.

... and since the brutal attack on six-year-old Rukhsana Khan of Bradford, the public has been calling for action to be taken against the breed.

Photograph of a small Indian girl with her swollen face stitched up like a baseball. Followed by video footage of a brown pit bull barking mad and murderously from behind a chainlink fence, its muzzle wrinkled back like an old lady's baggy stocking.

'Yeah, show the bloody rabies-job, why don't they,' says Mum, frowning.

And now, continues the newsreader, *that action is being taken. In a move that many will regard as extreme, the government is in the preliminary stages of planning a nationwide cull—*

'Mum, what's a—'

'Shhh!' Mum holds up a cigar-shaped finger. Now there's a grey-haired man on the screen.

... if plans go ahead we'll be looking at a, um, at a mass-banning of this breed and possibly others. And when I say 'ban' I mean that, uh, dogs belonging to the mentioned breeds will be destroyed.

I get down on the floor, wrap my arms around Rutger's neck and cry into his fur.

'... it's the owners that should be put down,' Mum is saying. In the rear view mirror I can see her 11 is up.

We're on the way to Hyde Park in London. A demonstration to stop the government killing all the pit bulls is taking place. Dad drives and twiddles with the knobs on the radio, making the song change from New Kids on the Block – 'Step by Step' – to boring man's voice to classical violins to INXS – 'I Need You Tonight'.

57

'All these arseholes using pit bulls as status symbols – all these scummy arseholes. Like Richard Frost, what he did to Judy. *He* should be put down.'

Dad nods.

Richard Frost lives in our street and is the older brother of my friend and classmate, Emma. He's a thug and a burglar. Mum is friendly in a love/hate way with their mother, Linda, who is also the street gossip and looks a bit like a meaner, fag stained version of Jeanette Krankie. A couple of litters ago, Mum and Dad gave one of Tugger's puppies to the family. They called her Judy. She had the same cow-like marks as her mum. She was soft and daft and lovely. But not for long. Richard took control of the dog, brought her up to growl at strangers. He turned her into a weapon. She's three now, and she's already bitten someone. Who knows – one day she could savage a little girl like Rukhsana Khan and all of Britain will call her a monster and say it's because of her breed.

'It's always the scum,' Mum says. 'Always the wankers in the council estates who wanna look hard.' Mum looks at Dad. 'I just wish we never gave her to them. Why did I do that? Am I that desperate to be liked by all the arseholes of the street?'

'At least we gave 'em the smallest one,' says Dad. 'Can't do so much damage.'

Mum nods. She's quiet for a while. Dad fiddles with the radio again.

'You know what I read the other day?' Mum says, and Dad glances at her to let her know he's listening. 'There was this little Scottish girl, only ten she was, playing in the woods. And these two Rottweilers came out from nowhere and attacked her. They killed her.' Mum raises a hand in Dad's direction. 'The news keeps going on about how Rukhsana Khan was thrown around like a rag doll – well, this Scottish girl, she was ripped to pieces. Listen to this, Neil…' her hand settles on the inside of his elbow and it twitches. 'The police found her voice box lying ten feet away from the rest of her.'

58

Dad stares at the road ahead. He opens a window and wind whooshes into the car, making a thwapthwap noise as it goes through the gap. Mum reaches for the Polos and goes quiet. I think about the Scottish girl. I imagine bits of body – hands and legs, the torso – and splatters of blood in the grass. Bits of bone and gristle and hair. But when it comes to the voice box, I'm stumped. What does a voice box look like? My mind shows me a little square music box, slivers of gore stuck to its shiny surface. I see it opening slowly on a mechanical hinge. But I don't hear musical notes tinkling out – just a small, shocked scream.

Hyde Park is full of people. Some carry banners or placards on sticks with slogans in marker pen or paint. 'DEED NOT BREED'. 'PIT BULL = SCAPEGOAT'. 'NO TO DOG GENOCIDE!' Some people have their pit bulls with them, strapped in to thick leather harnesses.

Mum and Dad are talking to a friend of theirs, Kimberly, who, like Mum, does paintings of pit bulls, but, unlike Mum, puts hers in nice frames and sells them fifty pound a pop. Kimberly is tall with wild red hair and she speaks like the people off *EastEnders* – *Nah, Neil, Ah spoke to tha' bloke in 'Ackney an' 'e tol' me all abah it.* She's nice, and she always brings presents when she visits us in Cardiff, but right now she's talking about 'legislayshun'. Me and Veronica stand around, bored and fidgetty. I wish Kimberly had brought John, her son, who once showed me his willy and let me poke it.

Soon a photographer from the *Mirror* comes over. He's gathering together a group of children for a photo. He's already got six. The girls look older than me and they're dressed nice – checked shirts, denim hot-pants, clean Reeboks.

I'm wearing bobbled cycling shorts and a T-shirt with a T-Rex on it. I have corned beef thighs.

The photographer squats down to mine and Veronica's level, hands on his knees. 'Can I have you two for my photo?'

Me and Veronica look at each other. Then we look at Mum. 'No,' we say.

'Oh, come on,' the photographer says. 'You'll be in the papers. You can show your friends at school.'

I look at my crap trainers. I can feel my face burning. Mum puts her hand on my shoulder and pushes me toward the group of kids. She does the same to Veronica. 'Pretend you're Madonna – strike a pose.' The photographer starts arranging us. He gives me and Veronica placards to hold. Mine says ££ CONSPIRACY ££, Veronica's says, DONT KILL OUR FAMLY. I hold mine so it's blocking the T-Rex. The boy next to me has his shoulder pressed against mine and I'm scared to move.

'Say cheese.'

We say cheese. The flash goes off.

In the distance I see a white pit bull squat down on its haunches and coil out a steaming shit.

That's gonna get stepped on.

The last time our dogs got into a fight was a year ago. A creeping Jehovah-dodging Sunday morning. Me and Veronica were watching *Labyrinth* for the millionth time. Slug and Tugger were downstairs in the room with us. Rutger was upstairs with Mum and Dad.

One minute, the Goblin King was dancing around with his goblins, his willy all obvious in his leggings, the next, Slug and Tugger were attacking each other in a vicious blur, spit and blood flying out, growls and snarls bubbling out of the mess.

Veronica jumped on the sofa and started screaming. I ran out to the hall and shouted up the stairs: '*Muum! Daad! Dogs are fighting!*' I went into the cabinet under the stairs and got the break stick then back into the living room. Slug had her jaws locked around the scruff of Tugger's neck and Tugger had her teeth deep in Slug's cheek. Veronica's screaming had got louder.

Mum and Dad thundered down the stairs and burst into the

room. Mum in her huge faded nightie, bleary-eyed, her curly hair a pile of rusty springs, Dad, still half asleep in just a white T-shirt, his bits hanging out like giblets.

I pointed. 'Dad! I can see yer willy!'

Dad looked down, made a small noise – 'huh' – and quickly cupped himself with his hands. He looked around the room, saw a pair of jeans hanging off the radiator and slipped into them, flashing his big white hairy bum cheeks. I passed Mum the break stick. She told Veronica to shut the hell up for Chrissake.

Mum grabbed hold of Slug's collar and Dad grabbed hold of Tugger's. Mum jammed the break stick between Tugger's teeth and prised her jaw open. Both collars were yanked. Tugger came away from Slug. Dad thumped Slug's face with his fist and soon she let go of Tugger. Dad pulled Tugger into the kitchen and closed the door.

Mum breathed out all raggedy. She grabbed Slug's face and checked the wounds. There were cuts on her muzzle, neck and cheek. One of her ears had a small chunk missing at the edge. The blood was a dark sexy scarlet against Slug's black fur. She sat there panting. There was blood in her spit, on her tongue. Mum stroked her head. 'Silly pair of bitches,' she muttered. 'What was it this time?'

'They just went for each other,' I said.

'You weren't giving them food, were you? Making them jealous?'

'No. They just went for each other. Din they, Vron?'

Veronica, still standing on the sofa, nodded miserably.

Dad opened the door a crack. 'She's all right. Er, couple of cuts, nothin' serious.'

'Good,' said Mum, 'Let's just keep them separate for the day. Rutger can stay upstairs.' She looked at her watch. Sighed. 'Sod it, Neil. Let's not go to the meeting today, my nerves are shot.'

Dad closed the door, leaving a bloody smudge on the white paint.

61

A journalist from the *South Wales Echo* came to our house. He wants to speak to Mum, who's been going round Cardiff with a petition. She's got loads of signatures, mostly belonging to friends and shop owners. Derek the local butcher is the only person who refused to sign it, and Mum is pissed off about this, because usually he goes on about what gorgeous dogs Rutger and Slug are, and gives them bits of pork scratching while Mum buys her barbecue ribs and tandoori chicken for the week, so why's he being such a chickenshit about a poxy signature?

'We want to show both sides,' says the journalist, sitting at our kitchen table stroking the cat. 'You'll be the voice of those who are pro-pit bull. Obviously.'

Mum finishes making his cup of coffee and passes it over. 'Don't you think everyone's heard enough from the other side?'

The journalist smiles awkwardly then sips his coffee.

'I hear you're going to speak to Linda Frost after me?' says Mum.

'Yes. You sold them a puppy a few years ago? I'd like to get her input too.'

'Gave. Not sold. We *gave* her a puppy worth two hundred pounds and her scummy son has raised her to go for people.'

'Scummy?' says the journalist. 'You want me to quote you on that?'

Mum picks a Jammy Dodger out of the biscuit tin. 'I don't give a gerbil's squeaky fart. He's a burglar and a shithead and he's ruined a good dog. If that makes him scummy, then yes, he's scummy. The lowest of the low.' She holds out the biscuit tin for him. 'I'd avoid the Rich Teas. They're stale.'

In the car on the way home from the vets in Swansea… Slug and Rutger are draped across my and Veronica's laps in the back seat, knocked out from the sedative. Slug is making a noise like a duck quacking in her sleep.

We couldn't afford to get Tugger done. Tattooing – thirty pound a dog. Registration – thirty pound. Insurance – forty. Microchip – fifteen. Neutering – thirty. Muzzles – twenty. Each dog. Dad wouldn't ask Nana for the money because she's only just bought us a new car and booked us a holiday to Disneyworld in Florida. It's illegal to sell or give away pit bulls now, and at six, Tugger was the oldest. It didn't help that last week Rutger did sex to her in the kitchen, his very own mother, and she was pregnant with psycho-incest puppies we couldn't keep or sell. She had to be put down.

'Why didn't they do them in pink or blue or something?' says Veronica.

'They're boring as anything,' I say.

Rutger has JW11007 on the inside of his thigh in crappy scrawly black ink. Slug has JW11008.

'You know what they look like?' says Mum. 'Like the tattoos Jews in concentration camps had. You'll learn about that when you go to High School, Christina.'

Mum's quiet for a bit. Then she turns around in her seat and looks at us. 'You know what, girls? People are stupid. Cruel and stupid.' She fixes her blue eyes on me, then Veronica. 'Try not to be cruel and stupid, OK?'

We nod. Mum turns back and grabs the Polos. I play with Slug's ear and look out the window at the multi-green blur of countryside. Sheep and cows sprinkle the long fields. Kate Bush sings about a man who has a child trapped inside his eyes for some reason I don't understand.

It's weird that Mum is picking up the dog poo. That's my job normally, my burden. I wear these old red leather gloves and use a small shovel to flick the bluebottle covered turds into a carrier bag. There are fewer poos now that Tugger is gone, but the job is still disgusting. Especially after rain. If Mum wants to take over for a while, that's great. I watch her slowly bending down over her stomach rolls to flick the shit neatly into the bag. She's got good technique. Quick wrists.

Night. Mum sends us to Pauline the Mormon's for a couple of hours. We take our shoes off at the door and watch TV with her three kids in the living room. Pauline is a nice lady but her obsession with house cleaning is nuts. She is married to Gregg, the window cleaner, who Dad reckons is a massive alcoholic, but not as bad as Suki Fisk because he is a 'functional alcoholic' who hides it well, and Dad only knows about it because he's done some window cleaning with Gregg and seen him sipping rum at the top of the ladder.

Mum and Dad pick us up at ten. I don't know where they've been or why they needed babysitters for us, but they have laughter in their eyes.

'They've been having sex,' whispers Veronica as we walk back up to our house.

'No they haven't,' I whisper back.

Mum and Dad don't have sex. I've never even seen them kiss or hold hands.

As we walk past the Frost's house I smell shit in the air. Up ahead, Mum and Dad start giggling. It's too dark to see anything because Linda Frost's scummy son is forever shooting the streetlamp outside his house with a BB gun. But my nose and brain work together and come up with a theory.

'They've put all our dog shit on the Frosts' front lawn,' I tell Veronica.

'They wouldn't.'

'They did. Bet you fifty pee.'

We pass the butchers on the way to school next morning. Me and Veronica stop and stare at the window front. Other kids are pinching their noses. 'Who would do something like this?' says Sheila, one of the mums.

'I heard he was a kiddie fiddler,' says another mum, lighting a fag. 'Maybe it's cuz of that. Get away from the road, Katie! Mind you, I bought a chicken breast from him a few months ago and it was on the turn. Had to chuck it in the bin.'

'What's a kiddie fiddler?' I ask Veronica.

She shrugs.

I point at a neat, beige-coloured log perched on the doorstep. 'That's Slug's. Bet you fifty pee.'

The Fat Bitch and
her Prostitute Daughter

Me and Jessica Fisk were walking up our street towards her house. It was a long, long Saturday. The clouds were grey. I could smell bonfire in the air.

Jessica Fisk was my best friend. We'd started playing together at the age of ten and now, at twelve, we were inseparable. We spent every minute of the day with each other, and even the night couldn't tear us apart – we slept over at each other's houses half the week, lying top and tail in our hand-me-down nighties, examining *More* magazine's Position of the Fortnight while listening to her older sister's rave mixtapes.

I didn't hang around with Veronica now. She was a moody, sulky mess and she ignored me at school. At home we argued over what music to play (we shared a ghetto blaster) and poster space on our wall and one day we had a physical fight because my Gary Barlow was touching the edge of her Dieter Brummer. She scrammed my face (she was a scrammer) so I punched her hard in the tit. After that I moved into the spare bedroom, and about time too.

Mum didn't like that I was spending so much time at Stonehouse Suki's house because she was afraid Suki would get too pissed one night and burn the house down, but me and Jessica would always find a way to talk her round. 'It's not like she could leave the gas on or anything, they have an electric cooker,' I would lie. 'Yeah, and my dad always keeps an eye on her,' Jessica would add, also lying. Charles Fisk spent his time watching war films while eating plateful after plateful of tinned pilchards on toast and smoking cheap cigars. He was almost as fat as Mum and he had tufts of bright red hair sticking up out of his angry head and a bushy brown beard that always had food in it. Mum looked down on him because he was fat *and* lazy, whereas she had simply suffered the misfortune of having a mother who raised her on chips and used cakes to comfort her at times of stress. Charles didn't keep an eye on Suki. He either ignored her or argued with her or had sex with her. Or all of these things, in that order.

'OK, but come straight home if she gets totally rat-arsed,' Mum would say, adding, 'no offence, Jessica,' and me and Jessica would high five and run off to grab my toothbrush and nightie.

Jessica was tall and skinny with mottled ostrich legs, a waist so tiny it looked abnormal and a long, bird-like face dotted here and there with succulent whiteheads. Her lips were plump, pale and forever chapped, and with her emaciated cheeks, she looked like she was sucking on a never-ending sherbet drop. She wore her carrot-red hair in a ponytail at all times. It was strawberry blonde, she told me, not ginger.

'I wonder if we'll be able to buy alcohol,' I said.

'Well, it says they sell cocktails on the tickets but they're probably non-alcoholic.'

We were talking about the upcoming Radio One Roadshow. It was being held in Astoria Nightclub, an actual nightclub, and Love City Groove and Michelle Gayle were going to be playing.

'I really *reeally* hope Michael McCrae comes,' I said, picking a leaf off a privet hedge and folding it.

'Ew, you're so desperate,' she said.

'No, I'm not,' I lied. I picked another leaf off the hedge, folded it, picked another. A habit. I liked the crispy crunchiness of the leaves snapping into halves.

An old-ish man appeared from over the top of the hedge. White hair, square glasses, pink, square face. 'Don't you pick my bloody leaves!'

We stopped. 'What?'

'You heard! Keep your bloody hands off my hedge. And it's pardon, not "What."'

I gaped up at his blotchy face. I didn't know his name. I just knew that he had a quiet, clean wife and they never smiled. 'It's only a leaf,' I said.

'I don't give a damn what it is.' He raised a stubby finger in the air. 'Just keep your bloody hands off, you little hussy.'

I looked at Jessica who was staring at him, her lip curled. I did the same look. 'Don't call me that, you *bast*ard.'

I walked off spitting out air.

Suki was sat at the kitchen table sprinkling messy curls of Golden Virginia into a Rizla, full of lipless concentration. A can of Strongbow instead of the usual Stonehouse at her elbow – must have been Dole Day. She had on a maroon woollen jumper. Her drippy blonde hair was clipped up and she wore an Indian scarf around her neck.

'You're not getting stoned already, are you?' said Jessica.

Suki did a pissed off blink and rumpled her lips. 'It's a rollie.'

Jessica opened the fridge, pulled out a jar of gherkins, and unscrewed the lid. She nodded her head at the can on the table.

'It's an empty from last night,' said Suki, meeting her eye all defiant.

Jessica said nothing. She pulled out a gherkin and munched the end off. I watched, jealously. I didn't like gherkins, but I really wanted to. I felt like there was something cool about liking gherkins because of that bit in *The Witches of Eastwick* where Susan Sarandon eats them in the supermarket without wearing a bra and that old bitch calls her a slut.

'I'm gonna need that money from Gran soon,' said Jessica.

Suki nodded. Licked her Rizla, sealed it.

'You've still got it, yeah?'

Suki nodded.

'You better,' said Jessica. 'If you've spent it on booze I'm gonna go fucking apeshit.'

'I haven't spent it,' said Suki, lighting her fag. 'Why don't you go over Christina's or something, Jess?'

Jessica screwed the lid back on the gherkin jar and returned it to the fridge. 'Let's go up to my room,' she said, walking off. I waited till she was out of listening range.

'Suki?'

'What, Cris?'

'What's a hussy?'

'A prostitute.'

My mouth went into an O. 'I'm not a prostitute!'

'I should think not, Cris.'

I walked out, spitting air again. I turned back to nod a goodbye to Suki just as she lifted the can of Strongbow off the table, smoke whispering out of her mouth.

Jessica's older sister, Sheena, came by. She was eighteen and gorgeous. She had ash-blonde hair which she'd got from her mum and very white perfect skin, which Jessica was jealous of. She had lovely shapely eyebrows which both me and Jessica were jealous of. She was a raver. She went out on the weekends wearing glow-in-the-dark bracelets and dancing to the Prodigy, and the next day she'd sit around on a come down listening to Portishead. I didn't know what a come down was, but I pretended to Jessica that I did, nodding with pouty lips all knowing and worldy-cool. Admitting to Jessica you didn't know what things meant was a mistake. It meant you were a spazzmatron and the whole school should know it.

Sheena came up to Jessica's room chewing chewing chewing on nothing, with big circle eyes. She hugged Jessica and then started going through her drawers.

'How's it goin'?' said Jessica. She always dropped her gs when talking to her big sister.

Sheena pulled a small white blouse out of the drawer. 'Ah, mate, things are kicking off at the mo. Mad shit.' She pulled off her own top. I quickly looked away, but not before seeing a flash of red bra strap. I felt weird. I looked down at my knee.

'Why, what's goin' on, Sheen?'

'Ah, don't worry about it, babe. Just the usual. Sound as a pound, me.' I sneaked a glance up and she was squirming her way into the white blouse. White white belly, flat and smooth as a Milkybar. She pulled the blouse down and took a fag out of her pocket and lit it, tilting her head.

Suki came into the room, can in hand. 'Sheena love, get your father to give you the money.'

'Fuck that, Mum.'

'Money for what?' said Jessica.

'None of your business,' said Suki.

'You're in my fucking room so it *is* my business.'

Suki glared at her. 'You're in *my* fucking house.' She took a grim swig of her cider and closed her eyes. 'Money for the taxi.'

'I'll just walk, Mum, it's OK,' said Sheena, chewing on smoke.

'Who's looking after him now?' said Suki.

'Looking after who?' said Jessica.

Sheena sucked on her fag and breathed out the smoke then sucked on it again. 'His mates are with him. He's fine.'

'Who's fine?' said Jessica.

'Mo,' said Suki.

Mo was Sheena's boyfriend. He had floppy black hair with ovaltine skin and beautiful Arab eyes. All these attractive grown-ups – and here I was with zero tits and a zitty best friend, who didn't even have pubes yet, because I'd seen a flash of white bald fanny behind her swishing bath towel last month, even though she'd sworn on Mark Owen's life she had pubes, *loads* of pubes. I wanted to be beautiful and worldly and red-bra wearing, like Sheena, with a handsome boyfriend and women friends who had pubes and nice eyebrows and spindly red bras of their own.

70

'He's put his bloody fist through a window,' said Suki.

'Why?'

'He was on bloody ketamine.'

'Tell the fucking world, Mum,' said Sheena.

She meant me. I sat and tried to look like I didn't exist, and even if I did, my ears did not. I hated being stuck in Jessica's family dramas, because no one wanted me there, but no one was cruel enough to say it. Like the time Sheena had taken an overdose and I was in the house when it all came out, and I just sat there trapped between all the tense silences, feeling like Baby in *Dirty Dancing* when Penny's bad abortion was being cleaned up, but less nosy.

'Is he OK?' said Jessica.

'He's fine,' said Sheena. 'Just stitches. The fucking dickhead.'

Sheena left the room, followed by Jessica.

'Suki?' I said.

'What, Cris?'

'What's ketamine?'

'It's horse tranquiliser.'

'*Horse* tranquiliser? Why would someone take *horse* tranquiliser?'

She shrugged. 'Fuck knows, Cris.'

'Does Jess know what it is?'

'I very much doubt it.'

I got up, went over to Suki, took her can, had a swig, burped and gave it back.

'Cheeky cow.'

I walked out the room. 'No, Suki. I am a cheeky *hussy*.'

There was Linda Frost at number eleven. The fag-stained Jeanette Krankie with the Judy-ruining thug-son. When I was five, Linda had walked into my classroom and shouted at me in front of the whole class for calling her daughter Emma a Stupid Face, because her head tilted to the side when she talked, like a broken jack-in-the-box, and her face was sort of flat as if someone had slammed a frying pan into it. And Emma had deserved it because she had two stupid faces; one of them had told the school my mum was a Big Fatty Jehovah and the other had told me I was her bestest friend. Linda Frost had stormed into the classroom like it was normal for parents to storm into classrooms and shouted her awful Krankie head off, turning the crayon picture in front of me into a watery blur while Mrs Jobbins stood all awkward, not knowing what to do with the gate-crashing Krankie and the crying blonde girl. Mum was so angry she chased Linda Frost all the way up Maerdy Road, her pit bulls straining their leads up front, shouting, 'You try shouting at *me*, you bloody bully!'

Then there was Mr Morgan who lived three doors down from us. He was an old guy with a head like a box, a grey buzzcut, no neck, and big Minotaur body. He was miserable because his son had died in some mysterious way a few years back. But that was no excuse for being spiteful to all the kids in the street. He shouted at me once for standing too close to his big ugly van. Said he'd knock my teeth down my throat. I was six. Mum had him later on his doorstep – said, 'Oh, you big strong man,' while poking his chest with a sharp-nailed finger and channelling anger through her 11. I didn't tell her I'd already dealt with it myself – scratched his van with my front door key, scratched it *loads*.

Next door to Mr Morgan was nasty old Tallulah May, who looked like she sucked on tiny pickled onions all day and lived with an old black man who wore a porkpie hat and looked like the guy who sings Zip-a-Dee-Doo-Dah from *Song of the South*. Tallulah May had called me and Veronica 'Jehovah's Knickers' in a poisonous voice. She hated that we were Jojos, which was crazy because her own daughters were Babette and Bernice, who were both die-hard Jojos. After 'Jehovah's Knickers', Mum went apeshit. She told me and Veronica to pinch our noses and say 'Pooey, whats that disgusting smell?' whenever we saw Tallulah May in the street. And that night, Mum had a screaming match with her in the pouring rain, both of them standing under massive umbrellas in their front gardens. Mum started throwing empty dog food tins out of a spilled binbag, so Tallulah May ran indoors and gave it two fingers from her front room window.

And the next day, Mum grabbed her pit bulls and chased Tallulah May up Maerdy Road, shouting, 'I'll fucking have you, Tallulah May!'

She didn't speak a word to Catherine Jones' daughters after that. Ever.

Mum ratt-a-tatt-tatted the lionhead knocker. The door opened. There he was – square glasses, square face. Brown cardigan.

'Yes?'

Suki stood at her front door from across the road, can in hand. Me and Jessica watched from behind the privet fence. I picked a leaf, folded it.

'So you like to pick on young girls?' said Mum, fists on her hips.

Understanding pink-blotched the man's face. 'She had no right touching my property.'

'Your property? It was a leaf.'

'It doesn't matter. It was my prop—'

'You petty arsehole.'

He flinched. Mum stuck her finger into the centre of his chest and jabbed him as she spoke, one jab per word. 'Big – strong – man – are – you?' Her old favourite. 'Having a go at a twelve-year-old girl? Make you feel big, huh? "Hussy"? She's twelve! You should be ashamed of yourself.'

'You tell him, Ca!' shouted Suki.

The man glanced at Suki like she was a mongrel bitch rubbing its fanny on the carpet. He started to close his door. Mum wedged it with a shiny Dr Marten. 'Yeah, you run away, you fucking hero!'

'Move your foot or I'll phone the police.'

Mum moved her foot. 'Go ahead. I'll have you done for harassment.'

He closed the door. Mum fired off a 'pathetic' into the shrinking gap.

Suki leaned out of her front door. 'He's a miserable *bastid*.' She leaned out further and waved two fingers at her neighbour's house. 'Smacks his wife round, Ca.' He's a *bastid*.'

'Get in the fucking house, Mum!' shouted Jessica.

Mum raised her hands in the air like a preacher in pain. 'This street! Paradise, my arse!'

When we got home, Mum cleared her paintings off the kitchen table, sat down and wrote a letter to the miserable square-faced bastid. It took her over an hour. A few times she made a mistake and had to crumple up the paper and start again. Finally she finished it and read it over, lips stern. She folded it, slipped it inside an envelope and handed it to me.

'Put it through his letterbox,' she said.

I nodded. Me and Jessica made our way to the front door.

'Hang on,' I said.

I ran up to my room and grabbed a marker pen. I came back down and drew a huge swastika on the front of the envelope. 'Cuz he's like Hitler,' I told Jessica, and she did a teeth-sucking nod.

We left the house and walked down the road. It was night now. The streetlight outside Linda Frost's house crackled on and off; the others glowed amber under the sleek powerlines.

'I wish we knew what she'd written,' said Jessica, glancing at the Nazi envelope.

'I bet she really bollocks him,' I said. 'I bet he'll need loads of horse tranquiliser after she's through with him.'

'Horse tranquiliser? Why the fuck would he need horse tranquiliser, you mong?'

I looked at her out the side of my eyes. 'Same reason Mo needed it, I guess. Ya know, ketamine.'

She went quiet for a bit, thinking, then she did an O-mouth

and slapped my arm. '*Horse* tranquiliser! I thought you said *whore's* tranquiliser. God, you talk like such a spaz sometimes, Cris.'

I snorted through my nose. Like a horse. 'Whatever, Jess.' I had her and she knew it and I knew it. But the whole school would never know it.

We reached the man's house. His curtains were closed. I imagined him sat inside his granny-house in an old brown armchair, talking angrily about the fat bitch and her prostitute daughter from number four to his small, silent mouse-wife. We tiptoed up his garden path and pushed the letter through his pretend-gold letterbox. We heard the thud as it landed and ran out the gate and up the street. We slowed to a walk and headed toward Maerdy Road. Up ahead I saw the dark figure of Suki Fisk fall sideways into a hedge. She stood up and stumbled through a pool of light thrown by a streetlamp. I could still smell bonfires.

Finger-me-sis

When most people looked at Nadeem they saw a scrawny teenage boy with muck all over his clothes. When I looked at him I saw a rippling god-boy. He was thirteen, a year older than me. His mum was white and his dad was Pakistani, but for some reason he looked like Daniel-San from *The Karate Kid*, who was Italian. Nasty old Tallulah May and her Zip-a-Dee-Doo-Dah manfriend had recently moved out of their pink-painted house, and Nadeem's family had moved in. He set my heart and pants on fire.

Here are some things about Nadeem:

He spat a lot. (After a day of football the square of our cul-de-sac would be so peppered with little globs of creamy white spit you wouldn't be able to sit down.)

Whenever he had a cold, instead of blowing his nose with tissue like a normal person, he would press a finger over one nostril and snort out a long stringy pendulum of pale yellow snot.

His bed was shaped like a racing car.

His little sister had a blood-coloured birthmark the size of a Jaffa Cake on her cheek.

His favourite bands were A Tribe Called Quest and Arrested Development.

We became friends, which is to say he bullied me and I let him. I called for him most days and we would play at karate fighting or kick a football around or climb the trees out my back. Because he set my heart and pants on fire, I wanted him to see me as a sexy-hot Lolita but I was a tomboy with miniature tits that could be supported by eggcups. Nadeem fancied Lisa, the flame-haired C-cup in his and my sister's class. I sat in hateful silence playing with my hangnails as he talked about how he was saving his pocket money to buy Lisa something from Bodyshop. Lisa couldn't do thirty keepy-uppies and she couldn't do a wicked roundhouse kick, but she could apply lipstick without looking like a rag doll, and that's what Nadeem was after in a woman.

It was night but we were still out. Me, Nadeem and Jessica. My mum was inside, working on a still-life painting – a peacock feather. Suki was stumbling around Gabalfa, knocking on familiar doors, asking to borrow money for White Lightning. Nadeem's mum and stepdad were watching TV. We could see the tops of their heads through the living room window, the screen-light flickering across their wallpaper. The black cul-de-sac square was lit up by a tall graffiti-covered lamppost, and we stood under the fuzzy glare, hands in pockets.

'Why don't we play Dares?' said Jessica, kicking a stone.

'All righ',' said Nadeem.

'Or Truth or Dare?' I said.

'Nah. Just Dares.'

I shrugged. I'd played Dares with Jessica a couple of years ago. She'd mooned out her bedroom window and I'd eaten chilli powder. Big deal.

Jessica folded her arms across her chest. 'I'll start.' She smiled craftily. 'I dare *you*, Nadeem, to snog Christina' – ominous pause – 'for a full minute.'

It was like winning the lottery on Christmas Day but I pretended it was the most grossest idea I'd ever heard.

'*Jessica!* You're such a slagbag.' Drawn out sigh. 'Well, if I *have* to …'

The kiss wasn't like I'd imagined it – no fanfare for one thing

77

– but it was kind of cool. I was too nervous to run my hands along the back of his neck like they told me in *Just Seventeen*, and Jessica counting one to sixty out loud like a metronome took away some of the passion, but still, it was better than when I'd kissed Anthony Vickers and his entire soggy mouth had closed over the lower part of my face like a surgical mask.

We finished. Wiped our mouths. I finally understood the implications of playing teenage dares with a boy. I dared Jessica to snog Nadeem for *two* minutes. She refused. I called her frigid. She told me to fuck off. I glanced at Nadeem. We moved to the dark corner of my driveway. We were shielded by the back of Dad's car and a couple of jagged rosemary bushes.

'I dare you to show me your tits,' Nadeem said to me.

I did.

'I dare you to grope 'em,' said Jessica to Nadeem.

He did.

It went on. We did some stuff – light stuff. Jessica turned away the whole time. She was our look-out. Every now and then she'd turn back and throw a dare in, followed by a smirk.

'I dare *you*, Nadeem, to finger Christina.'

Nadeem shrugged. 'OK.'

'Whatever,' I said, all casual, like I knew all about fingering. As Nadeem slipped his hand down my pants I tried not to look surprised. I heard Jessica giggling to herself in the dark. I looked at Nadeem's face. A film of gleaming snot like Sellotape on his philtrum.

The next step: 'I dare *you*, Christina, to give Nadeem a blowjob.'

I knew what that was. 'Eurgh, Jessica, you *twat…fucksake.*'

Within half an hour Nadeem and I had tried every single kind of foreplay we could think of. His penis was the colour of an old elastic band. And it was a proper adult penis with hairy balls and everything. I remember hoping nobody could see us. I remember holding on to his hair while he bobbed around down there, gazing

78

out into the square, past Jessica's skinny back, up at the star-soaked sky, and thinking, this is *lush*.

Then Jessica dared us to have sex. The biggie.

Nadeem shook his head. 'Nah. I want my first time to be, like, I dunno,' – he ran a hand through his thick black hair – 'special or something.' I don't think we should.'

He was saving himself for Lisa.

'Yeah,' I agreed. 'Not like this. Not in my front garden with *you*.' My heart and stomach felt all cold and achey.

'Then I dare you both to have *anal* sex.'

Nadeem thought about it. 'Er. Yeah, OK. We could do that.'

'OK. Whatever,' I said.

'We'll need a condom,' said Nadeem.

'I'll go get one,' I said.

I snuck into my house, went up to my room and got the silver Durex foil that had been hidden in my knicker drawer the past year. I tiptoed down the stairs. I could hear Dad listening to Frank Zappa in the front room. It was his bedroom now. Him and Mum had wanted their own beds. He'd started smoking again now that Jehovah wasn't around, and he had a drawer full of muddy mushrooms and herby stuff and he'd grown a goatee and clipped it all neat and fancy like George Michael.

Nadeem and Jessica were standing in the shadows talking in quiet voices. Jessica had one hand in the pocket of her denim waistcoat; the other hand twisting her ginger ponytail. I handed Nadeem the Durex.

He held it up to his face between thumb and first two fingers. Frowned. 'It's open.'

I nodded. Me and Jessica had had some fun blowing it up like a balloon a few months ago. But I'd rolled it up and put it back in the packet. Good as new. 'Duzn't matter, duz it?'

He lifted the side of his bumfluffy lip. 'Course it duz. It's probably gone off.'

I shrugged. 'All right then. Well, never mind.'

We stood there a bit longer. Silence. It was getting cold. Nadeem put his hands under his armpits and hunched his shoulders. I caught him looking at me. His eyes weren't as mean as usual. I smiled. He looked away.

'Fuck,' said Jessica, looking at her watch. 'It's gone nine.'

'I best go home,' said Nadeem. He slapped Jessica on the shoulder. 'Later, Jess.' He nodded his head in my direction, walked away. Hands in pockets, head down. He turned into his own driveway.

'So. Tell me about it, stud.' Jessica smiled up at me, shadows under her sharp cheekbones.

I told her all the details in a rushed flurry of words and half-words. Size, smells, flavours.

She listened, threw in an 'eurgh' or a 'gross' every now and then.

We concluded that it'd been a very interesting night. Then she went home.

I ran in the house and looked up 'anal' in the dictionary.

Gross.

'Thank *God*,' I whispered, hand fluttering to my heart.

That night I lay up for hours thinking about Nadeem. That look he gave me. Almost kind. As if he liked me. Finally, he's mine, I thought. Surely we would become girlfriend and boyfriend now. He'd stop being mean and we'd fall in love. We would hold hands on the way to school, share every Twix, every packet of crisps, and we'd have nicely lit adult sex like they do in the films, orgasming at the same time, in slow motion.

The next day Nadeem did a roundhouse kick to my head and threw me on the floor. Everything was the same.

A month later, Nadeem's front garden, twilight. I sat cross-legged on the dirty cement, my back to the gate, watching Nadeem eat a Pot Noodle. Spicy Curry. Nadeem didn't empty the sachet of spicy sauce into the pot and this shocked me. A Pot Noodle without the sauce? Why would somebody do that? And there was too much water in the pot so it was half noodle, half soup. Also he had a cold, and between slurpy mouthfuls he would press his finger against his nose and shoot out snot bullets which would land on the concrete floor with a splat and lie there quivering like mercury. I told myself the boy was gross, really flipping gross, and then I'd go back to admiring his nice strong legs.

He finished his Pot Noodle, stuffed the empty carton into the privet hedge that lined his front garden, and started on his favourite subject – funny things that the popular people in his class had said that day. He liked to pretend that he was in with the popular crowd though really he was almost as crap as me.

'So Miss Didd's got her back turned, righ'? And James, he goes up to her, yeah, and he goes – he does this thing, yeah, with his arms – he goes—' Here Nadeem stopped, froze. Puzzley-surprise seeped into his brown eyes. He twisted his head around and looked down at his baggy-jean covered arse. He jammed his hand down the back of his boxers, rummaged a while. The hand came out seconds later, grasping, almost delicately, between thumb and forefinger, a nugget of shit the size of a grape. Nadeem lazily flicked the shit onto his driveway then rubbed his fingers on his jeans.

'Anyway. So James is behind her and he goes—'

'Oh my God,' I said.

'What?'

'What ju mean, "what?"? I can't believe you just did that.'

'So? Who gives a fuck?'

'Nadeem, that's gross. It's just – it's fuckin' *weird* is what it is.'

I'd pushed the right button with 'weird'. He suddenly looked ashamed. But not for long. Shame turned into ember-eyed anger.

'So fuckin' what?'

He stamped his foot on the ground and lunged forward as if to go for me, pulling back at the last moment.

I flinched. 'Fuck *off*, Nadeem!'

'No, you fuck off, bitch!'

81

He spat on the ground a few inches from me and stormed into his house. I was left there feeling small and humiliated as if I'd been the one playing with my own shit.

That was it. Nadeem was the biggest wanker ever. He was a bully and a coward. He hit me because I was a girl and then he crept around the boys in school like some slimy, hunchbacked sycophant. He would probably be a wife beater when he grew up, I decided, and then one day his wife would reach breaking point and she'd stab him in the eye with a potato fork.

But really, his gravest sin was not falling madly, suicidally in love with me.

In school the next day I told Jessica all about it, knowing that she wouldn't be able to keep her mouth shut. She told some of the popular girls.

'What a twat,' said Christine Scott, sucking on her Lambert and Butler.

'Fuckin' gross,' said Soraya Hall, frowning out from under her huge perm.

And soon he had a new name. Shit Flicker. Hello, nickname. I had done my part. Now I could sit back and watch Nadeem get chewed up, swallowed and shat out by our disgusting monster of a school.

The next day I was walking down the corridor on the way to French. I passed a bunch of boys from my year. They were huddled together, laughing and pointing at me.

'All righ', Fingermesis?' said Danny Dolbear, who sort of looked like that little boy from the Yellow Pages advert who has to stand on the book to kiss the girl.

'Wha's 'appening, Fingermesis?' said Nick McCowan, who would be a jock if this was America.

I ignored them and went on my way. But it kept coming at me, this word, Fingermesis. Every other person I passed said it, laughing.

I saw Jessica's thick red ponytail in the distance. I caught up with her. She saw me and her face twisted with concern. She pulled me toward the wall and whispered, blissfully, 'Christina, Nadeem has gone round the whole school saying you finger your sister.'

'WHAT?'

'I know, I know, it's pure skank. It's cuz of Shit Flicker.'

I felt like I was going to faint. 'Jess, this is *aw*ful.'

'Don't worry. Everyone'll forget about it in five minutes, swear.'

They didn't. Everyone forgot about Shit Flicker. Nobody forgot about Finger-me-sis. Nadeem had been very clever. In High School a rumour about fingering always makes it. There was Sophy Garrow who got fingered by her boyfriend, Leon, except he accidentally put it up her bum and then told everyone about it. And Susannah Stoke. Gregg Champion fingered her at a party, and when he pulled his finger out it was covered in this smegma stuff which was probably down to her having eczema inside her fanny. And then he told everyone about it. And now there was Christina Jones who fingered her sister on a daily basis. It was beautiful.

My previous nickname had been Pissy Jones. That had been bad, because it wasn't a fun nickname made up by friends, it was a mean nickname made up by boys who didn't like me. But there was no dirty back story behind Pissy Jones.

I wasn't alone in this. Veronica was the other half of Finger-me-sis. The fingered. Though I got the brunt of the name calling, she was more deeply affected by it because teenage hormones had crazied her up. She was depressed and she'd started smoking and drinking and taking drugs. One morning around this time, Veronica came into school after sniffing a gram of 'whizz' she got off her friend. In maths class she threw a chair at a boy because he was teasing her, and then she stabbed the boy sat next to her with her compass, and he was just an innocent bystander. She spent the afternoon locked in the toilet, cutting herself. Veronica had been bullied and picked on all through high school. There was being a Jojo at the start. Then belonging to a poor family, which was stupid because everyone in our school belonged to a poor family, it's just they were in self-hating denial about it and threw themselves like starving jackals at anyone wearing Dunlops instead of Nike Airs. Then of course, Veronica was a bit weird and had grown massive tits before everyone else. And she hated those massive tits, wanted them chopped off. Every day the boys snapped her bra in the corridors and she screamed at them with fuckloads of crazy zapping out of her bulgy-blue eyes like a mental patient flapping around in an arse-less hospital gown, and they laughed and circled and it went on and on. Now she was an incestuous lezbo. So she snapped for real.

And now she was Chuck-a-mental as well as Finger-me-sis.

I wanted everybody who called me Finger-me-sis to die slowly, crying for their mothers, because they spoke the word with a mad joy in their eyes. But mostly I wanted to gut-stab Nadeem, slowly, with a cool, casual smile. Then cut off his stupid hairy man-balls and drop-kick them onto his roof with the mouldy tennis ball and the streaks of bird shit. I wanted to tell the school that I saw him cry once because his stepfather had grounded him. Or that, for all the 'fuck da law, smoke da draw' type slogans written on his pencil case in Tippex, when I stole that herby bud from my dad's drawer and brought it to him so that we could try it out, he got scared and pretended he could hear his mum calling him home.

But I couldn't do this because I knew Nadeem would find some way to hurt me. He might kick me a few times with his nice strong legs, or I might come into school to find that my name had changed from Finger-me-sis to Suck-off-me-dog.

Halloween. Me and Jessica walked up Maerdy Road. The moon, not quite full, shone silver-white in the blue-black sky. We were witches, the cheap sort – bin liner, white make-up with eye-liner wrinkles, ninety-nine pence plastic witch hat with scraggly green hair. Jessica held a pumpkin shaped bucket for collecting. I held a six-pack of eggs. Three of them missing. It was my second Halloween after quitting the Jojos and I was loving it.

There was someone running toward us.

'I think it's Nadeem,' said Jessica, squinting into the far-off, white face powder clinging to the downy hair on her cheekbones.

I pulled an egg out of the box and held it at my side.

The person got closer. Yes – Nadeem. He was wearing jeans, a black polo neck, a Spliffy jacket. He had an evil clown mask pulled back to his hairline. He reached us. Smiling, breathing heavily. I saw him bring his arm back. I saw something smooth and round in his hand. He whipped an egg at Jessica's chest. It cracked and splattered over her small humps.

Jessica looked down, mouth open, unbelieving. 'Nadeem, you fucking knob!'

Nadeem laughed and hopped around, waving the Vs at Jessica.

'Oh my God, you fucking dick! I swear!'

My first thought – It wasn't me. He didn't egg me. Maybe he *does* like me. I looked at him. I could feel the old love come back. So handsome. And he didn't egg me. Maybe he *does* like me? So handsome …

And then I swallowed it back down.

Don't be a stupid cow, Finger-me-sis. That's the devil, that is.

Nadeem turned round, pulled his jeans down to show his grey boxers, and wiggled his arse. 'Flick my shit, bitches.' He jogged away, shoulders laughing.

I aimed and threw my egg.

Everyone Loves Mayonnaise

I don't know what it was about Bianca that made two girls want to fight over her. She wasn't popular or hard or nice. Everything she said was followed by a high-pitched giggle that sounded like a child doing machine gun fire. She was half-black and half-white with massive tits and thick black wavy hair that she coated in coconut oil. Her tone was one of questioning, bemused stupidity. Sometimes she smelled like period. She'd uncross her legs and it would waft up your nose, musk and coppers and prawns and shame.

The first time I spoke to her properly we were in the annex that housed the headmaster's office, the nurse's office, and one of the science labs. In the middle of this enclosure were these two poles that ran from floor to ceiling, like you'd find in a strip bar. They'd recently been covered in gloopy blue paint to cover up all the graffiti. Waste of time: 'MR WILTSHIRE LIX MISS CARTERS HAIRY CANARY' was scrawled down one pole in thick black marker. Paint fumes still tinted the air. I was leaning against one pole and Bianca was swinging off the other, pivoting from the knees. She went round fast, head held back, long oily hair whipping my shoulder.

She stopped. 'Whoa, head rush.' She looked at me, cheek pressed against the pole. 'Who you waitin' for?'

'I got Chemistry.'

'Wiv Mr. Ball?'

'Yeah.'

'He's a wanker, in 'e?'

'Yeah. What 'bou' you?'

'I gotta see the nurse.'

'Why?'

'I dunno yet.'

'What ju mean, you don't *know*?'

She giggled. 'I 'aven't fought of nuffin' yet. I got PE next. So… I dunno. I'm gonna get out of it.'

'You're gonna pretend you're ill?'

She nodded. Her teeth were a bit big for her mouth. They dug into her bottom lip. She had eyes the colour of Marmite, thick eyebrows, clear brown skin. A slight moustache. With her wavy hair she looked more like a Spanish girl than a half-black, half-white girl. She started spinning around the pole again.

I kicked at a hard wad of gum on the floor. 'You could say you got period pains?' I had no idea what period pains felt like and nor did Jessica, but it was something all the other girls were going on about. Me and Jessica were in an unspoken race to start our periods first.

She stopped spinning. 'Nah. I've said that, like, the last two times. Maybe I'll say I've broken my wrist?'

'But yer wrist ain't broke.'

She shrugged. And then she raised up her arm and tapped it against the pole. Looked at me. 'I could break it now, couldn't I?'

I snorted laughter. 'As if.'

'Dare me to?' she said.

'Nuh.'

She raised her brows. 'Well I'm gonna.'

'Go on then.'

She rolled up the sleeve of her black bomber jacket, held out her naked wrist, veiny side up, and clanged it against the pole. She sucked in air.

I stared at her. 'Duz it hurt?'

'Course it duz.'

And she did it again. Harder this time. 'Friggin' 'ell,' she said.

87

'You're not *akshully* gonna break your wrist?'

'I dunno.' A laugh came out like vomit. 'I think so.'

And she went on clashing her wrist against the metal pole. A navy-blue blur of teenage traffic flowed past us. Some gaped with gobs hung open. A boy with a million zits on his chin scowled and muttered something.

Bianca went on clanging. She talked to me between strikes, her sentences punctuated by unsure titters and whistly gasps. I found out her name was Bianca Mayo and that some people called her Bianca Mayonnaise. She was in the same year as me but different sets. She lived in Llandaff North with her dad. Her dad was a total cunt.

The bell for next lesson went. Bianca stopped and twisted her arm up to her face. It was swollen and purple. The knobbly bump sticking out from the wrist was as big as a conker. I poked it. 'Razz.'

The door to the nurse's office opened and Nurse Williams, who looked like a friendly witch, came out, reading a yellow Post-it.

'Bianca Mayo?' she said, smiling.

Bianca glanced at me sidelong and grinned, her lips stretching over her front teeth. 'Yeah, thass me.' She walked up to the nurse, proudly holding out her plum-skinned forearm like it was an offering to the gods.

We'd been best friends for almost four years now, me and Jessica. Sometimes, when she wasn't looking, I would gaze at her cheek and connect the zits to form words.

Words like TWAT.

Jessica was jealous of me because my mum wasn't an alkie, and I had recently grown myself a pair of actual tits that could go in an actual bra.

I was jealous of her because she was funnier than me and she effortlessly got in with all the hard girls whereas I was still as unpopular and crap as ever.

She was mad at me because I'd given her ringworm after my mum took in a stray off the street.

I was mad at her because she'd given me nits. Twice.

I thought she was sly, false and manipulative and that she treated me like shit.

She thought I was a sulky bitch and a wannabe and that I copied her all the time.

In year ten me and Jessica were put in the same form group as Bianca, under Mr Martin, a huge ex-rugby player with ears like chewed up pork chops. Every morning and afternoon before class, we went to room 26 for registration. Mr Martin would do roll-call and then we'd sit around for fifteen minutes whispering about boys and writing on the desks in Tippex, and sometimes sniffing the Tippex and convincing ourselves it got us high, and making sure we left little white bits on our nostrils so people would see how twisted we were.

Bianca had this best friend called Sidney Trebor, only he was off school a lot with anxiety and panic attacks, so Bianca started to sit with me and Jessica during the fifteen minute tutorials.

'Oh, my God,' said Bianca. 'How lush is Shane?

We were huddled around a copy of *Smash Hits*. There was a picture of Boyzone from the set of the 'Love Me For A Reason' video. Wearing white shirts with huge collars and cuffs, standing by a candelabra.

Me and Jessica hated Boyzone. They were so sappy they made us wanna puke. Ronan Keating for some reason reminded me of Meryl Streep and Stephen Gately was a bit too cutesy-wutesy to be taken seriously. And Mikey? He was just shit.

We had loved Take That. But then Robbie had gone, Gary had gotten fat and Howard got those filthy dreadlocks that made you itchy just looking at them. They broke up, but by this point, we didn't give a shit. We were done with boy bands.

Now Bianca had come into our lives with her Boyzone pencil case and her swoony eyes.

'Oh my God – look at Keith's six-pack.'

'Apparently, Shane's got a donkey dick.'

'Isn't Stephen just like a little monkey when he smiles? Aww!'

She was wearing me down.

I looked at the picture. 'I think I like Keith the most.'

Bianca looked at me. 'Really?'

'Yeah. He's got sex eyes. Like, I can imagine him havin' sex just by lookin' at his eyes.'

'Shane's *waay* sexier. Shane's dickalicious. That's my new word.'

Bianca flicked through the magazine. I moved in closer. We looked out for pictures of Boyzone. When we came across them, I analysed Keith's face and clothes, the moody sex in his eyes, and Bianca did the same with Shane. 'Oh my God, how dickalicious is that one?' We imagined their cum-faces and what it would be like to kiss them. Bianca told me she wanted Shane to be her first blowie. I replied that I would like Keith to be my second and we laughed our loud and wise sexed-up laughter while the Somali girls up front argued over Tupac and Mr Martin drank coffee and did his paperwork.

Jessica looked on silently, her eyes twitching.

The next day she decided that Stephen Gately was gaaawjuss and she was going to suck his dick *dry*.

'Less call him Marmaduke,' said Bianca. 'Marmaduke Lynch.'

'Marmaduke Lynch *Duffy*,' I corrected.

'Yeah.' She cupped the cat's face in her hands. 'Ju like your new name? Eh? Ju like your lush new name?' She lifted the cat into her arms and cuddled it to her pillowy breast. 'We should get it some food,' she said.

'No money, duh.'

'Come on – let's go back to that Paki shop we passed earlier.'

She kissed Marmaduke's head and strolled off. I followed, feeling uncomfortable about her use of the 'P word' (I'd stopped saying it ages ago) but thinking that maybe it was OK for her to say it because she was, like, half-black and everything.

Me and Bianca were mitching off school. Jessica was home with a chest infection. We'd tried to visit her during lunch break but her miserable scowling father slammed the door in our faces. So we'd gone walking around Maindy and Cathays, and when lunchtime was over we just kept walking. Near Lo-Cost a small female tortoiseshell had started following us. Now she was ours.

I liked that she was ours and had nothing to do with Jessica.

The old Asian guy at the counter had dead eyes and a grizzly beard. A newspaper was laid out in front of him. At times his eyes would slowly glide up, like lava lamp bubbles up the glass, to the two teenage girls with the squirming cat, but mostly he read his paper.

Bianca passed me Marmaduke and shoved a tin of Sheba and a pink felt cat collar inside her coat. We pretended to look at the Kinder Eggs for a while and then we strode out as if the scuffed shop floor was a catwalk. We reached the street and legged it, Marmaduke jiggling around in my arms. We ran back to Lo-Cost and turned down Fanny Street, our laughter like glass bursting. Bianca ripped the foil lid off the cat food and put it on the pavement.

'That was wicked,' I said, dropping Marmaduke on the floor. 'He wasn't even watchin'.'

'I know,' said Bianca. She fastened the pink collar round Marmaduke's neck. 'It's dead easy. I've done it loads.'

'Really?'

'Yeah.'

I looked at Bianca like she was a goddess.

Marmaduke sniffed the food and walked away.

We walked back to Maindy arm in arm, keeping to the lanes. Gunpowder clouds were forming and the light was dying. We passed piles of binbags ripped open by rats and seagulls in the night, spilling teabags and potato peelings and empty dogfood tins.

'Ya know what we should do when we see Jess next?' said Bianca.

'Wha'?'

'Righ', next time we see her, I'll go like this –' she took a hold of my forearm and squeezed – 'an' then we both count to three in our heads, and on the three, we say, "What's the story, knickerbocker glory?" Like, at the same time.'

'Why?'

'Cuz it'll be funny. We'll pretend it was an accident. Like we're psychic or somefin.'

'But it's stupid.'

'It's like the Oasis album. *What's the Story, Mornin' Glory?*'

I frowned. 'I know that. It's just stupid.'

'So? Jess'll be well freaked out. Remember the signal. I squeeze your arm and we count to three. "What's the story, knickerbocker glory?"'

She tilted her head and smiled at me because we were amazing best friends with a secret.

Two days later, Jessica was well enough for school. I met her at the end of our street. Bianca was there too. We walked up Maerdy Road, talking about the upcoming Eisteddfod. We were going to sing in front of the school. Dress up in platforms and tiny button-down skirts, wear loads of make-up, choreograph some lush dancing. Everyone would, like, die of shock over how amazing we were. But we couldn't decide on what to sing. Originally it had been 'Zombie' by the Cranberries, which I was especially keen on because I thought Dolores O'Riordan was wonderful, even with her lesbian hair. Then Bianca changed her mind. 'Working My Way Back to You, Babe', by Boyzone, which I was against because I didn't think a love of Boyzone was something you wanted to admit publicly.

Now Jessica had a better idea.

'Bjork. 'It's Oh So Quiet'.'

She smiled, her lips pursed.

'Wow, yeah,' said Bianca.

'Cuz you look like Bjork,' said Jessica.

'No she doesn't!' I said. 'Bianca's black. Bjork's Chinese.'

Jessica scowled at me. 'You always have to shit on everything, Cris.'

'Wha'? I'm not shittin' on *any*thin'. I think doin' Bjork is a wicked idea *ak*shully.'

'Oh, how glad we are that you approve, Cris,' said Jessica. 'Now that we have your blessing we can sleep at night again.' She touched Bianca's forearm. '*I* think you look like Bjork. Like a black Bjork.'

'Aw, thanks.'

'And you could wear a little orange dress with pink knickers like in the video. We all could. 'Cept you wouldn't need a wig.'

'Yeah,' said Bianca. She did a little hop step and swung her arm in a circle. '"You fall in love – zin' boom – the sky above – zin' boom – is cavin' in – wow bam!"'

'It's gonna be wicked,' said Jessica.

Bianca bumped up against me. 'Oops, sorry,' she muttered. She glanced at me. Quickly grabbed my forearm and squeezed it. Nodded.

One, two, three …

'What's the story, knickerbocker—'

I stopped. I was on my own. Jessica and Bianca grinned at each other and creased up laughing.

I stood there.

'Gawd, Cris, you're *soo* sad,' said Jessica.

'You'll go along with anyfin'' said Bianca.

I rolled my eyes. 'It was your stupid idea.'

Bianca raised her eyebrows. 'Then why ju go along wiv it then? If it's so stupid?'

I had nothing.

Before Bianca there had been Amanda. Amanda Davis. Mousey-brown bob, greasy face, sharp nose. Amanda was small and mean and she lived in Rhiwbina. She had a boyfriend called Stefan who played Ice Hockey for the junior Cardiff Devils. He was ten. She was thirteen. She had told us once, while we were on the swings down Maindy park, that she 'sucked him off sometimes'. And then she had showed us how big his dick was – fingers and thumb curled into a circle: this thick. Hands spread apart a few inches: this long. Like she was proud.

Me and Jessica secretly thought it was gross that she was giving a ten-year-old blowjobs.

I don't remember how Amanda came into our lives. I just remember that one day it was me and Jessica and the next it was Amanda and Jessica, me trailing behind them in a tight-faced sulk.

One day Jessica was off school with the flu. The sneer suddenly left Amanda's voice and she spent the morning laughing at my jokes. During first break we walked round the schoolyard together, talking about boys and East 17 and obscure sex acts we'd heard of (Rainbow Kiss – a man puts his sperm into a cup and a woman puts her period blood into the same cup, then they mix it all up and drink). Near the bike sheds a fifteen year-old-boy with eyelashes like thatched roofs sold us a cigarette for twenty pence. We took it to the girls' toilets and went into the last cubicle – the smoker's cubicle. There was a used sanitary towel stuck to the wall at face level. It was streaked with brown, lumpy blood.

'Oh my God, thass proper clotty,' said Amanda.

Shoulder to shoulder we looked at the cigarette. It was a Lambert and Butler. Slightly bent where Amanda had clutched it in her nervous fist. Amanda got out some matches that she kept on her so people would think she was dangerous and sexy. She struck one with a shaky hand and lit the cigarette. She took a tiny wasp breath, her lips white and wrinkled around the tan filter. Quickly she blew out a thin bloom of smoke and passed the fag to me.

'Are you sposed to, like, breathe it all the way in?' I asked her.

'Duh! No, moron. Just suck the smoke into your mouth and leave it there for a bit.'

So I did. And I didn't even cough.

'Oi! Ooz smokin' in there?'

Amanda's grey-green eyes grew huge and fixed themselves to mine. It was the fifth-formers.

'Come out and share, bra!'

'There's two ov um. I can see their shoes.'

Wha'? They're lezzin' off, in they?'

'Haha! Fuckin' lezbos!'

Amanda closed her eyes and tensed her brows. I stared at the rust-red smear on the jamrag next to her head.

'Girls! Why you hidin'?'

Amanda leaned in. 'Less wait until they go,' she whispered.

I nodded. Sucked some more smoke into my mouth, blew it out. Amanda angrily snatched the fag out of my hand, her long nails scraping my fingers, and stubbed it out against the wall.

'I bet they're 'avin' a whachucallit – a post-coytal fag. Dirty dykes.'

Their laughter bounced off the grubby walls. Amanda's face was the colour of Philadelphia cheese spread. 'Wha' you 'fraid of, girlies? Come on out, innit?'

The bell for next lesson trilled. We heard a clumsy arpeggio of footsteps and the door to the toilets swing open and bang shut. Silence. The pink came back into Amanda's face. She put the stubbed out fag into her purse and opened the door to the cubicle. We stepped out.

We were not alone.

A tall girl with a black, greasy perm stood smiling. She pointed a finger at us and laughed, her head tilted back, open mouth a kidney.

'You lezbionic twats.'

And she walked out, her platform heels clicking against the cold tiles. Me and Amanda looked at each other miserably.

Later, in History, we laughed about it.

At lunchtime we smoked the rest of the cigarette in smoker's alley.

By home time we felt like we'd survived something big. A coming-of-age drama. It had bonded us.

The next day Jessica came to school and I was back to walking behind the pair of them in a tight-faced sulk.

Bianca wanted to go shopping with a 'five finger discount', which was an amazing term she made up all by herself.

Jessica looked unsure. 'I'll come along but I ain't nickin' nothin'.'

I sidled up to Bianca. 'I will.'

We left school at lunchtime and walked to town. We started off in Bobangles. I got away with a red gingham scrunchie and a Yin and Yang pendant. Bianca managed a silver bracelet. Jessica stuck to her word and took nothing. I showed them my stuff when we were a safe distance from the shop.

'Razz,' said Bianca, running a dirty fingernail over the smooth glass of the pendant. 'I wish I'd seen that.'

'Lush, innit?' I said. My hands were shaking.

'Mmmm. How ju do it?'

'Stuck 'em up my sleeve.'

'Yeah, me too. They got all those mirrors but no one bovvers lookin' at 'em.'

I nodded. 'They're probably just there to try an' stop people doin' it.'

Bianca jabbed me with her elbow. 'Well it din stop us!'

We laughed heartily, the leftover adrenaline giving us extra volume.

Jessica glanced at our jewellery. She was trying to look bored but I could see the jealousy hiding there like a fat person behind a tree. 'I'm gonna nick something from the next shop,' she said.

The next shop was Boots. Bianca grabbed a Forest Fruits

Fruitopia and started drinking it in the shop. Jessica dropped sixty pence worth of perfumed bath balls into her pocket. I managed to stuff fifty pounds of crap up my sleeves. Key rings, a Parker cartridge pen, Exclamation perfume, a Sylvester the Cat fridge magnet.

We left the shop.

Two security guards wrapped their spidery hands around our arms and smiled down at us.

We were taken to the surveillance room. They searched our bags. The tallest security guard told us to empty our pockets and sleeves, a wry smile on his stubbly face. Jessica delicately placed her bath balls onto a table. I released the end of my shirt sleeves and let loose an avalanche of trinketty crap. Bianca had long since finished her Fruitopia and left the empty bottle in the deodorant section. She was allowed home. Me and Jessica sat in the corner of the room as the security guards called the police. We were led to the back of a riot van and sat next to a dreadlocked drug dealer called Macayla-Lee who smelled like boiled eggs.

At the station we were stripped of all jewellery and personal belongings. We were each left in a cell for a couple of hours while our mums were called. We had our fingerprints and mugshots taken. I crossed my eyes when the flash went off, Jessica did mongface. At least that's what we told each other later.

Suki arrived at the station sober and serious. My mum arrived angry. She told me I was having a laugh if I thought I was still going on the school trip to Oakwood next week. Suki doled out the same to Jessica. We left the station and headed for the bus stop.

'Pair of fuckers,' said Suki.

'Criminals,' said my mum. 'Look at them. Criminals.'

Mum and Suki looked at each other and burst out laughing.

Me and Jessica walked ahead.

'I can't believe Bianca only nicked a bottle of Fruitopia,' I said.

'*I* can't believe we were treated the same even though I stole sixty pee's worth of stuff and you stole fifty *quid's* worth.'

I laughed. 'I know.'

'Oi, you two – no laughing,' yelled Mum. 'Pair o' crims.'

I looked up from my drawing.

'I just don' get why they call it a lunchbox.'

Bianca rolled her eyes, exasperated. Jessica smirked.

'What? Is it, like – does it have something to do with blowjobs?'

'It's the size,' said Bianca, staring at me like I was the dumbest animal ever.

I frowned, my eyes on the crumb-dotted carpet. 'What? Shane's knob's the size of a lunchbox?' I thought of the little red lunchbox I had when I was five. The one with He-Man on it.

'Duh,' said Jessica.

'I'm not flippin' stupid, Jess! How am I s'posed to know what it means straight away?'

She pursed her lips. 'Well *I* didn't think it was that hard to work out.'

I looked at her. 'Good for you.' *Anorexic, acnefied whore*, I thought, going back to my Damon Albarn drawing. *Emaciated carrot-headed prick, grow some fucking tits.* She was just jealous because I'd started my period, so now she was the only one out of the three of us who couldn't talk about tampons and period pains with any real knowledge. *Stupid skinny bitch with your child's womb.* I'd won *that* round.

'Well I don't think it matters anyway,' said Bianca, a sly smile on her downy lips. 'It's not like he's ever gonna brin' his lunchbox anywhere near *you*, Cris.' There was a pause. Then she broke into harsh peals of laughter, her eyes squinting shut into thick black crescents. Jessica joined in, burying her face in the copy of *Smash Hits* that had started all this.

'Oh har fuckin' har.'

The laughter eventually trailed off. Bianca threw a green Skittle at my head. 'Oh, take a joke, will you?'

'I know, she's so *serious*. Like, chill.'

I ate the Skittle and looked back down at my picture. I'd fucked up the eyebrow. I hated Jessica. So. Much. She'd already spent the earlier part of the evening accusing me of copying Bianca just because we were both wearing Sweatershop jumpers. 'First you try to copy how I do my y's,' she'd said, 'and then you get into green jeans just because I like green jeans, and now that you're done copying me, you've started copying Byank.' Such bullshit. So I'd started doing my y's with a straight line instead of a curl, big deal, it was just a fucking letter in the alphabet. And me and Jess had gotten into green jeans at exactly the same time, only her nan had bought her a pair before I could get my nan to buy me a pair. And Sweatershop jumpers? Fuck off. Everyone had Sweatershop jumpers. In fact, Jessica was probably the only person in school who *didn't* own one. Jealous, blatantly. OK, and maybe I was wearing white leggings and Bianca was wearing cropped white trousers. So we kind of looked the same. But it was pure coincidence. Jessica had worn white leggings the other week too. Did that make her a copycat?

I tried making one of the other eyebrows bigger. No. See, now he looked more like Liam Gallagher. I tossed my pen on the floor, stood up.

'Running home, are you?' said Jessica in a little girl's voice.

'I'm going to the loo.'

'Try not to block it.'

I stormed out, slamming the door on their breathless giggles. I passed by the toilet and went down the stairs. Through the hall with its many Buddha statues. Past the living room where Ali, Jessica's five-year-old sister, was watching cartoons on the floor cross-legged and Charles was eating a plate of hotdogs. I came to the kitchen. Suki was cooking lentil soup. It was the only thing she ever made. She was standing in front of the stove, a wooden spoon in one hand, a half-smoked rollie in the other. She was wearing slightly flared jeans and a purple gypsy vest.

I slumped down at the table that was overflowing with junk. 'Hiya, Sook.'

She turned her head slightly. 'Oh. Hiya, Cris. Those two being bitches again?'

I leaned forward and sniffed the plant that smelled like lemon flavour Turkish Delight. 'Yeah. As usual.'

'Leave them to it, Cris.' She picked up her mug of cider from the counter and sipped. 'When Bianca goes home tomorrow, you watch – Jessica'll be all over you.'

'Yeah, I know.'

Suki dipped the spoon in the soup, brought it out, blew on it, tasted it. She grabbed the pepper pot and sprinkled some in. Then some salt. Stirred it. Sipped her cider. She wasn't drunk yet but there was an easy wateryness to her movements. She'd probably had a ganja-spliff.

'D'you still see that Amanda?' she asked me.

'No,' I said, resting my cheek on the heel of my hand. 'She hangs round with Lucy Singleton now.'

'Good riddance.' She brought her lighter out of her pocket and re-lit her rollie. 'Mind you, that bloody Bianca's no improvement. She's a bad influence on Jess.'

Before Bianca, Jessica had been in all the top classes with me. Now she'd fallen to middle class for English and History, and bottom for Maths and Science. It was deliberate. She'd stopped trying in class so she could be moved down to the same group as Bianca. She'd expected me to do the same, but I liked getting good grades too much.

'She's not so bad. Nicer than Amanda,' I said, picking up a white shell from the ornamental bowl in front of me and running my finger over its jagged ridge.

'Can I have some cider, Sook?'

Suki passed me her mug. 'Just a sip.'

I downed half of it. Burped.

She took it back, looked inside. 'Cheeky cow.' Had a sip. Re-lit her rollie.

'Are those Jessica's jeans?' I asked.

She dipped her spoon in the soup, blew on it.

'They are, aren't they? Jessica's gonna go ape shit.'

'Oh, fuck her.' She licked the edge of the spoon, turned the hob off. Jessica and Bianca came down.

'Oh. You're down here,' said Jessica.

I nodded.

Bianca opened the fridge, looked inside, closed it.

'Dinner's ready when you want it,' said Suki, busying herself with cutlery.

Jessica looked over, nibbling on a fingernail. 'We'll have it in a – are those my fucking jeans?'

'Christ,' muttered Suki, shaking her head.

'For fuck sake! What have I said?'

'Oh, fuck off, Jess.'

'No! Don't tell me to fuck off. What. Have. I. Said?'

Suki brought some dishes out of the cupboard. 'I didn't have any clean ones.'

'I don't care! Don't wear my fucking clothes.'

'Don't be so selfish, Jess.'

'Selfish? We know what happens when you wear my clothes, don't we?' We did: the last time Suki had borrowed a pair of Jessica's jeans she'd left behind a wine-coloured period stain in the shape of a flower. 'I don't want your crusty fucking fanny all over my new jeans, know what I mean?'

Bianca smirked into her hand. Suki shot her a dirty look. 'I am *wearing* knickers.'

'Well that makes a change.' Jessica glared at her mother for a moment, and then sighed crossly. 'Come on, Bianca,' she said, turning to go. 'Let's go back up.' She looked at me coldly. 'You coming?'

I glanced over at Suki and the giant pan of soup. Looked back at my two friends. I'd have a better time with the alcoholic and the soup. But the longer Jessica had Bianca to herself, the deeper she'd get her hooks in. I followed them up.

Jessica had something on me. Nadeem. Any time I attempted to break friends with her for real, she'd play the old blow job card.

'I bet your mum would *love* to know about her dick-slurping daughter.'

'As *if* you'd tell her.'

'I ain't joshing, Cris,' she'd say, raising her eyebrows and puckering her lips in a way that made me want to ram my elbow into her nose.

I was also afraid of being alone. It was OK at home. I had my mum and the dogs. Television, drawing. But in school, a lonely person was automatically a shit person. Nibbling on a sandwich alone in the canteen, floating like a depressed ghost through the corridors. Tragic. 'Hang around with your sister,' Mum would say. '*You* hang around with her,' I'd say back, and Mum would give me this look as if to say, point taken.

One day I just didn't care any more. The night before Bianca had told me on the phone that Jessica was an ugly cow. Her zits were so big they had their own zits growing out of them. Anorexic *and* titless – gutted! And she was *blatantly* frigid. She preferred me, Bianca said, always had. I was in raptures. But the next morning it was the usual thing – Jessica and Bianca making fun of me, their spiky laughs merging into one. I followed them around, scowling at their backs as they whispered and giggled together. Everything that came out of my mouth was met with a smirk or a frown or a 'Yeah, whatever.' At lunchtime I told them I wanted to learn kung fu and they called me a lesbian. When I told them I was serious, they started acting out karate chops and doing mong faces. Bianca kicked my thigh and called me a lesbian spastic. I felt like crying. So I walked off. Just like that. I wandered the corridors, the yard, kept my eyes to the ground.

Eventually I went to my form room, hoping it would be empty. It wasn't. Arpita Aktar was cross-legged on a table with her friends, Hasumati and Sharifa. Arpita was a clever Bengali girl who got

As for everything. She was skinny and yellowish and she wore nerdy glasses. Her upper lip was exactly the same shape as her lower lip, like two orange slices. She wore her hair in a long, fat plait. Her brother was the nasty teasing boy who Veronica threw a chair at that time she became Chuck-a-mental.

'Hiya, Christina,' she said.

I nodded self-consciously and smiled. Sat down near them.

'How come you're on your own?'

'I've argued with Jessica and Bianca.'

She rolled her eyes. 'You three...'

We got talking. I remembered speaking to Arpita when I was in my first year of High School. She'd just come over from Bangladesh and her English was shit. We made the most boring small talk. The weather, where we lived, the weather again. Now here she was, talking like a proper Cardiff person, swearing and everything.

The bell for end of lunch rang. 'Hang round with us for a while if you want,' Arpita said. 'Until you make friends with those silly mares.'

'Thanks, I will,' I said, all casual, like it was nothing.

Inside I was punching the air. Arpita was really funny and I pissed myself and had to go to the toilets to spray my crotch with body spray and tie my jumper round my hips.

I saw Jessica and Bianca on the way home. I stared at the ground and walked faster. They caught up with me at the North Road traffic light.

'Oi, slag,' said Jessica. 'Coming over mine?'

I shook my head. 'I just wanna be by myself tonight.'

Bianca frowned. 'Why?'

I shrugged. 'I dunno. I wanna do some drawin'.'

'You can do drawing at mine,' said Jessica.

'Nah. Not tonight.'

Bianca turned to Jessica. 'She wants to be alone wiv her sister, innit? Less leave Finger-me-sis to it.'

They laughed.

'Fuck off, Bianca,' I said.

Bianca stopped laughing abruptly. She glared at me. 'Make me.'

'No.'

'Go on. Make me fuck off.'

'Leave me alone.' I glanced at Jessica. She was smiling, eyes small and mean. I checked the traffic light. Red man.

'I said, make me.' Bianca shoved my shoulders. I could see in her flickering eyes that she was playing a part, trying on a new persona. She was enjoying it.

I felt my face go hot and tight. I didn't dare blink because tears would spill out.

'Oh, look. She's crying,' said Jessica.

'No, I fuckin' ain't.'

'She so is.'

Bianca smirked. 'I know. She's *so* hard.'

I tried to frown away the tears but it didn't work. The cars sped past in a watery blur. Rush hour. I wanted to throw myself in front of one. The biggest and the fastest. Just to make them feel guilty. I imagined how it would feel, having a car run over your head, splitting the skull, brain squelching out – like what happened to Grandad. I imagined Jessica and Bianca shrieking out hot tears onto my coffin lid as I lay inside with a tyre-track watermelon head. And then the traffic lights were beeping and the little green man was neon. I ran across the road, Jessica and Bianca's laughter on my back like nails.

I ran all the way home. I didn't look back. I went in the house. My mum was in the kitchen washing dishes. Suki was swaying next to her, a can of Stonehouse in her hand.

'Mum,' I said.

She turned round. 'Oh hiya, Cris.' She flicked soap suds off her hands. 'Look,' she said, lifting her foot up. She was wearing my navy-blue Converse All Stars. 'They fit. Your mother is cool and youthful.'

'Mum, I need to tell you somethin'.'

She wiped her hands on her hips. 'What is it?'

'It's bad,' I said.

'What is it?'

Suki took a swig of her cider, pink puffy eyes peering at me from over the metallic rim.

'I did oral sex with Nadeem.'

Cider exploded out of Suki's mouth like a geyser and splashed the oven door.

Mum blinked slowly.

I went out the garden, climbed the laburnum tree and sat with my damp ammonia pants squished against a branch for an hour.

'Oh my God, did you see Moesha last night?' said Hasumati.

'Yeah, man. Hakeem was lookin' *fiiine*,' said Mishti.

Hasumati lifted her hand and Mishti slapped it.

'Eurgh,' said Arpita.

'Who's Hakeem?' I said.

'Hakeem is my future husband,' said Hasumati.

'Hakeem is beautiful,' said Mishti.

'Hakeem is a dog,' said Arpita.

Hasumati gasped and looked at Arpita like she'd been slapped.

Mishti got a tube of mascara out of her bag. I watched her comb black gloop through her superlong lashes, eyes half-closed, chin stuck out.

'Sure you don't need a rake for that?' asked Arpita.

Mishti stopped and stared at Arpita. Blinked. Went back to applying mascara.

It was lunchtime. We were in the form room, sat on top of the tables. The sky outside the windows was dark grey. Rain spat at the glass.

The Somali girls came in, water dripping off their leather jackets. Zaynab, who looked like Shug Avery from *The Color Purple* but darker and with worse teeth, was singing 'Ready or

105

Not' by the Fugees in a gorgeous, gravel-scraped voice. They sat with us. Sara got out some Vaseline and started rubbing it into her skinny, hairless ankles. Sharifa, who was fat and half-white with red-dyed curls, elbowed me. 'Oi, Scully, where's Mulder?'

I had an auburn-dyed bob and a thing for *The X-Files* and I thought Scully was an absolute bellend ... but for some reason I couldn't stop thinking about her or trying to be her.

I smiled. 'Up yer arse, Beast.'

Sharifa's nickname was The Beast because she was hard. Just two days ago I'd watched her get into a fight with a six-foot tall Somali girl called Fatima. She'd thrown Fatima over a table, grappled with her on the floor. Fatima had tried to run away but Sharifa grabbed her and booted her hard in the fanny. She'd hit the floor like a dropped piano.

Sharifa flopped onto a table and burped loudly. 'Probably.' She lay down and closed her eyes.

Zaynab finished singing. Glanced over at Hasumati, did a double take. 'Shit, girl. What's wrong with your eyes?'

Hasumati fluttered her eyelashes. She had bright indigo contact lenses in. 'Like them?'

'You look like a scary bitch.'

'Fuck you, kalu kutti.'

Zaynab laughed, head tilted back, tremulous mouth wide open.

The Bengali girls were going mental for coloured contact lenses. Emerald green, topaz, indigo. It was a way of expressing themselves without dressing like white slags.

Jessica and Bianca came in dripping wet. They saw me and smiled sarcastically. 'Alrigh', Streaky Bacon Head?' said Bianca.

This was their new nickname for me. Because the auburn dye job had initially gone wrong.

I waved two fingers.

'How rude!' said Jessica.

They sat in the middle of the room. Huddled together over a

piece of paper, giggling archly. Every few seconds they'd glance over at me.

I ignored them. Listened to Arpita and Hasumati's conversation. They were arguing over who was the lushest member of 3T.

I heard chairs scraping the floor. 'Hey, Cris,' said Jessica. 'We got something to show you.'

'No thank you,' I said.

'It's nuffin' bad,' said Bianca.

I went over and was handed the piece of paper.

'Whass this?'

'It's a petition,' said Jessica.

At the top of the paper, in Jessica's neat, contrived hand, was written: 'Do you like Christina Jones? Do you dislike Christina Jones? Do you hate Christina Jones?' Three columns for ticks. A fourth for signatures. There were a few ticks in the dislike column, around twenty in the hate column.

'They're all real,' said Bianca, tapping the signatures with her nail.

They both smiled at me.

I felt sick. 'I don't even know who most of these people are.'

Jessica raised her eyebrows. 'Well they know you.'

'How?'

'Come on – everyone knows who Finger-me-sis is,' said Bianca.

The paper was shaking in my hand. Bianca's eyes looked like centipedes.

The door opened. Sidney Trebor, Bianca's old friend, the one with anxiety, came in carrying a soggy umbrella. He was a girly boy with blond curtains. He had long, sweeping lashes and big pouty woman's lips. Just a little chubby in the face. Arpita reckoned he was gay. She called him Timotei because of his hair-swishing prettiness. I kept insisting he was just *sensitive*. I thought he was gorgeous.

'Hey, Bianca,' he said, high-pitched and nasal. 'Hiya, Jess.'

'Sidney, darling,' said Bianca. 'You can do our petition.' She handed the piece of paper over to him. 'Tick one. An' sign your name.'

Sidney took a hit off his asthma pump, frowning. He looked down at the paper, glanced up at me, looked down again. 'How come you have two negative ones and only one positive one?'

Bianca rolled her eyes. 'Just tick one, Sidney Trebor Mint.'

'Well, I quite like Christina.' He smiled shyly at me. 'She's always been nice to me.'

My heart did a little dance. But it was a brief lonely dance in a dead bone desert. Jessica snatched the paper out of Sidney's hands, rolling her eyes. She went up to Zaynab, dragging Bianca along behind her. Smiled her most charming-bitch smile. 'Hey, Zaynab. Will you please sign our petition and pass it round?'

Zaynab took it, read it. 'What the fuck is this?' Looked at me. '*I* like you, Scully.' Looked at Jessica and Bianca. 'What the fuck is this?'

Arpita came over, read the paper. Tutted. 'That's not a petition. That's fuckin' bitchy.'

'Yeah, that's *ruude*,' said Zaynab.

The paper was handed to Hasumati. 'Oh my God.' She giggled nervously.

Mishti leaned over and read it. Her hand fluttered to her mouth. 'That's rude, man.'

Beast, still laid out on the table, stuck her hand in the air. 'Gimme.'

Arpita grabbed it and passed it over, shaking her head and clucking like an old Bengali grandma.

Beast sat up to read it. She frowned. Glared at Jessica and Bianca. 'What the fuck, man?' She slid off the table and went up to them. 'Why would you do something like this?'

Jessica and Bianca looked up at her. They had their chins tucked in and their eyes shimmered like mirages. 'I dunno,' said Jessica, in a quiet voice. 'We just—'

'Why would you go to all that trouble to make someone feel shit?' She looked down at the petition. 'It's proper skank, man.' She shook her head like a disappointed mother. Then she ripped the petition up and dropped the pieces on the floor. 'You better say sorry to Christina.'

Jessica and Bianca looked at each other. Faces clammy.

'I mean it.' Beast took a step closer to them. She looked angry. I wondered if she'd hit them.

'Apologise to her before I make you. Yeah?'

Don't apologise, I silently willed. Resist. Tell her to fuck off. Call her fat. Give her an excuse to kick you in the fanny and rip your fucking face off.

'Sorry,' said Jessica.

'Not to me, to *her*, dhillo.'

Jessica's terrified eyes swivelled over to me. 'Sorry, Cris.'

'Yeah, I'm really sorry,' said Bianca.

Sharifa's shoulders relaxed. 'OK.'

She turned around and lay back down on the table.

Jessica and Bianca walked out of the room, heads hung like damaged swans.

Mum's Men

Dad

He sways between the door frame, his glacier-blue eyes lit up with a lazy sort of excitement. He can't take his drink because he's not used to it. Alcohol never interested him. Probably because it's legal. I'm twenty and just back from uni' for the holidays.

'Thing is though, Cris, thing is, she takes it *personally*.'

'I'd say it's quite a personal matter. Make some chips, will you?'

'Yeah, in a bit.' He waves his hand, then lights up the rollie that has burnt down to a floppy centimetre of yellow-brown paper. A Frank Zappa song spills out into the kitchen. 'Cris, thing is, like, it was the wrong time.'

'Dad, make some chips.'

'Keep your knickers on. I will.' He won't. He's pissed and he wants to talk to his daughter. I settle for crisps.

'I don't know why she's so pissed off anyway. I could've been worse. 'S'not like I beat her up or anything, like, uh, wossissname? Suki's husband. Wossissname?'

'Charles.'

'Yeah. Like Charles. 'S'not like I smacked her around.'

'Well. You didn't love her and you cheated on her.'

He clomps his way over to the small kitchen table and sits on a chair. 'So? Doesn't mean she shouldn't speak to me for ten years.'

I just look at him and eat my crisps.

'And I did love her.'

'No you didn't.'

'Well, I wasn't *in* love with her. But I did love her.'

'You were fond of her.'

'No, I loved her. I wouldn't have stayed married for fourteen

110

years if I didn't love her. Thing is, Cris, until I got to forty I wasn't that interested in women. It was like, it was like, I was only interested in drugs; they were my, what-ju-call-it? My passion. And then I was a Jehovah's Witness for a bit and that was my passion. And then I got to forty and it was like, hello girls!' He does a horsey laugh, his eyes wrinkling up at the corners.

I run back into the living room and come back with our tobacco and drinks. Jack Daniel's and Coke, made the way he likes – too strong. He's still yacking away like I'd never left the room.

' – wrong time. I reckon if I'd met her when I was forty, you know, it would be, it would be… ' he trails off, his drug-addled brain unable to come up with an ending.

I make two rollies, pass one to him. He pops it in a tight, lipless mouth.

'You miss her, don't you?' I say.

'Yeah. We were good friends. We got on.'

'I know. But think – she felt unloved for fourteen years. That's gonna sting. Imagine it was the other way round?'

'Unloved. I dunno what she's talking about. Look, right. Next time you see her will you tell her, tell her, uh…' he makes grabbing gestures with his chunky hands as if he's literally trying to pluck words from the air 'tell her it was cuz of the drugs. It was the wrong time. Tell her I *did* love her, but I was more – more – tell her *drugs* were my passion, like. Uh. Tell her it was nothin' personal, like.'

'OK, Dad. Now will you make some fucking chips?'

Melanie Hall. Wife of his workmate and friend, Mark. Melanie was a scrawny, skanky woman, known throughout certain parts of Cardiff for fucking men in pub toilets. A real woman-hater, she loved stealing men from the bosom of their family. She'd already broken up three marriages. Time for a fourth.

Mum found out through Mark. He and Dad had spent the day

painting and decorating. Afterwards they went back to Mark's. Melanie suggested they get their dinner from the local chippie. Mark went to pick some up, and when he returned twenty minutes later, his wife was pulling down my father's paint-splotched jeans on the living room floor.

Mark rang and told my mum, his words grief-garbled. She put the phone down and calmly told my sister and me what our father had done.

'What's gonna happen?' I asked.

'Divorce,' replied my shock-dead mum.

Veronica ran upstairs, crying. Not me. I'd seen it coming. Mum and Dad had been sleeping in separate rooms for God's sake. In all my childhood I'd only seen them kiss once. And that was only because they were on magical mushrooms. It hadn't even been with tongues. I was only twelve but I wasn't flippin' stupid.

When Dad came home that night he didn't deny it. Mum told him the score, accentuating each word with her famous finger-jab. He walked straight back out of the house, climbed on top of his coffee-brown Cortina and sat down on the roof, drawing his knees to his chin. He stayed like that for hours, looking out into the street, or further beyond, to the night-smudged mountains of Caerphilly. Mum stayed inside, walking from room to room. She was pale; I remember her round glowing face floating around the dim living room like something from a Hammer Horror.

I went outside and watched Dad for a while. I asked him questions – 'Why ju do it?' 'Ju think Mum really means it?' – But I just got a few quiet 'I dunno's'. He was ashamed. He felt sorry for himself. He was sore over being caught.

The next day he left and that was the end of that.

The Pen Pals

She handed me a small, square snapshot. 'This is Clancy.' Bulging muscles. White vest. Short, spiky hair.

'Hunky. Ju think you'll ever meet him?'

She laughed a little nervously. 'I hope not.'

'Why?'

'He's a murderer.'

'Oh.'

Since Dad left, Mum had got some pen pals, most of them prisoners from the US.

'He's nice though. We talk about a lot of things. Well, we write – you know what I mean.'

'Do you fancy each other?'

'Well, I don't know if he fancies me ...' She'd lost a lot of weight since the break-up, but she was still big.

'What if he comes to see you when he's let out of jail?'

'That would never happen. It's nothing serious. We just chat. It's nice.'

Clancy had shot three people in an armed robbery. Two of them had died. He felt very sorry about this now, wished he could go back in time. He was a dumb son-of-a-bitch. He had a lot of time to think about that now.

'Who's that one?' I said, pointing to another envelope, this one covered in turquoise writing.

She pulled a photo out, passed it over. 'This is Mitchell Freeman.'

Mitchell was a middle-aged black man with short, bronze-tinted hair. Thick skin, wide smile. A pink and purple tinselled Christmas tree drooped in the background.

'Is he a murderer too?'

'Yes. He stabbed someone. He said it was in self-defence.'

'Ju believe him?'

'I don't know. He's a Christian now. He found God in prison.'

'Is he nice?' I asked.

'Yes, he's really nice.'

'Who ju prefer?'

She thought about it, her eyes gleaming with lust. 'I don't know. Mitchell's had a really interesting life, he's got more to say, but – I don't know.'

'Is James still your favourite?'

Mum nodded. James Duffy was another American prisoner. San Quentin, first degree murder, acne-scarred face, scruffy goatee. Mum had been writing to him the longest, and she and him were close. James' letters didn't make Mum go all embarrassed and giggly – it wasn't like that. His letters had helped her through the worst part of her break-up with Dad.

I reached for the small stack of envelopes on Mum's lap. 'Can I read their letters?'

She snatched them away and laughed in my face.

A few months later, in the living room…

'What do you think of this?' she said, a little embarrassed.

She was wearing a large, baggy top, open neck, midnight blue. Black lycra leggings and heeled ankle boots. She had lost some more weight. Size twenty now.

'Nice,' I said, just relieved she wasn't wearing those ugly tent dresses any more. 'Lycra's a bit tarty though.'

'So?' she giggled, her face a paradox of doubtful rebellion. Mum had re-discovered her sexuality; it had been hidden underneath all those folds of fat. 'Nothing wrong with looking a bit tarty. I'm only thirty.'

She went out to the large oval mirror in the hall. I could hear her scrabbling around with her make-up. 'Get my camera, will you?' she called. Lips smacked together like a jar being popped for the first time.

I got the camera.

Mum came back in, her lips glossy – Heather Shimmer,

Rimmel – a smudge of grey eyeshadow, some mascara. 'Call the dogs, will you?'

'Why?'

'I want you to take some photos of me with Rutger and Slug.'

'Why?'

'For Clancy. He used to breed pit bulls.'

I called the dogs. They gushed into the room, their thin tails whipping back and forth. Mum calmed them down, made them congregate in the middle of the room. She stood behind them, bent forward to hold their collars.

'Rutger,' I whispered, to make him look. Then I took the picture.

'Couple more,' said Mum. She bent a little closer to the dogs. Her top sagged down.

'Mum, I can see your boobs.'

'Can you?' She looked. 'It's only cleavage.' She didn't adjust it. 'Last one.'

'OK,' I said.

At the last second she pulled a face that stank of hussy.

'Mum!'

She let go of the dog's collars. 'It's only a bit of fun!'

I put some cheese on toast under the grill and sat down to wait. There was a pile of *Take-a-Break*s and *Bella*s on the kitchen table next to a bundle of my dad's post that Mum had yet to mark 'Return to sender'. Dad was living in the YMCA. I visited him every Sunday. We'd sit in his small box room – white walls, brown carpet, a giant Pink Floyd poster, not much else. Sometimes we'd barely speak. He was depressed. He'd stare at a spot on the floor, sometimes looking up to ask me how school was going or, uh, how were the dogs? I didn't like being here in this tiny room with my miserable dad and all the weird men knocking on the door to ask for a fag-end every ten minutes.

I picked up a *Bella* and flicked through it while I waited for my food to cook. An envelope fell out of the bottom of the pile. Turquoise writing, addressed to Cathy Jones. Oh, mother, you've been careless.

I read the letter while I ate.

I get so lonely at times ... blah blah ... *guy next door is being released Friday, and I just know he's going to re-offend ...* blah blah *... perhaps you wouldn't mind answering some questions of mine, miss! ... 1) Have you ever done doggy?*

Whoa! Jackpot. Following this were nineteen more sexual questions addressed to my mother. Anal? I knew what that was. Oral. That was a blow job, right? Swallow? Swallow what?

Mitchell signed off with his love and some kisses. And then:
P.S. Thanks for the pubes ☺

Mark

Mark Hall was visiting my mum a couple of times a week. They were friends. They confided to each other their feelings of loneliness.

The thinner Mum got, the more he came over.

'I think he fancies you, Mum,' said Veronica, one dinnertime, through a mouthful of lettuce.

'Nah.'

'He does, Mum. It's like, *duh.*'

'He's still in love with Melanie.'

'Euurgh,' I said. I'd never seen Melanie, but Mum had described her. A scabby prostitute with a scabby fanny – that's what Melanie looked like.

Mum carved a slice of grilled chicken breast and dipped it in some low cal mayo. The fork paused at her mouth. 'Mark Hall is a weak man. I don't want any more weak men.' The fork went in. She chewed neatly, swallowed. 'I had fourteen years of it with your dickhead of a father.'

When Dad had left, Mum promised us she would never

116

badmouth him to us or around us because he was still our father no matter what. But she was seriously pissed off with him lately. It was the drug bust that did it; I'd come home from school one day to find a squad of uniformed men searching our house. One of them had been bitten by Slug but they couldn't do anything about it because that's what you get when you kick the door in like an FBI agent.

They didn't find any drugs, not even an ashtray.

Afterwards, Mum rang my nan and told her about the ordeal. A lightbulb went off above old Eileen's head – her 'useless' son had been spending a lot of time in her garage lately. She went to investigate. In the garage was a huge cupboard made out of chalkboard. Inside were fifteen or so marijuana plants. Eileen poured bleach over the lot and watched them die.

'My babies,' Dad said later, after being let out on bail. 'She killed my babies.'

Mum wasn't speaking to him now. He was a 'dickhead' and an 'arsehole' and a 'knobhead' and if he ended up in jail it was his own stupid fault. It was open season.

'I think Mark's a really nice guy,' I said now, squeezing out salad cream onto my potatoes. I wanted Mum and Mark to get together because I fancied Mark's fourteen-year-old son. He could start out as my stepbrother but over time I'd make my feelings known and we could fall in love and keep it all a sexy secret. 'I mean, how ju know he's weak?'

'Look how many times that woman has cheated on him and he still wants her. He'd take her back if she asked. He's a weakling. And anyway, he doesn't fancy me.'

But he did – it was in his eyes – and deep down Mum knew this. Something had to be done.

The next time he came round, eyes a-smiling, she took him out the garden, had a word. Me and Veronica watched from under the apple tree. Mark stood with his hands stuffed in his jeans pockets, his eyes on the floor. He looked like he was about to cry. I saw him nod his head. Then he left. I'd have to do without a sexy stepbrother.

Harry

Mum didn't just write to murderers. She also wrote to bikers. One of these was Harry. He came from somewhere near Birmingham. Close enough to visit.

One night he decided to pop by. Mum fluttered around the house, billowing perfume behind her. Size eighteen, now.

'You're staying over Jessica's tonight?' she asked me.

'Yes. I'm staying over Jessica's so you can have sex.'

She laughed. 'Is that what you think of your dear mother?'

'Yeah.'

'Oh, you cynic. Veronica won't go with you?'

'No way!'

Mum waved her hand, dismissively: Veronica wouldn't present a problem. She spent most of her time locked in her fishy bedroom, sulking over her fast-growing monster-tits.

Soon I heard the rumble of a motorbike climbing the driveway. Mum steered the barking dogs into the spare room and ran to open the front door. In stepped a denim-clad man with a helmet tucked under his armpit. He was medium-build with a scruffy mop of curly brown hair. He looked around twenty-five.

'Harry,' said Mum with a friendly smile.

'Catherine,' he said, nodding his head.

Mum didn't know what to cook for Harry. We'd been living on grilled chicken breasts and salad or low fat curry for the past year. That's not what you cook a man. What do you cook a man?

Mum decided on sausage, egg and chips. It didn't go to plan. We didn't have a deep fat fryer so Mum filled a saucepan with oil, dropped the chips in, and later, scooped them out with a fish slice. They all got stuck together in the pan, and were half-burnt, half-raw.

'Mum, these chips aren't cooked properly,' I said.

'I'm out of practice,' she said with a nervous laugh.

Harry nudged the worst chips to the edge of the plate. He looked embarrassed. I hadn't seen him smile once.

I finished the sausage and egg and went over my friend's house.

Harry's motorbike wasn't there the next morning.

Marcus

She met Marcus through our neighbours, Sherry and Tyrone. He was single. Mum was single. How about it? When he came round for the first time she decided to stick to what she knew – Marcus would be having a low-fat balti with us. We sat in the living room, plates on our laps. Mum wanted this to be casual, informal – *Oh, you've just caught us about to have dinner … why don't you have some? Plenty to go around. No, it's fine …*

Marcus seemed comfortable straight away. He talked about himself easily between clumsy mouthfuls. Rice fell from his plate to the freshly hoovered carpet. He didn't notice. Talked, scooped, scattered. Every spoonful at least a quarter of the rice fell on the floor. I stared, my spoon frozen in mid air an inch from my hung-open gob. He didn't notice. I caught my mum's eye. She quickly shook her head. Shush.

'Thanks, Catherine, that was lovely,' he said, standing up to pass my mum the plate. He patted his stomach. 'First decent meal I've had in ages.'

Mum beamed.

Marcus was a small man. Short and lean. His features were black but his skin was like extra milky coffee. He wore slacks and a polo shirt and a gold watch. He had a strong Cardiff accent.

They went to the pub together for a drink, and next morning he was still in the house. Maybe Mum had found herself a man?

'He's an alcoholic, Christina.'

119

'What? How do you know?'

'He drinks all the time. He relies on it. He can't spend a night sober.'

'Maybe he could if you asked him.'

A slow shake of the head. 'You know what alkies are like, Cris. You know what Suki's like.'

'But Marcus ain't like Suki.'

'He's still an alcoholic. He doesn't have to fall asleep in the street to be an alcoholic. Remember all the rice on the floor? That was because he was pissed as a fart. I practically had to carry him home that night.'

'But—'

'Look. I know he's *nice* enough, but it's not going to work. We're not suited to each other. He's too skinny. And he wears slacks for God's sake.' She rolls her eyes.

'I just think people can change.'

'I wish he'd change out of those slacks!' She laughed. I didn't join in. 'Oh. He's coming back.' She straightened her face, carried on wiping the work surface.

Marcus came in from the garden stinking of smoke. 'Come on then, Ca', let's go to the pub.'

Idris

Mum was in college doing Access to Art. When she wasn't walking the dogs or starving herself she was painting. She loved it. The kitchen table was always covered in charcoal sketches, watercolours, papier mâché models. She would sit there late into the night painting nudes while mumbling along to the Cranberries or Nirvana.

One morning I decided to pull a sicky from school. I was long overdue one. Hopefully Mum would have no other option but to leave me at home while she went to college. She'd recently started hosting Ann Summers parties to earn some extra money and I wanted to root through the huge box of dildos and posing pouches under the stairs to see if I could find any porn.

Mum wasn't having any of it. 'I'm not leaving a fourteen-year-old home alone. You're coming to college with me.'

Mum's art class was held in a hut. I walked inside. Paintings, drawings, sculptures everywhere. Around fifteen people were busy with their work. Most were in their twenties, a few in their thirties, one in his seventies. Most of them were kind of grungy. And I noticed something: Mum fit right in. She'd lost even more weight – size sixteen – and was dressing young. She wore lots of silver jewellery and dangly gypsy earrings. A stud in her nose. Her hair was at its curliest and she'd started putting henna on it so that bits shimmered copper in certain lights. She bought baggy hippy tops that were beaded, tie-dyed. Sometimes a dress with tights, sometimes leggings. Always Dr Marten boots, black with rainbow laces. She looked good. She wasn't a sexless, ageless, frump-lump hidden by tent-clothes anymore. I felt proud of her.

I hung round while she worked on her piece – a brightly painted dalek with tits. She concentrated on her brushwork with the focus of a dentist. Started painting lasers coming out of the nipples. But sometimes her attention wavered and she grew distracted. I soon found out why.

Idris had long, white-blond hair. A nice face, bit of a hooked nose. Long, slender body, pale sun-starved skin, artist's fingers made for holding floppy rollies. He had holes in the knees of his jeans, his boots were paint-splattered. He looked like he belonged in Alice in Chains or Pearl Jam.

Mum had competition. At lunchtime, as the class sat in a loose circle and started eating their sandwiches and smoking their rollies, I watched the other women prowl. There was Rachael, the beautiful half-Egyptian man-eater with the gold eyeshadow, who would soon swear off men and turn into a morbidly obese bull dyke. She flirted with pretty Idris, touching his knee and making crude innuendoes. There was Suzie, my mum's friend with the long red hair, who in a few years time would end up with a violent man with spiderwebs tattooed on his neck – even now I see her wandering around Tesco with plums for eyes. Suzie knew my mum liked Idris but she was in her thirties and time was running out. She vied for his attention by acting ditzy and helpless. Then Vienna, long blonde hair, nose ring, hairy legs. She merely hovered.

They were wasting their time – he liked my mum the best. When she talked he listened thoughtfully. He gave her his full attention. And he offered her half his KitKat. There was chemistry.

It never happened. Mum would come home from college, love hearts in place of irises.

'Is he your boyfriend, yet?' I'd ask.

'No. That bloody Suzie keeps flirting with him. "Oh, Idris, I think I've messed up my painting, would you have a look for me? Oh Idris, I can't find my pastels!"'

'But she's your friend.'

'Sometimes I wonder.'

'Why don't you go for a drink together?'

'I don't know. 'I'm a single mum with two kids. I've got all this loose skin. I don't—'

'So? He fancies you.'

'I thought so. But he won't ask me out, will he?'

'Give it time.'

She did. Nothing happened. You could say their romance had fizzled out, except it had never started fizzing in the first place.

I asked her about Idris a couple of years later over coffee and toast. I was writing an essay for English Literature (GCSE) and the topic was romantic desire. We were doing *Romeo and Juliet*. My argument was that Romeo was a romantic idiot. I intended to draw parallels between him and my mother.

'Remember that guy from college you fancied? The one with

the long hair?'

'Idris. Yes.'

'Didn't you almost go out with each other?'

'I don't know. That was…strange. It was like, we both fancied each other but neither of us had the guts to do anything about it. Ya know? And sometimes I wondered if I'd got it wrong and I'd been mis-reading all the signals and in actual fact he thought I was an old heifer. But I don't know. This one time I thought it was on the cards. We were in Bogies. Just when it looked like we might do something – you know, kiss – Suzie started puking everywhere – very convenient – and we had to take her home. So no, it never happened.'

'He was nice though, wasn't he?'

'Oh yes. You know, sometimes I wonder what my life would've been like if we had gotten together.'

She gazed into her cappuccino, a small, ambiguous smile curving her lips.

Dad II

Mum eventually forgave Dad for the drug bust. She started talking to him again and soon they were friends. She stopped writing, 'Not at this address … *It's fun to stay at the YMCA*,' on his post. He visited the house every couple of days and they would have tea in the kitchen. Me and Veronica got our hopes up. So did Dad.

Dad had dated a couple of women since the break-up. The only one I met was Alys. She was a small, thin woman with a big mop of dark hair. She looked a bit like Siouxsie Sioux, but rougher. One Sunday, Dad took me and Veronica to her house in Adamsdown. She promptly gave us each a can of strong, cheap cider and yanked my dad upstairs. They didn't come down for an hour. I asked her for another cider and she said no.

It didn't last. Nor did the others. Dad was hankering after Mum. She was making a life for herself; she'd gotten thin and trendy; the house was looking nicer. Dad wanted in.

They spent New Year's Eve of '94 together, drinking and laughing in the living room. The next morning Dad was still there. Veronica ran downstairs like it was Christmas morning. *Dad and Mum are back together! Back together!*

But no. According to my mum, they had started to, *you know*…but it hadn't felt right, so they'd stopped. And that was the end of that.

Russell

'You dated some right nightmares after Dad. No offence, but you did.' I'm helping Mum chop onions for a turkey mince bolognese (turkey breast mince is low-fat). I've written most of my essay on romantic idiocy over the last week but I've still got another five hundred words to burn. And I know the best is still to come. She can't know I'm writing an essay that draws anecdotally on her dating failures, so I have to casually wheedle the information out of her. 'Which one was worse, ju reckon? Out of all of them?'

'Magnus! Without a doubt.'

I haven't got to him yet. I'm doing it chronologically. 'That army guy before him, what was his name again?'

'Russell.'

'That's it. Russell. What was he like?'

'Nutcase.'

'And what happened with him?'

'Right. Basically, what happened was, I met him one night in – lemme think – oh, yeah, in the Old Market Tavern, where O'Neill's is now. You know, opposite Poundstretcher? Anyway. I was out with some friends from college. And I remember, it was December the twentieth. Last day of my art course, and mine and your father's wedding anniversary. *And* it was also the day my divorce papers came through. December the twentieth. Triple whammy.' She wipes away an onion tear with the back of her hand. 'So anyway, this guy comes up to me and he starts coming onto me, hard. Really trying it on. And of course Idris was there and he got really pissed off and went off in a huff. He ended up sleeping with someone from our class that night. Julianne, I think. To spite me probably.

'So. I'm stuck with this cockney lunatic. Russell. He drags me along to some pub on Westgate Street. And we're drinking, having a nice time and he's introducing me to all his friends. He seems really into me. I quite like him too. He ticks all the boxes. Big macho bastard, in the army, quite charming – you know my type. He stayed over, as you'll remember. And that was that. He said he'd call me.

'But he didn't. He'd just finished with his wife, see. He wanted to spend Christmas with his kids and I thought maybe he was going to wait till after Christmas to call. But obviously he went back to the wife, didn't he? It's obvious now. I got a phone call from him two weeks later, and he was all, "Sorry, it's been manic." And he said we should get together again soon. Said he'd ring me. But he didn't. I was quite hurt actually.'

She puts her knife down on the counter, scrapes the onion into a plastic bowl and takes a red pepper out of the fridge.

'Anyway. He rings me up a while later pretending to be someone else. He puts on this awful Irish accent. I won't do one. "I'm a mate of Russell's. Look, you need to keep away from him, he's bad news." And I was like, "What kind of mate are you, telling me that?" And he goes, "Look, I'm with the IRA and I happen to have information on him. He's into some bad stuff. Terrorist groups and that." So I say, "Yeah, what else?" And he says, "He's a drinker." And then I thought, right, enough's enough, this is ridiculous. So I say, "Look, I know it's you, Russell," and he puts the phone down.

'Clearly he felt bad about leading me on so he wanted to put me off. Fucking nutcase.'

I nod, reaching for the mushrooms. Russell the nutcase and Mum the idiot. I can use that. After all, Romeo was both a nutcase and an idiot. How else to explain the ending?

Magnus

It's Magnus's last day with us. We're in the garden, enjoying the start of the spring weather. Clear skies, cold sunlight. Magnus is mowing the lawn. Making himself useful, perhaps, since he's spent a full week living off Mum. He's in faded jeans, the only pair he owns, and nothing else; I'm watching his lard-white torso as he works. Purely out of interest. No definition, a wobbly belly, five or six orange chest hairs. Rubbish DIY tattoos up his arms, the main piece an inky scrawl that says '100% muff diver'.

Mum has lowered her standards for this one. But I like him. Because of that chat we had in the kitchen on his third day here.

'Sorry – what was yer name again?'

'Christina.'

'Aye, Christina. Listen.' There followed a few words I couldn't understand. His accent was so thick that half his speech turned to mush in my ear. I got the next bit though. 'And I'll niver take over your da cuz he's your one and only da, like, but if anyone ever fucks with ye, come to me, aye?'

Nobody had ever offered to stand up for me before, except Mum, and she was a mum so it didn't count. Dad certainly hadn't. Having a big, ginger, sweary-mouthed biker offer his manpower was comforting. Finger-me-sis was still doing the rounds at school.

I bring him glasses of lemonade while he mows, and do keepy-uppies all over the garden in the hope he'll see. Soon he's turned pink, either from the exercise or the weak sunlight. Mum's

126

sketching him from the bench, the cat by her side.

Magnus turns off the lawnmower. 'Fuckin' scauldin',' he mutters.

Mum hears. 'You should cut your hair off.'

'I should cut my hair off, should I?'

'Maybe. I don't know. You wouldn't get so hot.'

He turns to me, his eyes screwed shut against the sun. 'Christina. Go and get some scissors, will ye?'

'Really?'

'Yes. I'm gunny cut the whole fuckin' lot off. Fuck it.'

I run in, get the scissors and take them to Mum. She puts her sketchbook down and comes over to Magnus, smiling. 'Now are you sure?' she says.

'Aye. Just fuckin' do it, woman.' He gets down on his knees.

His hair is long, red and wild. Mum grabs a chunk and shears it off. 'Get the camera, Cris.'

When I come back thick wads of hair are lying on the grass. Small tufts stick to his freckled shoulders. I take some photos. Magnus smiles with teeth and sticks his thumb up for the camera.

Suddenly he frowns, jerks his head away from Mum's hand. 'Ow, be careful, for fuck sake.'

'Oops,' says Mum. She brings the sharp scissors back to his head and starts cutting again.

'Leave a wee bit at the bottom, Cathy.'

'Like a pigtail?'

'Whatever the fuck ye call it.'

She takes a while tidying up the uneven bits with cautious little snips. Then it's done.

Magnus grabs a thick handful of his shorn hair and hands it to my mum. 'Keep this. So you'll always remember me.'

Mum smiles.

Magnus offers his cheek and she kisses it quickly.

He'll be back. He's got to meet up with some friends in Bridgend to pick up his bike. He'll definitely be back – he's even left his bag with us, and it's got his only possessions inside it.

He gives my mum a kiss on the lips. No tongues. I get a kiss on the cheek and Veronica gets a little nod. He leaves like a cowboy, walking off into the sunset. We watch him get smaller and smudgier. Mum smiles and waves. Then he turns right and he's gone.

I look at Mum. Her smile has fallen off. 'Thank God for that,' she says, blowing air out of her cheeks. She walks back to the house.

'What ju mean?' I say, following her.

She slams the door behind us. 'Christina, Veronica – he was a lunatic. Thank God for Slug, that's all I can say.'

On hearing her name, Slug runs up to Mum, wagging. Mum bends down on one knee, something she wouldn't have been able to do a couple of years ago, and strokes the dog's smooth, black head. 'Who's my little feminist, eh?' Slug wags harder: *I'm your little feminist.* Mum gets up. She sees the bundle of ginger hair on the kitchen table. Picks it up warily, like it's warm shit. Dumps it in the bin. Briskly wipes her hands on her hips.

She met Magnus in The Dog and Bone, the pub where she worked. It was a typical bloke's pub – pool table, dartboard, skittles for the ladies – but every Thursday was biker night. Mum made sure to look good on Thursdays.

One Thursday, Magnus turned up. Mum didn't recognise him as a regular. Nor did anyone else. All the other bikers – especially those from the cliquey Taff Riders, turned a cold, leather shoulder. Magnus sat on his own, talking to Mum when she wasn't serving people. She felt sorry for him, so when he said he had nowhere to go at closing time, she invited him back to hers. But only for one night.

Before she left, Bob, her boss, took her to one side. 'Careful with that one,' he said. 'He says he's a biker, but where's his bike?'

'It's all right. He's going on the couch. And I'll be kicking him out in the morning.'

'Give me a call if you have any trouble.'

She left Bob to lock up and walked home with Magnus. She soon started to regret her kind offer. Was bringing a stranger back to her two teenage daughters such a good idea? Was she being too trusting?

Luckily there was a man-hating pit bull in the house. Rutger had gone to live with Dad, leaving just Slug. Mum liked to joke that Slug was a lesbian: the only time she and Dad tried to have her mated she grabbed the stud by his neck in a blur of spit, teeth and rolling whites, and shook till he howled. Slug didn't like many males.

'Slug! Shut up,' said Mum, yanking the barking dog away from Magnus's ankles.

'Fuck me! She'll not bite, will she?'

'No, no. She just needs to get used to you.'

Mum didn't sleep with Magnus that night. She didn't fancy him. That's what she told me two years later, when I was probing her for my essay. As far as she was concerned she was helping him out and that was all. He was going in the morning.

The fuck he was. As Magnus ate his breakfast at the kitchen table that first day he knew he was on to a good thing. Free food, a free bed, an insecure woman. Fuck aye.

Magnus charmed me straight away. He had lots of stories.

'So how come you've got nowhere to stay? Where's your house?'

'I don't have a house. I've just got back from Nepal.'

'Where's Nepal?'

'Smack bang in the middle of India. Fuckin' beautiful place.'

'What were you doing there?'

'I was teaching the children. Look.' He opened his small green canvas sack, pulled out a dented copper flute. 'I played the flute to them.'

'Can you play some now?'

His brow furrowed. 'Not now. Some other time.' He quickly put the flute back in his sack. Brought out a video. *Highlander*. 'See this? Fuckin' great film. My favourite. The story's based on my family history. The McLeods. It's filmed in the same spot my clan's from. We'll watch it some time. Look.' He shoved his arm in front of my face. Tattooed underneath 100% Muff Diver, in the same spidery writing, was his name: Magnus McLeod. 'I'll tell you all about my clan. The McLeods were fuckin' warriors.'

Slug walked into the room, slowly, head stooped low as if she was hunting. She sat down and watched Magnus as he packed the video back in his bag.

Magnus noticed. He drew away nervously. 'Get that fuckin' dog away from me.' This would become his catchphrase for the week.

'She won't hurt you.'

'Fuckin' vicious fuckin' thing.'

I grabbed Slug's studded collar and pulled her out of the room. Veronica was in the hallway mirror putting concealer on her chin zits. 'Is he still here?' she mouthed, frowning. She hated Magnus. But then, she hated everyone. 'You and Slug should get married,' I whispered, closing the door on them both.

Mum was getting as wary as the dog. If Magnus had just come back from Nepal then why was his skin so pale? How come he didn't know any Nepalese? And why did he tell everyone that Nepal was in the middle of India, when in fact it lay between India and China, or so her world atlas had told her? And those tattoos! Certainly prison tattoos. He had his name sewed into his underwear too. Yes. Probably just let out of prison. Thank God for Slug.

Mum tried to get rid of Magnus with strong hints but he had no intention of leaving. He made up new excuses, said it would just be another day. He decided that Mum needed sweetening up so he kissed her, hugged her. As Magnus sensed, Mum was grateful for any sort of affection. On the third night he slept in her bed. When Magnus couldn't get it up Mum questioned him. Is it me? Magnus got angry – he was fuckin' tired, all right? He turned his back with a jerk, went to sleep.

By the fourth day, Mum was more than wary. She wanted this leech out of her house. But how to break it? He might get violent. Thank God for Slug, thank God for Slug. This became her mantra.

On the fourth night, Magnus met Suki. They got on brilliantly.

'We have a bonny Scotsman in our midst!' said Suki, sitting down next to Magnus on the couch. She grabbed his wrist and moved in close, her drunken head nodding. 'My friend,' she said in her deep, slow voice, 'you are in good company.' She fished a can of Stonehouse out of her plastic carrier bag and pushed it into his hand, smiling.

Magnus glanced down at her sun-sizzled cleavage, eyes twinkling. 'Ah can see that.'

They drank to their health. From across the room Mum noticed how their thighs touched. She noticed Suki's skinny arm drape around his shoulders, her fag ash speckling his back. They laughed together. Magnus didn't mind inhaling her rotting cider breath at such close quarters because Suki was his kind of woman – skinny, wild, easy. And Mum noticed. She's an alcoholic, she's pissed, she doesn't know what she's doing, Mum concluded.

Suki knew exactly what she was doing. She came over on the fifth day, still pissed, and headed straight for the man on the couch. Warm thigh pressed against warm thigh. Hand skimmed knee. Arm draped shoulder. The burst capillaries on Suki's cheeks flamed red with lust. She wanted this man, this Highland warrior.

It was a nice day, clear and bright. Magnus came out the kitchen to see my mum. 'Coming for a walk, Cathy?" he asked.

'No, not now. I told you – I have to do my UCAS form.'

'I'll come with you,' said Suki, lurching over to him.

They stayed out all day. That night, in bed, Mum questioned Magnus.

131

He looked at her, dead serious. 'Yes, I fucked her, Catherine. We fucked in the woods.'

'You're joking.'

'No. I'm not going to lie to you. She seduced me.'

'Get out of my house,' said Mum.

'Calm down, woman, calm down,' he said, his hands fluttering around her shoulders like moths. 'Take a fuckin' joke, will ye? I wouldn't put my cock in that woman.'

'I want you gone tomorrow,' she said, turning her back and pretending to go to sleep.

The sixth day. Magnus used the phone to ring his friends in Bridgend. We heard the conversation that may or may not have been real. Course. Tomorrow. Sure. Fuckin' aye. See ye then. He put the phone down. 'I'm meeting my mates tomorrow, Catherine. Will ye put us up till then?'

'Just one more day. I mean it.' She called Slug over and smoothed her head. 'I mean it, Magnus.'

That night they went to the Dog and Bone to see a band. Magnus got drunk, chatted with some of the locals. Mum sat with her friends, drank Diet Coke. Toward the end of the night Bob came over. Bob was a strange contradiction of a man, in that he was kind and decent but also a white supremacist. He had shaved white hair and a short white beard, no moustache. If it wasn't for the leather waistcoat and bulky biker boots, he could pass for a peasant in a Robin Hood film.

'Catherine, you've got to get rid of this prick,' he said, sitting down next to her.

'I've been trying, Bob.'

'Some of the boys have overheard the conversation he's having. He's talking about how sweet he's got it over yours. Free food, two virgin daughters.'

These last two words sliced through Mum's ears like a scream. 'Bob, what do I do?'

'Look. I can personally have him taken out of Cardiff. And I can make sure he never comes back. Cuz he'll have two broken legs. Or worse. Know what I'm saying? I can take care of that for you.'

'He said he'll go tomorrow. I'll wait till then, OK? We've got the dog, she doesn't leave my side. And if he doesn't go, then... Thank you, Bob.'

'No problem, darling.'

Day seven. Magnus had some bad news. He'd popped into a phone box to call his friends on the way to the shop. The bike was waiting for him but he didn't have a helmet. He'd have to wait a few days till they could sort one out for him. Just another couple of days, Catherine, and he'd be out of her hair, what's two fuckin' days?

Mum slowly put down her magazine, placed her elbows on the kitchen table and looked at him. It was a look so cool, so mean, that even Slug, bristling, could sense the shift of energy in the room. 'Today, Magnus. You're going today.' She stroked down Slug's hackles, her eyes never leaving his.

Magnus nodded like someone had poured ice cubes down his back. 'Aye. Fuck the helmet.' He flapped an almost girlish hand. 'Ah don't need a fuckin' helmet.'

Magnus enjoyed his last day with us. We had salad and barbecue pork for lunch. We watched *Highlander*. Then the clouds drifted away to reveal a small, yellow sun.

'I'll mow the lawn before I go,' he said, spilling squiggles of tobacco all over the kitchen table as he rolled up a skinny prison cigarette. 'Aye, it's the least I can do.'

'I wish I was a lesbian,' Mum told me, slumped over the kitchen table.

'Eurgh, don't be gross,' I said.

'Well, I keep meeting losers, don't I?'

'It's just bad luck.'

'No, I attract them like a magnet.'

'What about Seamus?' Seamus worked behind the bar with

Mum. He was broody and quiet and she fancied him, and there was chemistry, but it was like Idris all over again, and nothing was happening.

'No. It's all bullshit, Cris.'

'That's a shame,' I said. But it wasn't a shame. Ten years in the future Mum would see Seamus on *Trisha*, sitting broodily and quietly under the TV lighting while his wife cried because he beat her up all the time.

'What about this Jeremy guy?'

Mum had met Jeremy a week or two after Magnus left. On Biker Thursday. He was a member of the Taff Riders. A gentleman apparently, nice, but at twenty-five, a bit young.

'I doubt anything will come of it.'

'You never know.'

It was at this time Mum started painting her best piece. It was inspired by a recent incident. She'd been walking Slug down the woods one Sunday. Passing Freddy's House, she noticed a man in the trees a short distance away. He was standing there, watching her. Smiling, he unzipped his flies and a big pink dick fell out.

This was the third time Mum had been flashed in her life. The first two times had been when she was a young girl, down Roath Park Lake. Trampy men hiding in bushes while she played with the ducks. And of course there was Norman Glengerry, old smarmy nostril-face, and though he hadn't flashed Mum personally, he was the worst because of his hypocritical disfellowshipping ways. Jehovah would *not* approve of such a representative. Enough was enough. Full of fire, Mum ran toward the flasher, Slug straining the lead up front. 'My dog'll fucking kill you,' she screamed. 'She's a pit bull, she'll bite your fucking dick off!'

The man quickly tucked himself away and fled, his smile gone.

'Yeah, you run away, you pervert!'

So Mum decided to document this experience with her oils. She painted the flasher amongst trees that were dabbed on in greens and browns. She left his face an alien blur, unable to

134

remember it. She made sure to make his penis look obscene, like a fat-headed worm. Then the finishing touch – a firing squad in old-fashioned red guardsmen cloaks, their bayonets trained on the man's bulbous knob. She took a lot of care painting this scene, using delicate brush strokes, though her hand was guided by rage and bitterness. It was a good picture.

She decided she didn't like the face being blank. She painted some features in. Now he looked like Magnus. No. It didn't work. She wiped the paint off with a sponge, laid down some more peach-white, then started again. Now it was Dad. No, that wasn't right either. She left the face a blur. There was no point trying to pinpoint a particular vile man. They were all as vile as each other.

Jeremy

I'm in my favourite chair in the living room, reading Stephen King's *It*. Slug is curled up on my lap, snoring quietly. I've just turned fifteen. Hormones haven't been kind to me: I'm getting fat and depressed. I've recently been hit by an overwhelming and unexpected wave of chronic shyness that makes me too scared to leave the house, and even my nice Muslim friends don't want to know. All I do is read Stephen King and eat crisp after crisp.

Mum comes in, followed by Jeremy. They stand in the middle of the room conspicuously.

'What?' I say.

Mum looks nervous and girly. Marriage? It wouldn't surprise me. Jeremy's already moved himself and his dog in. It's got to be marriage.

Mum looks at Jeremy, nods. 'Go on,' she says.

He titters. 'No, you go.'

'All right.' Mum turns to me. 'Christina. I'm pregnant.'

I put my book down. 'Seriously?'

'Yes.'

'Whoa.' A little baby around the house. This is brilliant.

Jeremy wraps his arms around Mum. 'Tell her the names, Ca.'

'Oh yeah. April for a girl. Garth for a boy.'

'Garth? You can't call it Garth, that's a horrible name!'

'I think it's a great name,' says Jeremy.

'It's not. Garth. Why would you call it *Gaarth*?'

Mum hesitates. 'Because that's where it was conceived. On top of Garth Mountain. In April.'

'Too much information.'

They giggle again. Mum and Jeremy have been having sex all over the place. He takes her out on his motorbike for long rides and al fresco sex. Mum's having the time of her life.

I drop Slug to the floor, get up and give out some awkward hugs. Veronica isn't around to hug anyone. She moved out in a riotous cloud of hatred and anger a few months ago. Her last words to Mum: 'You fucking bitch, I hate you.'

'So who's making the tea?' says Jeremy, sitting down with a proud, fertile smile.

I make my way to the kitchen. I like Jeremy, have done since he first came to the house in his ripped Metallica t-shirt and leather jacket. He's all fun and laugh-happy energy. Mum reckons he's genuine. And he gives her all the affection that Dad didn't. Leaves cringy love notes around the house, holds her hand everywhere, tells her he loves her every day. Physically he isn't her type. He has this strange body. From the back he looks like Michaelangelo's David – toned, wonderfully proportioned. He has strong muscular legs from cycling to work every morning. His rippling back is dark-tanned from working outdoors. He's got a good arse. But then turn him around and it all goes wrong – he is pigeon-chested and the colour of raw tofu. A few lonely-looking chest pubes. It's odd. Like Mr Muscle and Mark Wahlberg got smooshed together.

Still, Mum has fallen in love.

Soon they'll get married and I'll have a stepfather.

Jeremy did all the things my dad said he'd do but didn't. He fixed the house up, had Sky installed, a shower installed, landscaped the garden (re-turfing most of the grass areas, digging up borders, planting shrubs and flowers, placing paving slabs in attractive patterns, getting some nice benches in). He soon had our huge backyard looking like something from a magazine. The man was a whirling devil of energy and productivity. He woke up at five when it was still dark and went out the garden to do some work. At eight he cycled to whatever construction site he was working on and spent all day doing manual labour. Then he came home and carried on with the garden. Sometimes he'd fix a motorbike up from scratch and sell it.

It was a nice change. Dad'd had us living like gyppos with his skip-scavenging ways. Finally we were looking like a respectable family. Our next door neighbours on both sides started talking to us over the fences, asking Jeremy about the best place to buy garden furniture, telling Mum laughingly that she had herself 'a keeper', asking me how I was looking forward to having a younger sister or brother. We had a place in Paradise.

Jeremy didn't like Dad. His visits to the house had become painful, strained. Dad was depressed: Mum had found someone and he had not; he was lonely; he had a court case coming up and the outcome would probably be a prison sentence. 'Back when I was with your mum,' he told me, 'I thought the grass was greener on the other side, like. But it's not.' He was taking these tablets for his bad back – Dihydrocodeine it said on the box. He'd sit in his shitty new Splott flat in his underpants, sometimes with a bulb of pink testicle poking out ('For God's sake, Dad, why don't you go out and buy some boxers?'), drinking endless cups of tea (made with two teabags and three sugars) and popping out those little pills from a foil packet. When I told Mum about the pills she shook her head with pursed lips and said, 'Your father is not someone who should be flirting with opiates.' I didn't understand what that meant, but I knew it was bad from the pursed lips so the next time I visited Dad I took him a packet of Paracetamol for his back pain and a three pack of Hypervalue boxer shorts. 'Uh, cheers,' he said, doing a small, glassy-eyed smile.

Rutger was also depressed. Dad hardly walked him and he was putting on weight – he missed Paradise Place too, the big garden and the rest of the family. He was buzzing with fleas. One Saturday I slept over Dad's flat (I had the settee) and the next morning I counted ninety-two flea bites on my body.

The worst was when Dad came to visit us at our house. He'd sit in the living room sipping the dumpy bottle of beer Jeremy gave him, his knees pressed tightly together, his face empty of expression. Jeremy would make an effort with his falsely cheerful small talk, call him Ne', call him mate, but Dad would give nothing back.

Jeremy didn't want this melancholy ex-husband stinking up his new life like an eggy fart. He convinced Mum it would be best to ban him from the house.

'That's not fair, Mum – he's my dad, he should be able to visit me.'

'Jeremy gave him all the chances in the world.'

It's not like Dad had done anything terrible, I thought. He was just a sad man that was all. But I left it. I could always visit Dad and Rutger. He'd had the place fumigated and got Sky installed. Sometimes Veronica would stay over too and he'd buy us cider and make us fancy soup with lots of basil stirred in. 'The night before my court case,' he told us, perched on his windowsill, 'I'll make a moussaka like I used to when we wuz Jehovah's Witnesses. The last meal.' He took a long drag on his spliff, blowing the smoke out of the open window and looking up at the stars sadly.

One Saturday morning I was looking through our video collection for *Highlander* because the night before I'd had a blowjob dream about Christopher Lambert and now I kind of fancied him. But I couldn't find it. Later, in the kitchen, I asked Mum about it.

'Oh, Jeremy threw it out. He threw out all Magnus's crap.'

'He'll be making you throw away all your pen pal letters next.'

She didn't look at me. Carried on folding clothes on the table. 'Well, I already have thrown them away.'

'Mum!'

'I know, I know. But they were filthy. Jeremy's right. Any man would feel the same.'

'What about James Duffy?'

'I'm not writing to James anymore.'

'Why not?'

'Jeremy doesn't like it.'

'But that's not fair. He probably really looked forward to your letters.'

'I know.' She finally looked at me. 'I feel really bad about it. Jeremy has issues.'

'Well, duh.'

She stopped folding. 'He's jealous, Cris.' Especially of your father.'

'Dad? That's stupid.'

'I know. Convince Jeremy of that, will you? Your dad was there first, wasn't he? He got there before him. And Jeremy was a virgin before he met me. You know what men are like. Ridiculous.'

She picked up a pair of Jeremy's faded jeans, folded them.

Jeremy's jealousy grew faster than the baby in Mum's uterus. She had recently accepted a place in UWIC. A BA in Art and Design. It was crap, the course, half the students were doing experiments with string and toilet roll, but she wanted to stick it out, wait and see if it got any better. It was her dream, university. A degree after leaving High School at fifteen… Moira and Oscar would have been proud. Maybe she could end up teaching like them?

Jeremy was so paranoid about her mixing with creative young

men that he made her life hell. He whined about it, he cried about it, he shouted about it. After just a couple of months she gave in and left the course.

'Oh, it was a load of shit anyway,' she said. 'And it's not like I could carry on when the baby comes, is it?' She placed a hand on her growing stomach.

Jeremy threw away anything that might be linked to Mum's past. Anything that Dad had something to do with. He cut down all the trees in the backyard, even the Laburnum, my favourite. 'It was diseased,' he said. Mine and Veronica's childhood photographs were going missing. Dad's sound system was sold and replaced with a new, cheap one from Argos. Records that Mum and Dad had listened to together – Devo, Fleetwood Mac, Kate Bush – were sold and replaced by Cannibal Corpse and Iron Maiden. This was Jeremy's house now. Erase the past. Squeegee it away like grime on a window. Maybe then he would be Mum's first.

Mum confided in me sometimes, usually after arguments. Jeremy was convinced that Mum was screwing Dad. Jeremy was convinced that Mum was screwing everyone. His jealousy ate away at him, gave him bad stomachs. He couldn't help it; his own mother was a whore. He was fucked up. He didn't want to be like this. Mum was going to help him get through it.

Soon the baby was born. April, a girl. Mum and Jeremy started to worry that Slug could be dangerous. A pit bull around a baby. And hadn't Slug made a funny yelping sound once, when April was crying? She had to go. You just didn't take any chances with a baby. They couldn't sell her because of the Dangerous Dog's Act. I suggested they give her away to someone. No – what about The Dangerous Dog's Act? It wasn't allowed. Fuck it, I said – no one cares about the Dangerous Dog's Act anymore. Mum said no. She'd spent nine years with us, it would be unfair to take her to a new home now. No. It would be kinder to have her put down. She was right but I didn't like it.

I belonged to the past too.

They come back from their shopping trip with pale, angry faces. Mum is clutching April tight to her chest. 'Fucking arseholes,' she says.

'What?' I'm sat in my chair with *Misery*. No dog.

'Someone's been tampering with the car.'

'What? How?'

Jeremy dumps a carrier bag on the living room floor, his eyes the colour of thorns. 'Someone put air in one of the tyres. Could've killed us. Lucky I noticed when we were drivin'.'

'*In* the tyres? Why would someone put air *in* the tyres?'

'I dunno. To kill us.'

'How could having too much air in the tyres kill you?'

'It's dangerous, Cris. You can skid. We were on a duel carriageway an' all. That was when I noticed there was somethin' wrong. Wasn't it, Ca? So I went to have it checked in a petrol station. One tyre was way over. That's dangerous, Cris. We could've been killed.'

'Who'd want to kill you?'

Jeremy pauses. Looks at my mum.

'Don't, Jeremy,' she says.

'What?' I say.

'I think it's your dad,' he says.

'Jeremy—'

'What? I'm just sayin' what I'm thinkin'. Who else would do somethin' like that? It's gotta be Neil.'

I stare at him. 'Dad wouldn't do that.'

'Well, you know he likes playing pranks,' says Mum, laying April out on the changing mat. 'That time I was at hospital in labour and Jeremy got that phone call… '

'What, you don't believe this, do you?'

'I don't know.'

'So you think Dad's a potential murderer?'

'I don't *know*, Christina. But I wouldn't put it past him.'

'For God's sake. You were friends with him a little while ago. And now you're saying—'

'Look,' says Jeremy. 'I know he's your father but—'

'It's the kind of thing he'd do,' says Mum, lifting up April's tiny legs with one hand.

'I think you're forgetting one thing,' I say.

I wait for them to say 'what?' They don't.

'Dad knows that I'm in that car half the time. Do you think he'd want to risk my life?'

The question hangs in the air.

'Bloody hell, April,' Mum murmurs, 'how can one human produce so much shit?'

Dad laughs. 'Who'd put air in someone's tyres? If I wanted to mess around with his car I'd take air *out* of the tyres, like. Can you imagine me sneaking around the front garden with a big car pump?' He acts out a desperate pumping with his hands and arms. 'Why'd I do that?'

'I dunno.'

Dad has a think, his eyes to the ceiling. 'You know who he reminds me of? Jeremy?'

'Who?'

'Grima Wormtongue. And your mum is King Theoden. And he's there, Grima, whisperin' poison into her ear. Controllin' her, like.'

'I don't know what you're talking about,' I say.

'*Lord of the Rings.*'

'Never read it.'

Dad nods and is quiet for a while. 'Well anyway,' he finally says. 'He's a dickhead.'

St. Mark's Church. A spacious hall filled with toddlers, babies, family. The smell of pastry and sandwiches. Underneath this, subtle, almost indecipherable, the musky damp scent of large, cold halls. Tinny music spills out of a cheap ghetto blaster. Steps – Five, six, seven, eight. My boot scootin' baby is driving me kerazy.

It's the first birthday of Veronica's daughter, Chantelle. Veronica is engaged to a young mechanic called David who is fun and sweet but will grow up to be potato-faced and joyless. Chantelle was conceived when her parents were sixteen; Veronica is her mother's daughter.

I'm seventeen. I'm hovering by the buffet table, piling mini sausage rolls and sandwich quarters onto a paper plate. I will eat this and then not eat anything else for twenty-four hours. Nothing tastes as good as starving yourself senseless feels. I take my plate over to Dad. He's standing on his own looking uncomfortable. This is the first time him and Mum have been in the same room since he was banned from the house. It's been over three years. Veronica's insisted that all of Chantelle's grandparents be present (she made up with Mum shortly after giving birth). Jeremy has promised not to cause trouble.

'How's it going?' I ask Dad through a mouthful of tuna.

He shrugs. 'OK.' He glances at Mum and Jeremy. 'She's gotten big again.'

'Yeah. Shame.'

'I bet that's him, that is. Feeding her up.'

'She reckons it's baby weight,' I say.

'He's got a bit chunky himself, mind.'

'Yeah. It's the anti-depressants. He's on a really strong dose.'

Dad smiles, nudges me with his elbow. 'Crazy old Jeremy.'

'Shush, you. He's doing therapy and anger management.' I ball up my sandwich crust and throw it at Dad's face. It bounces off his chin. 'God loves a tryer.'

Dad shrugs his eyebrows. He drinks from a white plastic cup and looks around the hall. 'I had a dream about Jeremy the other day,' he says. 'He was standin' by an open grave down Thornhill. I crept up on him and pushed him in. Then I filled the hole.' He laughs with real pleasure, his chin jutting out.

We watch the toddlers smear food and gluey saliva all over their faces. 'So you're OK then?' I say.

'What ju mean?'

'Not too awkward?'

'Well, it is awkward, like, but there we go.'

'OK. Cuz I'm gonna go and speak to Mum for a bit. OK?'

He nods. Before I go he quickly grabs the last sausage roll from my plate and stuffs it in his mouth.

'Bastard.'

He nods, chewing.

Mum and Jeremy are on the other side of the hall, drinking squash. I make my way over. Jeremy is glancing at my dad, little sparks of hate flickering his retinas. April is clinging to his leg, all blonde curly hair and blue eyes and chubby loveliness. She too glances over at the solitary figure of my dad but it's fear, not hatred in her eyes. Jeremy has brought April up to believe that my dad is the Acky Man, a monster. Her Freddy.

'I see he's in his Sunday best,' says Mum.

I look over. I hadn't noticed before. His old Jehovah trousers – the television pixel ones – and a white shirt. 'God. How long's he had them for?' I say.

'Years. Do you think he's trying to impress anyone?'

'It's a church, isn't it?'

'Hmm.'

I notice Dad crouch by a fat child of unclear gender. He hands it a toy – then my view is blocked by Veronica, carrying a pink birthday cake. We all sing Happy Birthday, while Chantelle, oblivious, chews on a plastic frog, her chin and neck sopped with dribble. I look back at my dad but he's gone. I scan the hall. Gone. Probably nipped outside for a fag.

Outside it's grey and chilly. I can't see Dad. I look for his car. It's still there and he's sat in it. He looks sad.

I roll up and light my fag. 'All right, Dad?'

He nods, but he's not all right.

'What's wrong?'

He mumbles something.

'What?'

'I've split my trousers.'

I laugh, swallow a mouthful of smoke and break down in a coughing fit. It passes. 'How ju do that?'

'I was playing with a kid. I bent down – it's these trousers, it is. They're too small.'

'How bad is it?'

He looks down at his hands like a little boy who's been told off. 'All the way up the crack of my arse.'

I laugh again. 'Sorry.'

'Make a rollie, will you?'

I nod, start rolling one up, just the way he likes it – fat, no filter.

The Curse of Gwendolyn

Mum, fifteen. Sailor jeans, orange baseball top, a pair of blue, bolshy eyes searing the kitchen table top. 'I'm not listening to you, you old bitch.'

Gwendolyn slowly shakes her head. 'Moira didn't raise yew to talk like that.'

Mum glances up, eyes nervously defiant.

'I'm not. Fucking. Listening to you.'

'Iesu *Mawr*!' Gwendolyn stares at her chubby granddaughter.

'Catherine Winters, mark my words:' she begins, approaching the table, 'one day *yew* will have a daughter and she will treat yew like yew've treated *me*.' She stands over Mum, head high, jaw wobbling with rage. 'One day yew'll be in *my* shoes, girl.' She stares with those crooked eyes, then, satisfied, walks to the tall Frigidaire and takes some ham out.

Sixteen years later. Dad's car is parked at the end of the drive, behind Jeremy's motorbike. Dad stands by the driver's side, expressionless in the dark as Veronica throws bin liners stuffed with clothes into the boot.

'Take her, take her!' shouts Mum from the bright doorway, doing 'shoo!' gestures with her hands. 'Take her!'

Veronica throws the last load in – a C&A shopping bag filled with rolled-up socks. She slams the boot shut. Her big blue-frog eyes are fierce. She has such a scowl, Dad has always said, you could park a bus on her forehead, a truck on her bottom lip. She gets into the car, slams the door. Dad gets in his side and starts the engine.

Veronica opens her window and sticks her head out. 'You fucking bitch, I hate you!' she screams, wisps of blonde hair fluttering.

I look at Mum. Her eyes are as fierce as Veronica's but shiny with tears. Jeremy drapes an arm round her shoulder as Dad's car disappears round the corner.

At sixteen I bought a Nirvana hoodie and took up smoking. Suddenly I had a social life, starting with lunch-break conversations in Smoker's Lane with the school metalheads. 'You like Nirvana, issit? You should come out to Metros with us on Friday.' Metros was a grimy rock club notorious for its bad smells, sweaty walls and cheap, watered down drinks. I had dreamt of it the way American kids dream of the prom.

I starved off all the weight I'd gained from puberty and depression, became a vegetarian, shaved most of my hair off, got my lip, nose, eyebrow and tongue pierced, and started wearing army boots and combat trousers.

Georgey Porgy, pudding and pie …

Mum has finished the hoovering. She's wrapping the cord up.

'Mum, I want to talk to you a minute.'

'OK.'

We're both standing there in the middle of the living room, her with the plug dangling.

'Um… ' How to phrase it? 'So here's the thing. Um…'

The plug is just dangling there.

'OK. OK. So. I think I might be gay. Or bi.'

She starts blinking rapidly. It's just like that time I told her about Nadeem, except there's no alcoholic around to listen in. The plug is still dangling there. Like some idiot.

'But you must know this already,' I add.

'What? No, I didn't know. I had no idea.'

'Oh, come on. How could you not know? I've been dropping hints. Look at me. I'm wearing dungarees.'

'I just thought…I dunno, I thought you were just being *alternative*. Like that Skunk Anansie. You used to be so boy-mad.'

'Well, not anymore. And newsflash – Skin from Skunk Anansie is bent as anything.'

'Is she? OK. Um.' Her face is very earnest. 'Well, I'm happy with whatever you do, as long as you don't start smoking.' She scoops up the plug and starts wrapping it up in loops around her wrist. 'Anything but that.'

Jeremy is haunted. That's what Mum says. He has bad energy stuck inside him. It's like rotten meat stuck between clean white teeth.

Sometimes, when he gets angry with his rotten meat thoughts, you can feel the energy in the room frazzle with nastiness, and a couple of times, when he's been fully charged up, the electricity flickers on and off.

Once, when Jeremy was having a nightmare, Mum saw an alien-green glow on the wall above his head. It grew like a cluster of bacteria and moved slowly across the wall. It couldn't have come from outside – the curtains were shut.

Another time, he was sat on the couch watching TV with a pint of Caffreys on the windowsill next to him. He'd been in a bad mood all day. Suddenly the TV flickered and the pint jumped off the windowsill and landed on him, drenching his boxers. The windows and doors were shut. Not that a breeze could knock over a full pint anyway. If it had been only Jeremy who told me this story, I wouldn't have believed it, because Jeremy is the king of exaggeration – the-fish-was-*this*-big – and a prankster. But it was Mum who saw it all, and her Freddy Krueger days are well over.

Mum reckons it's a mixture of his bad energy and the ghost of his stepdad, Geoffrey. Geoffrey was a mean abusive brute, and after he died, his ghost tore through Jeremy's house, opening and slamming and opening and slamming cupboard doors like something from a horror, making the radio play backwards without being plugged in, filling the rooms with icy breezes in the middle of summer.

Maybe Geoffrey followed Jeremy to Paradise Place?

Jeremy has a dark, dingy past. His mother won't tell him who his real dad is. Also there is madness in the family, including whispers of an auntie who set herself on fire after a mental episode and an uncle who kicked a dog to death because he didn't like the look of it. Jeremy's mother has tried to kill herself five times, and one of these times he found her drooling on the sofa, almost dead, when he came home from school. Infant school. Too young to know how to use a phone. He'd had to call the next door neighbour for help.

'I'm glad he told me all about this *after* I got pregnant with his child,' said Mum. 'Oh yes, it all came out *after* he'd got me knocked up. Before that, he was just a nice, happy guy. You remember that, when he was just a nice, happy guy?' Yes, I told her. 'Never lasts,' she said. 'People only show their best side at first. Then they get their hooks in you and all their shit just splurts out like diarrhoea. Remember that.'

Jeremy is still on a strong dose of anti-depressants and they help with his anger and jealousy, but every few months he secretly comes off them and goes mental. Genuinely sick people never want to be on their meds, says Mum. Jeremy no longer has the crazed energy he once had, and he's put on weight, at least three stone. He tried anger management group sessions for a while, but hated it and felt like he didn't fit, and just got even angrier sat there listening to men talk about breaking their wives' ribs and bashing Pakis and fags and putting their kids in hospital, because these are things he would never do.

Jeremy can go months working on his issues and behaving himself, but then, bam, suddenly Mum is a whore and she is fucking Neil Jones all over again. A whore, just like his mother. Mum hasn't spoken to Dad in ages but somehow she is still fucking him.

'Typical insecure male behaviour and mummy issues,' says Mum. 'You know, Cris, sometimes I think about his stories, the ones about Geoffrey's ghost. And I know they're not just stories because his sisters back them up. And I think about them, and I think, maybe it wasn't Geoffrey's ghost? Maybe it was all Jeremy? All his psycho puberty energy.' She sighs. 'I've really landed myself a good one here, Cris. You're lucky, being gay. Men are no fun.'

'This is just what people are like in the real world,' says Jeremy, cutting up his Fray Bentos pie to let the steam out.

I wipe April's gooey chin with a tea towel. 'What, racist?' I say.

'No, not racist, Cris,' he says, forking meat into his mouth. He chews. 'It ain't racist to say Somalis are trouble.' Swallows.

'I think you'll find it is, Jeremy.'

'What, so ten Somalis from Cathays High start actin' up on the bus and it's not OK to say somethin' about it?'

'White kids from Cathays always act up on the bus, big gangs of them, and no one comments on their colour, do they?' I push away my untouched food and put my elbows on the table. 'I mean, if a group of white kids start misbehaving, you'd say, "Fuckin' teenagers," or something like that. But if Somali kids misbehave, it's "Fuckin' darkies, comin' over here, blah blah blah."'

'Stop swearing in front of your sister,' says Mum.

'Sorry,' I say.

Jeremy rolls his eyes. 'You don't live in the real world, Cris, that's your problem.'

'Good. I don't wanna live in the real world if it's full of racist homophobes like you.'

Jeremy's knife and fork freeze. 'Why you bringin' homophobic into this? I'm not homophobic, Cris. Tell her, Ca.'

Mum does a little shrug and carries on eating.

I spoon some potato into April's mouth. 'You are homophobic.'

'I'm not. I haven't got a problem with you, have I?'

'You think gay men are disgusting.'

'I never said all of them. Just the ones who go cottaging. Turns my stomach.' He shudders, eyes on his plate. 'That's just how most normal men feel about it, Cris.'

'In the real world?' I say, brows raised.

Jeremy nods.

'It's not the real world, it's *your* world,' I say. 'There's no such thing as only one version of reality, Jeremy.'

Jeremy drops his knife and fork on the plate. 'Will you tell her, Ca? I've just come home from work and I'm knackered. I just wanna eat my dinner without your smart-arse bloody daughter—'

'You started it,' I say. 'You know what my views are. If you're gonna start slagging off Somalis, knowing some of my friends are Somalis, I'm obviously gonna argue with you.'

Jeremy kicks his chair back and stands up. His bulgy-out eyes are crackling with anger. 'I've lost my appetite now. Thanks, Cris.' He goes out the garden, slamming the door.

Mum looks at me.

I get my Rizlas and tobacco out. 'What? It's not my fault you've married a bigot.'

Mum shakes her head and carries on eating.

Men so *are* fun.

It's Mum I can't stand arguing with. She's smarter than Jeremy and she knows how to make me feel shit. Arguing with her makes my temples throb and my shoulders bunch up like arthritic hands. But the worst is when I argue with Mum *and* Jeremy. The pair of them together, hip-to-hip on the sofa, backing each other up. Four righteous, confident eyes on me.

This is their case against me:

It is a non-smoking house and yet I continue to smoke out of my bedroom window. No amount of joss stick will hide the smell, Christina!

I'm not eating and I'm probably anorexic, and if I carry on like this I will have to be institutionalised or something.

I treat this house like a hotel.

I'm smoking cannabis and God knows what else – I'm going to end up just like my bloody father.

I'm going out drinking and coming back in the early hours in a right state, leaving the key in the front door lock. I won't be happy till I've got the house burgled.

I'm going to end up like Suki bloody Fisk.

I'm moody and argumentative and horrible to have around.

My education is going down the drain.

I don't bathe enough and I smell.

I always have an answer or a justification. Sometimes a strong one – 'How the hell can you say *I'm* moody and argumentative and horrible to have around when Jeremy's smashing glasses and having jealous rages every time he comes off his meds?' Or, 'How many nine stone anorexics do you know, Mother?'

The subtext underneath my every parry is this:

Mum, you've changed since you met Jeremy.

Jeremy, you won't be happy until I'm out of your house because a) you want my mother all to yourself, and b) I am the daughter of Neil Jones.

But maybe it's just me wanting my mother all to myself?

They've had enough. Bloody curse of bloody bastard Gwendolyn. They want me gone.

Time to live in the real world. Mate.

I stay at a youth hostel called Danescourt House, filled with problem teens. Most of them are chavs – yellow-haired girls from Ely who slob around the house in their Kappa tracksuits smoking Lambert and Butlers, boys with gelled-forward fringes and thick gold chains who say, 'origh', bra?' I'm terrified of them, and sit quietly smoking my rollies in the common room, but they turn out to be friendly and they don't call me a 'stinkin' fuckin' mosher', like the chavs in school did. I learn a valuable lesson about prejudice. And then I forget it.

Soon I'm given a flat in Canton by Single Women's Housing, an association that helps out fuck-ups, mentals, addicts and prostitutes.

Jeremy helps me move my stuff in. It's a small flat with a living/sleeping area and a kitchen and bathroom. Upstairs lives a skinny girl with a brown ponytail who gets beaten by her boyfriend a lot, and downstairs there's Michelle and her drug dealer boyfriend, Rico, who I will spend the next five years buying weed from and who, when I'm twenty, will want a threesome with me, which I will reject. After a week Michelle and Rico give me their black cat because they're sick of him, and I name him Meegs the Bastard. Meegs the Bastard used to live upstairs with the girl who gets beaten up all the time, and that's probably why he's such an aggressive shit. I have big plans for Meegs the Bastard. I'm going to train him, pacify him, give him stability and love

Instead I spend the next six months getting him stoned and giving him dirty looks.

Just before my eighteenth birthday I ask Mum if I can move back in. I can't afford to pay my bills, and I've just spent three days sick with a stomach bug, lying on my sour sheets, alone, too scared to eat anything while Meegs the Bastard sporadically attacked my bare feet in the darkness.

Mum says yes. I take Meegs the Bastard to the animal shelter, crying but relieved, and the next day, Jeremy helps me move my stuff back into Paradise Place.

'It's going to be different this time,' says Mum, standing in the hallway as I drag in my heavy, blood-stained futon. 'You're going to have to follow our rules.'

'OK, Mum, I will.'

Four months. That's how long I last. I move in with Nana. Who is now Nan, because I'm not a child any more. She has a big house in a nice area. She lives on the ground floor with her cats and dogs, and lodges out the second floor to Kev, a middle-aged, chain-smoking milkman from London who has watery-blue Sid James eyes and a Rottweilian cough. He has these sleazy black and white pictures up in his living room; women with big pale-nippled knockers and sticky-out ribcages, in thigh-high leather boots. The sort of pictures that are trying to be arty but are the very opposite of arty. He takes them down every weekend when his grandkids visit and the walls are nicotine yellow with perfect white rectangles. I stay in the attic room. I'm not allowed to use Kev's toilet, since I'm not paying rent, so I piss in pint glasses and empty them out the window, making the roof below me smell like rancid chemicals in the summer time. I cut down on weed and take up a coffee habit. I go back to college and start four new A-levels.

I miss family life – April is four now and adorable, and Jeremy is making the house nicer and nicer each year with his colour schemes and varnish jobs. I ask Mum if I can move back in again.

She says OK. OK. But this is my last chance.

A warm afternoon. April is in my bedroom twirling around to 'Daydream Believer' by the Monkees. She has on a denim skirt and a lilac t-shirt. She's got honey-blonde hair like mine at that age and Jeremy's sharp nose. Eyes a mixture of Mum's and Jeremy's – light blue like Mum's, deepset like her father's. I have a couple of photos left on a camera film. I give April my electric guitar to play with. She pretends to play along to the song. I show her how to do rock 'n' roll devil horns with her hands and I take a photo. One picture left. I have some cigars wrapped in tissue in my knicker drawer that I kept from Veronica and David's wedding party. I take one out and hand it to her.

'Do a Popeye face,' I say, puffing one of my cheeks and squinting.

She laughs and tries, blowing a spitty raspberry, the cigar held between her tiny thumb and forefinger.

Flash goes off. Snap.

I wind the film and take it downstairs. Give it to Mum. She works in Asda now, developing photos.

'I'll see if I can get you a discount,' she says, putting the film in her pocket.

Mum comes home from work late. I'm in the living room revising for my exams. Mum walks in wearing her horrible navy blue and flower-puke Asda uniform and drops the photos into my lap. 'I'm not happy with one of these,' she says.

'Which one?'

'The one of April with the cigar.'

'Really? It wasn't lit or anything.'

'You know how I feel about smoking, Christina.'

'Oh come on. I was only messing around. I was getting April to do a Popeye impression.'

'Popeye smokes a pipe.'

'Does he? Oh.'

Mum kicks her work shoes off. 'I want you to get rid of that photo. Rip it up or something.' She starts going through her waistcoat pockets.

'What?' I laugh incredulously. 'Why?'

'You know how I feel about smoking. I lost both of my parents because of smoking.'

'I'm not ripping it up.'

Mum's hands freeze mid-rummage. She looks at me. 'I want you to rip it up, Christina. You've got your four-year-old sister posing with a filthy cigar. I don't like it. Especially after all that Monica Lewinsky stuff.'

'Oh my God. How could you say that? As if I had that in mind.'

'I hate smoking, it killed my parents, and you know this. I don't *like* it.'

155

'Well *I* don't like being told what to do like that,' I say, standing up. And I walk out of the room.

I go upstairs to my bedroom and look through my photos, which are mostly boring. Get dressed for bed, brush my teeth, read some of my book. As if nothing has happened. As if I haven't just started a war that will end in my third and final ejection from Paradise Place.

It takes three days. The first day I avoid Mum and Jeremy. Stay in my room eating tomato sandwiches for tea and revising. The second day Mum again tells me to rip up the photo. I refuse. Because I'm not asked, I'm *told*. Because I'm stubborn. Because I'm too old to be dictated to.

By the end of the second day Jeremy is in on it too.

'Just rip it up, Cris, for your Mum,' he says, when she's in the kitchen.

I shake my head.

'You know how we feel about smoking—'

'It's just a photo! You're making such a big deal about nothing.'

'It's not nothin' to us. Just do this thing for your mother.'

Mum comes back in the room with her elevens deeply engraved. 'Don't waste your time with her, Jeremy. She doesn't give a shit about me.'

'Oh, don't be so dramatic.'

Mum looks at me sadly. 'First Veronica, now you. It's the Curse of Gwendolyn. Daughters from hell.'

'More like the fucking mother from hell!' I storm out of the room. My arm scrapes hers on the way out.

Mum gasps. Rubs her flabby upperarm.

'Oh, come on. My arm just touched yours. It was an accident.'

Mum looks at Jeremy. 'She hit me!'

'That's your fuckin' mother,' says Jeremy, rising from his chair.

156

I shake my head in disbelief. 'Why don't *you* fuck off?'

I run up the stairs, Mum's hysterical voice fading as I reach my bedroom.

By the third day they want me out. I refuse. This isn't about the photograph, I decide. This is about power. Two lardy egos slamming against each other like sumo wrestlers. Mum can play the Dead Parents card all she wants – this is about me not submitting to her.

This is what all our arguments have ever been about.

I hide in my bedroom. Mum and Jeremy shout at me through the door. They threaten to call the police. When April tries to come into my room to play, Jeremy snatches her away with a harsh whisper, as if I'm a smelly old man sat on a park bench watching the children play. I lie on my futon looking at the photos. I feel stupid. It's just a crappy photo, I wouldn't miss it. I should have ripped it up as soon as she told me to. But it's too late.

I'm being sent to live with Freddy all over again.

Around lunchtime I tiptoe to the toilet. I'm two minutes at the most. When I come back I find Jeremy dumping my stuff into bags. The photograph of April is on the floor, torn into glossy rag-strips. He doesn't look at me. Just keeps bagging my stuff.

I pack a night bag, quickly adding my diaries and vibrators when Jeremy's back is turned. I go to my nan's and phone Veronica, crying. She tells me I should've just torn up the photo and I say, 'It's not about the fucking photo, Vron! It's never been about the photo!' But I'm not sure any more.

After the call I make myself a cup of tea and smoke a rollie in between gaspy sobs. Nan pats my shoulder with her small awkward hand and tuts. 'Fancy throwin' you out a week before yer exams!' I nod and smoke.

The doorbell rings. I answer it and see Jeremy's hatchback pulling away from the kerb. In the street outside are six or seven stuffed black bags, a guitar and a rolled-up, bloodstained futon.

I see Stonehouse Suki near Roath Park. It's been a long time. She looks like Iggy Pop. Her blonde hair is in plaits, lots of them and her skin is like cooked bacon. She's pissed as a fart. She grabs me and hugs me for a long time and there's that same old smell – booze fumes and fag smoke and patchouli. We sit down in the street and smoke. Just opposite us is the street Mum grew up in with Moira and Gwendolyn and Henry. The house Oscar died in. It would be worth half a mill now, easy.

She asks about Mum and I tell her we aren't speaking. 'Oh Cris, my *friend*, you must speak to her, she's bloody great, your mum.' And she pulls me in close and stares at me all grave and wise, or at least tries to, but her lids are sinking and her irises are like floating scum. 'Cris. Cris. Don't be a twat.'

I tell her Mum is still with Jeremy. She smirks and shakes her head. She'd once tried to come on to Jeremy the same as she'd come on to Magnus, and he pushed her hand off his thigh disgusted and walked out of the room and asked Mum later why she was friends with that horrible woman. And Mum didn't let her in the house after that.

The pair of us, banished.

Before we part Suki pulls me in close again, that strong hand on my arm, the hot breath in my face. 'My friend, don't be a stupid cow. You speak to your mum. She won't be around forever.' And I just shake my head and stub my fag out on the clean pavement.

Veronica's house is neat but gross. Bad fourth-hand furniture, shit decor. She has a pantry full of skinny dead spiders. There are these two black cats and they're morbidly obese because they have cat flu and they just lie there on the stairs, the size of armadillos, sleeping all day. They still go in the litter tray and the house stinks of piss. Veronica's house is the place I come to when I'm broken-hearted or on a come-down and need to mend. Or when I want a break from sleeping on Nan's leather couch (her spare attic room is uninhabitable at the moment because of a leaking ceiling and damp on the walls). There's always a bit of weed and a tin of biscuits and Tesco Value crisps and pirate movies. Veronica will flutter around doing housework around me, sometimes shouting at Chantelle ('She is *so* fuckin' busy!') or David, who just sits there with black grease in his fingernails, watching TV while slowly and patiently smoking a weak spliff. Apart from the weed, it's just like Paradise.

She's talking on the phone to Jeremy now. I scowl like I always do when Veronica talks on the phone to our Wicked Stepfather, or the Bitch Queen herself. I haven't spoken to them for a year and a half. A year and a half of dreaming every night about Paradise Place. Always the garden for some reason. Every dream. Set in that fucking garden. It's hard to stay angry for a year and a half. But I manage it. I let my bitterness brew like coffee grounds in a percolator. Suddenly she puts the phone in my hand and says, 'He wants to speak to you,' and I put the receiver to my ear without thinking. A year and a half. And here's his high-pitched Gabalfa Boy voice talking words in my ear while I smoke a roll-up on my sister's threadbare couch.

She misses me. That's what he says. 'Just speak to her, Cris.'

So I do. I go to see her and we sort things out, apologising for our respective sins. April is shy of me now, but it's OK, we've sorted things out. 'We're a right pair of silly stubborn cows, aren't we?' And we smile and laugh and we do not look into each other's eyes, not quite.

What is *wrong* with us?

She'd paid for a weekend to New York with her annual Asda shares. Just the two of us. Officially it was a graduation present. I'd managed to finish a degree in Bristol UWE. Drama and Film Studies, 2:1, whoop-de-doo.

Unofficially it was blowing away the old stink of a cigar.

It was a Big Deal for Mum, being away from her youngest daughter and husband for the first time, and it was an even Bigger

Deal for Jeremy, letting her out of the country on her own. 'You're not just going on a trip,' I said to her, as we sat on the plane sucking Polos, 'You're going on a guilt trip.'

But he did OK. The guilt drops he dribbled down the 3,340 mile long phone line every night were tiny and not too bitter. Mum would come away from the phone at the hotel lobby sadsmiling. She missed her family. But I was there. And the whole point of this holiday was to prove that I was family again.

Mum was shocked by New Yorkers. She liked her Americans Disney-friendly or at least brassy and colourful, like they are in the films. She wanted Danny DeVito taxi cabbies with hairy arms hanging out the side windows, honking and shouting 'Get awf tha road, punk!' then turning round and smiling and saying, 'Sorry about that, laydeez, these roads is crazy, now where can I take yuz?' Instead we got African drivers with shit English and eyes full of dark glass. Dead-faced white people serving us burgers. Not even snapping bubblegum or rolling their eyes like they were supposed to. In the East Village I got my septum pierced. Mum got pissed off because the piercist told her to take her bottle of water outside for hygiene reasons, and she bitched about it for the rest of the day because the piercist had 'filthy bloody dreadlocks' and was therefore a hypocrite and an arsehole. When we were walking through the clumped sidewalks and hundreds of apathetic grey-soul natives knocked and jostled me, I'd stick out my elbows and knock back, charging through, all vicious triangles and mean Welsh eyes, while Mum followed like a nervous sow at market.

But we had a nice time. We tried Krispy Kreme and chilli dogs. We looked out for places that had been in *Home Alone 2*. In Greenwich Village we went to a small gay bar, right out of *Will & Grace*, called Rosie's Turn, where a neat old queen sang charming songs at a piano and Mum sat there with her proud, My-Daughter-Is-Gay-And-Look-How-Cool-With-It-I-Am face on. We were doing so well.

We were in a cab on the way to the airport, late and stuck in traffic. I was hung over. The back of the driver's neck looked like a slab of gone off pork and his blond hair was nitted with dandruff.

'It just makes no sense, the utter stupidity of it.'

It was the dreadlocked piercist again. Tenth time that day.

'I just had no idea people here could be so unfriendly. I'm really shocked, Christina.'

I stared at the rotten pork in front of me.

'Wouldn't it just be our luck to miss the plane and be stuck sleeping in the airport with the rude bloody New York airport staff?'

'Oh God, don't say that,' I said.

'I really am taken aback by the rudeness of these people, Cris. Remember that man in the tube station when we asked him for directions? Ridiculous! I can't believe these people…'

And she went on and on, both chirpy and negative, I don't know how she managed it, and the cars around us beeped their horns again and again, like monkeys in zoos who spit and piss out of their cages because they are safe in their cages, depressed and safe, and my brain screamed for silence but my lips said nothing. Those New Yorkers! Weren't Americans supposed to be friendly? It was just astonishing.

'God, Mum. I think we've established by now that New Yorkers are rude. End of.'

'I know, Christina. But I just didn't *expect* it. That man with the dreadlocks! How could he bitch about my poxy bottle of mineral water when he's there with his dirty dreadlocks swinging all over the place? A poxy fucking bottle of water? But it's that man at the tube station who really takes the prize for rude arsehole of the year.'

I rolled my eyes. 'You know what? This is *Trains, Planes and Automobiles*, and you are John Candy and I am Steve Martin.'

She looked at me. 'So you're saying I'm fat and annoying?'

I opened my mouth and nothing came out.

'Well, thank you very much, daughter. Thank you very fucking much.'

'I don't mean it like that, Mum! You're John Candy because you're sort of relentlessly cheerful and talkative, and I'm Steve Martin because I'm the uptight, cynical one. I'm having a go at myself too.'

'I know what you meant.' And she pulled her book out of her bag and placed it on the desk of her belly and read it with her 11s deeper and darker than cracks in a drought, and I bet she wasn't taking in the words.

Silence the rest of the way home. Rushing through the airport, departing, seven hours flying, collecting the luggage, finding the coach, waiting for the coach to depart, four hours on the coach. Silence, finally. A horrible, drum-tight silence. Half an hour from Cardiff, Mum called Jeremy on her mobile and talked to him. 'I've missed you,' she said. 'I wish you were here with me,' and I felt the subtext of those words and they made me feel like the biggest, baddest apple of all.

I called her an hour after I got back to my (newly decorated) attic room at Nan's. I wouldn't normally apologise so soon, but I could smell the smoke of a musty old cigar. I squeezed out a quiet sorry. 'Pardon?' she said, coldly. She didn't want that sorry yet, she wasn't ready for it. She hadn't had enough time to roll around like Bacchus in the wine-like glory of her resentment. But she must have smelled the cigar smoke herself; she eventually took that sorry and a couple of icicles dropped off her voice and smashed.

'Thanks for the holiday,' I said. 'It was cool.'

'That's OK. Well done on the 2:1. Moira and Oscar would be proud.'

And we said good night and hung up.

Close.

Me, Mum, Veronica and her daughter, Chantelle. We're walking down Maerdy Road, heading back to Paradise Place. Chantelle is five. She's got bright blue eyes, a large red mouth and a lion's mane of brownish-blonde hair. She's a little chubby and she dribbles a lot and I reckon she's going to grow up gorgeous.

Suddenly Chantelle starts running. Veronica lunges after her and grabs her by the arm. Yanks her back.

'Stop running off!'

Chantelle violently squirms, bottom lip sticking out. 'Muuum, get off.'

'Stay here!'

Chantelle intensifies her struggles. Starts crying.

'Oh shit,' says Mum, looking at me.

Chantelle starts screaming, full-on screaming. She thrashes around, angry red elastic lips stretched around her enormous gob.

Veronica's gone red. 'Shut up! Shut up! Shut the fuck up!' She glances around to see if anyone's watching. They're not. She whacks Chantelle on the bum.

Chantelle's hysterical. Snot and dribble drools down her chin. She looks like she's having a fit.

Mum, looking at me with bemused eyes, curls her lips in. She does a deliberate 'I don't know this person' side step away from the screaming child. Then another. I follow. We end up a good ten feet away.

Chantelle falls on the floor. Lies there still. Veronica tries to grab her arm and pull her up but she's totally limp.

'Oh dear,' says Mum. 'She's doing the corpse again.'

Veronica looks like she wants to give her daughter a good hard kick. She walks towards us. 'Fuck it, I'm just gonna leave her.'

A woman leans out of her front door. 'Is she OK?'

Veronica glares at the woman, blonde eyebrows almost white against the pink of her face. 'Yes! She's just having a tantrum. She does it all the time.'

'Ooh-kay. Sorry.' Woman closes her door.

'You can lie there all day,' she tells Chantelle. 'I'm going.'

No response.

Veronica starts walking drearily down Maerdy Road. 'Fuck her,' she says. 'She's a little bitch.'

Mum, still bemused, follows, glancing back at the corpse-child. 'You know what this is, don't you?' she says to Veronica.

'What?'

'It's the Curse of Gwendolyn being passed down to you.'

Veronica looks at Mum.

'And one day Chantelle will have a daughter and she will treat Chantelle like Chantelle treated you. Same for you too,' she says, turning to me.

'Not me,' I say. 'I'm not having kids.'

We hear a child's high wailing and turn to look. Chantelle is running towards us, arms outstretched.

'Muuuuum!'

Veronica scowls. 'Oh, go and play with traffic!'

Twelve-year-old Lesbian

I called her Leo, but that wasn't her name. I didn't know her name. It would take me a year to find out.

The first time I saw her she was leaning against the shop window of Blue Banana, fag in hand. She was in her early-twenties. She had slick, blonde curtains, the hairstyle of choice for heartthrobs and lesbians at the time.

I slowed down and stared. Elbowed Sidney. 'Look at her.'

He swept his gaze over her face. She was breathing out smoke, looking down at her trainers.

'Oh my God.' I could see most of Sidney's iris instead of the usual slate-blue sliver under thick doe lashes. 'She's beautiful.'

I nodded.

We stopped. I leaned against a lamppost, got out my tobacco and started rolling up, eyes flickering from Rizla to the woman.

'Ju reckon she works there?' Sidney said.

Blue Banana was a piercing and tattoo shop which also sold bongs and joss sticks and over-priced clothes.

'I dunno. Let's wait. See what she duz.'

'She's really androgynous,' he said. '*I* almost fancy her.'

I licked the Rizla. 'She's blatantly gay, isn't she?'

'Oh yeah. Defo. She looks like Leonardo DiCaprio. But a lesbian version.'

She dropped her fag and rubbed it into the ground with a scuffed trainer. Then she went into the shop.

'I bet she works there,' said Sidney. 'Sha' we go in and look?'

'Nah. It might look really obvious if we go in now.' I lit my fag and stared at the shop front. 'Let's go in tomorrow.'

We walked home through the woods, talking frantically about the woman. Sidney called her Leo and it stuck.

Just before Pontcanna playing fields we passed a topless teenage boy with a rippled torso and acorn-smooth skin. A couple of minutes later Sidney had to sit down.

'He had the most perfect nipples,' he said, getting out his asthma pump.

We were on a bench facing the gurgling River Taff. Sidney had his bag on his lap. I watched coffee-brown scum glide the surface of the water and thought about Leo. I was seventeen. I would think of fuck all else for the next few months.

Me and Sidney had become best friends when we were fifteen. He'd lost his plump cheeks and grown into a beautiful young man with long eyelashes and full lips. His anxiety was still bad but he masked it with Valium and fake coolness. During the summer holidays we went to town almost every day. We met in the woods, by Freddy's House, and then we followed the Taff trail all the way to the city centre, holding hands and singing early Madonna songs in loud, earnest voices.

We walked around town, browsing in shops and people watching. We never had money and rarely ate – by the end of the day we'd be so weak our incessant giggling would take on a hysterical edge, like someone being tickled for too long. We'd walk home, again through the woods, and when we got to Freddy's House we'd stop and go over the day's events, Sidney talking out of the side of his mouth like Drew Barrymore and waving my fag smoke away with his pale thin hands. Then we'd hug awkwardly, say, 'Phone you later,' and go our separate ways, him past Freddy's house, down the Taff trail to go home to his agoraphobic mother with the Farrah Fawcett swept hair, and me up the hill past Talybont, to return to Mum and Jeremy in Paradise Place (I hadn't been kicked out yet).

Now there was Leo. A visit to Blue Banana became part of the daily routine. Usually near the end of the day – a delayed treat. As I walked through the doors my heart would be banging. If she wasn't there behind the counter I'd get this horrible hungry feeling in my stomach and a rush of sadness so dark and abrupt it was as if a dog had just died.

But if Leo was there I'd get a different kind of hungry feeling and it wouldn't be in my stomach. I'd stay in the shop as long as possible, pretending to examine each tattoo design on the wall like a connoisseur. I'd sneak glances at the till. Just seeing her face would give me electricity.

I always bought something in Blue Banana. Novelty tobacco paper that smelt like old mushrooms if I was especially poor, a packet of pink-tipped Joss sticks otherwise – Fantasy, the same incense they burned in the shop. So my bedroom would smell like love.

Once I asked Leo about the price of a tragus piercing even though I knew the answer. When she went to double-check, Sidney leaned in close, full girlish lips curled into a grin, and whispered, 'Ya should've asked how much it costs to get yer flaps pierced,' and I elbowed him, and she came back and told me, 'Twenty pound,' and she smiled – she had clear blue eyes and dark eyebrows – and I took home with me a clear mental snapshot of the smile and never let it fade.

One Saturday Leo was standing outside the shop talking to a skinny, butch woman with spiky bleached hair. She was dressed in faded denim and had at least eight piercings in her face. They were smoking and laughing. Instead of going in the shop me and Sidney carried on walking down Caroline Street.

'Thass not her fuckin' girlfriend, issit?' said Sidney.

'I fuckin' hope not.'

'She's horrific, Cris.'

'I feel sick,' I mumbled.

We sat on a bench near the bus station. I burst into tears and buried my face in Sidney's shoulder. He smelled of rosewood and static.

I first met Jan down the castle grounds one Saturday, six months later. It was sunny and a large group of us were sat inside the stone circle, passing round spliffs. She was sat at the edge of the group with a friend. Not quite included. Jan was tall and heavy and dressed in black. She looked like she had some Egyptian or Iranian in her. Her hair was a messy raven nest. She had big bulbous eyes and the iris floated in the middle, small and black like a curled up woodlouse.

Me and Sidney got talking to her. Her friend, Sally, sat there looking at her trainers and casting out nervous little glances like a miserable squirrel.

'So, you obviously live in dykesville,' Jan said to me.

I laughed. 'How could you tell?'

'Hmm, it was a toughie.' She looked at Sidney. 'Poofsville for you?'

'I dunno.'

'Yes,' I said. 'He pretends to be bi, but really he's grossed out by vaginas.'

Sidney gave me a dirty look. 'Yeah, yours.'

Jan leaned forward, eyes gleaming, like she had a secret to tell. 'You ever seen that lush lesbian who works in Blue Banana?'

Me and Sidney looked at each other. 'Oh my God,' we said at the same time.

I said, 'Yes! Fuck. I used to go in Blue Banana every day just to look at her.'

Now Sally was leaning forward too. 'We still go in every day,' said Jan. 'We're in love.' Sally pulled a swoony orgasm face.

'I used to cry over her,' I said.

'I still do,' said Jan. 'She's, like, a gay icon or something. Every Cardiff lezzer worth her salt wants a bit.'

'Ju know what her name is?' said Sidney.

'Yeah, it's Gail.'

Sidney laughed. 'Gail? Ew.'

'We always called her Leo,' I said. 'Like Leonardo Dicaprio. Ju know anything else about her?'

'Yeah. Apparently she's a total bitch.'

'I can *so* see that,' said Sidney. 'And she obviously knows how lush she is.'

Jan nodded. 'Blatantly. We're going to see her later. Sally's getting her belly button pierced. Should give us around twenty minutes in the shop.'

I sucked in my stomach and lifted up my top. Pointed to the butterfly tattoo on my navel. 'See that? I had that done just so I could be in the shop as long as possible. It was the cheapest design they had.'

Jan and her friend laughed. Me and Sidney shook our heads incredulously. Small world. We carried on talking about Gail, whose real name felt like an olive pit coming out of my mouth. The sky clouded over. I ran out of tobacco. A girl in a Fear Factory hoodie gave me a pinch of her Old Holborn. Sidney sucked on his asthma pump and made daisy chains.

Sally spoke to me for the first time. 'Ju know how old Jan is?'

I shrugged.

'Guess.' Sally was bone-thin and had a long pram-face and droopy, bovine eyes. She had the air of a world-weary barmaid.

Jan hit her on the arm. 'Shut up, Sal. Fuck sake.'

'I dunno. Sixteen? Seventeen?'

Sally shook her head. Small smile. 'She's twelve.'

Jan gave Sally a sour look, her eyes dark slashes.

'Twelve?' said Sidney. 'You're lyin'.'

'Seriously?' I said.

Jan nodded grimly. Hitched her eyes to the sky. 'Yes, I'm fucking twelve.'

'That's shocking,' I said. 'You don't look twelve. Duz she, Sid?'

'No way. You look our age. And you're dead mature.'

Jan smiled. 'Thank you.' She gave Sally another black glare. Turned back to us. 'I'm surprised you haven't heard of me before actually.'

I shook my head.

She raised her brows sardonically. 'Well apparently *every*one's heard of Twelve-year-old Lesbian.'

Sally snorted out a laugh.

Twelve-year-old Lesbian hammered a fat fist down onto her friend's skeleton-bone thigh.

Castle grounds. Four in the afternoon, September. I was sitting on some grass near the edge of the stone circle with my friend Dennis and a bunch of stoners I didn't know very well. Dennis was a blue-eyed gay boy with pierced nipples and a beautifully sarcastic voice. He had a bottle of poppers and we were passing it round. Heady, fragile laughter went round like a Mexican wave. Cardiff Castle wobbled and blurred like a watercolour in front of me.

'Look, it's Twelve-year-old Lesbian,' said Bonehead, who was skinny as a starving boy but apparently had a ten-inch dick.

Jan and Sally were walking toward us. 'Hey!' I shouted, waving. 'Twelve-year-old Lesbian!'

She didn't wave back.

'How was school?' I shouted. It was seventh of September, the first day back.

'Yeah, how was *schoool*?' said Bonehead.

'Didja sing kumbayah?' said Fred, a scruffy, handsome guy in massive, filthy Dr Martens.

'Hey!' said Bonehead. 'Didja play hide and seek in the playgwound?'

Jan and Sally changed direction and veered toward the big flat rock in the middle of the stone circle. They sat on it and huddled together.

'Aw, I think we upset her,' said Bonehead. He stuck out his bottom lip, made it go like a slab of sashimi.

'Twelve-year-old Lesbian's a dickhead,' said Fred, saying 'dickhead' in a Liverpudlian accent. That was the new big thing, saying 'dickhead' in a Liverpudlian accent. Dickhhhead.

'She's only young,' I said.

'She's a dickhead,' said Fred.

'Well, I don't think so.' I got out my tobacco. 'Did you see Trenderella's new piercing?'

Trenderella was the name Dennis and I had given to Sally. She was in the middle of a clumsy cross-over from chav to mosher. She wore baggy trousers and Green Day t-shirts, but she also scraped back her hair into a Croydon Facelift and was dripping with gold jewellery from Elizabeth Duke.

Bonehead snorted through his nose. He was so alternative that he didn't need piercings.

We carried on with the poppers for a while. Then we got headaches and nausea and dropped out, one by one. Me and Dennis got up and headed for the gates. I stopped as we were passing Jan and Sally. Jan was bent over a piece of paper, furtively writing. She had her arm wrapped around it like a prisoner at mealtime.

'Hey, you all right, Jan?'

Jan looked up, eyes bald of expression. 'Yeah. Fine.'

'Seriously, how was school?' I couldn't imagine her in school with other twelve-year-olds.

'Oh, ya know. Shit.'

'What you up to?'

'Nothing. Writing a letter.'

She gave me this cool look. Raised her brows a little. It meant, 'Was there anything else?' Trenderella gazed at me from cow-heavy eyes, her chin on her knuckles.

I nodded a goodbye and walked on.

'I don't think Twelve-year-old Lesbian likes me any more,' I whispered to Dennis.

He sucked on his rollie. 'Twelve-year-old Lesbian's a dickhhhead.'

Two months later I got a phone call from Jan. She had gossip, she told me, really huge, dramatic fuckin' gossip.

Trenderella had been arrested for stalking Leo.

'*Stalking?*' I said.

'Yep. Stalking. She got her bedroom searched by the police this morning. At seven o'clock. They had a warrant and stuff.'

'Searched? What for?'

'I dunno. Stalking paraphernalia?'

'Oh. My fucking. God. Has she actually been stalking her? Like, full on stalking?'

'Well, it looks that way.'

'But what about you? Aren't you, like, the ringleader of your little gang?'

'"My little gang"? Thank you, Christina.'

'Your little twosome then. Whatever.'

'Well. The police haven't come to me yet.'

'Are you afraid they will?'

'Blatantly.'

'How embarrassing.'

'I know. I dread to think.'

We went on talking. We arranged to meet up the following Friday at half five so she could give me more details. She lowered her voice to a whisper. 'My mum's in the room, I gotta go.'

She didn't turn up for our meeting on Friday. I rang her house and her mum answered. She said that Jan was ill in an odd, strained voice with silences that felt like nervous glances.

We're in town, me and Dennis. We're going to Blue Banana. I want a new tattoo. Dennis wants some incense cones for his mother. Also, he has a blinding crush on Rick, a small guy with a Jesus beard and dark, fuck-me-violently eyes. Rick is Blue Banana's piercer. Dennis is in love with him. Like, *actually*, literally in love with him.

I am wearing a small dress and fishnets and Dr Martens and a fur coat (so long, George, till next time). No knickers. I think I look lush. We walk through the doors, into the shop. We're there for just two seconds and then Gail calls my name.

Leo says my name.

Heart jolts like a gun going off.

She's going to offer me a job, I think. I sent in an application form once. She's going to give me a job. My crush will re-form, become fresh and substantial again, like a shrivelled-up pea thrown in boiling water. We'll work together. We'll fall in love. I'll fuck her on the tattooist's chair after closing time.

I spin round to face her. There she is. Her skin's bad – rough and blotchy – and her roots need doing, but she's still beautiful.

'Yeah?' I say.

She looks at me seriously, her perfect jaw fixed. 'Christina,' she says, 'I am now barring you from this shop.'

Everyone in the shop turns to look at me. My insides drop and shudder. I suddenly feel foolish in my fur coat and slutty dress. Like a dickhhhead.

'*What?*' I say. 'What for?'

'I don't have to explain my reasons. I'm the manager, and I'm barring you.'

'Christina, what've you done?' says Dennis.

'Try stalkin' for a start,' says Kurt, the tattooist.

'What?' says Dennis. He's casting little petrified glances at Rick the piercer.

'But thass fuckin' *stupid*,' I say.

Gail raises her brows and tilts her head. 'Yeah? Well it'll be stupid to not leave this shop.'

'I don't understand,' I say.

She just looks at me, brows still raised. I turn abruptly, mouth snarled, and walk out of the shop, Dennis close behind me.

Outside our hands fly straight to our tobacco tins and we roll up with nervous, fluttering fingers.

'Oh my God,' I say. 'This is awful.'

173

'I can't even cope with how embarrassing this is,' says Dennis.

'Embarrassing as *fuck*,' I say. 'Obviously it's got something to do with Twelve-year-old Lesbian.'

He nods. I light my roll-up and suck on it with eyes that fizz with histrionic zeal.

'I can't believe my biggest crush ever thinks I'm a stalker. I can't wait to tell Sidney about this.'

Dennis shakes his head. '*Soo* embarrassing. What's Rick going to think? Oh my God, I can't believe it. What are you going to do, Cris?'

'I'm gonna go to the police.'

'The police?'

I nod and suck on my fag, grim and resolute, like a soap opera matriarch. 'I wanna find out what's going on and clear my name.'

We find Dennis's car and drive to Central Police Station, ranting and chattering all the way, our tone switching back and forth between mortification and amusement.

We go in. Reception is grubby and bare. Couple of grey plastic chairs, an old plywood table coffee-ringed and key-scraped, several empty Styrofoam cups on the floor, most of them dented, chewed or picked to pieces. I speak to a policeman who looks like a fat Michael Keaton. I tell him the situation. 'I just want to sort this out,' I say.

The policeman gets out a pocket notepad and asks for our names. We tell him, he writes them down. He looks at us and seems to come to a decision. He goes away, consults another policeman, comes back. He turns to me.

'Christina Jones, I am now placing you under arrest. You do not have to say anything, but it may harm your defence if you fail to mention when questioned anything you later rely on in court.'

He turns to Dennis. 'Dennis Webster, I am now placing you under arrest. You do not have to say anything, but it may harm your defence if you fail to mention when questioned anything you later rely on in court.'

'What?' Dennis's mouth opens to the size of a tangerine slice. 'Oh my God. Oh my fucking God.' He is obviously worrying about his mum being called to the station, even though he is nineteen. 'Why?'

'A letter of harassment was sent to the shop called Blue Banana and it's got your names on it. That's why.' He slips his pen in his breast pocket. 'Come with me.'

We are made to take off all our jewellery and accessories except for piercings. We have a lot. Spiky bracelets, spiky belts, rings, chains, chokers, dog tags, sunglasses, hundreds of black bangles. Shoe laces.

'Why d'you need our shoe laces?' says Dennis.

'So you don't hang yourself.'

Dennis sets his mouth and frowns at a spot on the floor.

Another policeman comes along. He's old and has a heavily lined face with wobbly jowls. A grey-specked goatee. His small, grey eyes peek out from mounds of overlapping, wrinkled skin. Kind of like ball bearings wedged into bald vaginas. His nose is fat and lumpy. He has the sort of face it would be fun to recreate with clay.

'I'm Sergeant Greeves,' he says. And he starts on a bundle of paperwork.

'I can't believe I've been arrested for stalking,' whispers Dennis. 'What if Rick finds out?'

'No talking to each other,' says Fat Michael Keaton.

Dennis looks at his laceless shoes like a scolded child.

I press my legs together and cross my arms; it's cold and drafty. I wish I'd worn knickers now.

Sergeant Greeves leads us to separate cells. Mine is a stark, dirty room with a ledge sticking out of one wall. It might be the same one I stayed in when I was arrested with Jessica four years earlier. I sit on the ledge and read the graffiti. 'PIGZ BURN IN HELL'. 'Olly waz ere 98, same old shit'. 'OINK FUCKIN OINK, PC

175

FARNHAM SUCKED MY DICK AND HE <u>LOVED</u> IT'. I count the tiles on the ceiling. Twenty-six.

After two hours I'm let out and brought to the interrogation room. I sit down at a small table opposite Sergeant Greeves. He looks tired. He slurps coffee from a plastic cup. There are little white blobs of foam in the corner of his mouth.

He gets a Dictaphone out and presses play. He tells me that I've been arrested for stalking, except he gives a long-winded technical term for it. The victim is a Miss Gail Richards. The days of Leo are long gone. He tells me to give my statement, and as I talk, he writes. Now and then he interrupts to ask questions.

'So who are Twelve-year-old Lesbian and Sally?'

'Twelve-year-old Lesbian is Jan. I don't know her surname. Then there's Sally. Jan told me her surname once but I don't remember it. It sounds something like bollockboobs.'

'It's Challacomb,' he says, dryly. 'Sally Challacomb.'

'Oh.' I look down at the table. 'No, that doesn't really sound much like Bollockboobs.' I clear my throat very quietly.

'No it doesn't,' he says. He watches me squirm for a while, his eyes tiny and still in their many skin folds. 'Please, go on.'

I tell him about my crush – its beginning and end. I tell him about my relationship to Twelve-year-old Lesbian. Just some girl I sort of knew and liked.

He reads out the letter that has implicated me and Dennis. '"To Gail the Bitch. We don't fancy you anymore. We think you're a bitch, a beautiful bitch. But we've moved on to someone else. Did you like the postcard? See you around. The Castle Dykes. Jan, Sally, Seren, Dennis, Christina, Elined, Sidney, Aled, Fred, Richard, Chloe and Tina."'

He looks up from the paper in his hand. 'What do you know about this?'

I let out a hollow laugh. It echoes. 'What the fuck?' I say. 'You're arresting me over *that*? You really think there's a gang of – how many are there? Ten, twelve? You think there's a gang of ten, twelve people stalking one bloody lesbian? She's not that fucking great.'

'I'm not saying I think anything about it.'

'And listen, I applied for a job at Blue Banana a while ago, right. Ju really think I'd be so fucking stupid as to put my name on a letter like that?'

'All right. Calm down. Like I said, I'm not thinking anything. I'm just trying to get down all the facts.' He shows me the letter. It's torn out of an exercise book. The words are scrawled on in blue biro and the writing is fat and curly. 'So you've never seen this letter before?'

I shake my head.

'Suspect is shaking her head,' he says. He looks at the letter himself. 'It's dated the seventh of September.' He raises his brows questioningly. It stretches the skin around his weird vagina eyes.

'Oh! That's the day we upset Twelve-year-old Lesbian. Seventh of September – that's when everyone goes back to school.'

'Can you tell me about it?'

I do. The words spill out, he writes them down. I interrupt my own narrative with incredulous laughter. I've been arrested over a twelve-year-old's tantrum.

He passes me the statement. Asks me to read it. 'Are you happy with everything that's been written?'

'Ecstatic,' I say.

He raises his brows again.

'Yes. I'm happy with what's been written.'

I sign the statement. He switches off the Dictaphone. Leans forward, elbows on the table. 'Now this is off the record. It's fairly obvious who's responsible for the harassment. Has been all along. But your name was on the letter and we had to follow it up. You'll be let out on bail and given a date for a court hearing, but don't be surprised if you get a letter in the post telling you the court hearing has been cancelled and all charges dropped.'

'OK. Good.' I watch him scratch his armpit. 'So how bad was the stalking?'

'Um.' He rubs a hand up and down his tired old face. 'We've seen a lot worse. But it was quite serious. She's suffered a lot of stress over the last few months. Miss Richards, I mean.'

I think about her bad skin.

'There were letters, postcards. And there was something spray-painted on the shop windows of Blue Banana. "Gail the bitchy dyke." That was probably the worst thing.'

'I had no idea,' I say.

'Well. Now you do.' He shuffles his papers. 'It's your friend's turn now. Thanks for your co-operation, Miss Jones.' He smiles, and for a nano-second it reaches his eyes, flickers there like a fly at the corner of your vision. And then he's tired and serious again.

Sergeant Greeves leads me out of the interrogation room. I'm taken back to my cell. After a while a woman opens the hatch by the door and asks me, in a kind, mumsy voice, if I want a cup of tea, and how many sugars?

I say yes thank you, and two, and I ask her if I can have my tobacco. She says she'll see. She comes back a few minutes later with a styrofoam cup of hot, weak tea and my Cutter's Choice. I sit and smoke.

It's dark when me and Dennis are let out of the station. The sky is starless. We walk slowly to the car park in our loose, flapping shoes, the laces dripping out of our fists. We reach his dark plum Ford. I sit in the back. We're still for a while.

'I actually counted the tiles in the ceiling I was so bored,' he says.

'Me too,' I say.

'Twenty-six,' he says.

'Me too.'

He drives to my horrible Single Women's flat, where Meegs the Bastard is probably waiting in the shadows flexing his claws. We're silent all the way. He parks. Our tired eyes meet in the mirror. Hysterical laughter explodes out of our mouths, filling the cold car.

Lentil Soup

A quiet Sunday, nineteen ninety-five. Me and Mum were in the kitchen. She was at the table, working on a self-portrait in oils and I was making toast. The house was silent save for the tinkling of Mum's paintbrush in the turps glass and the gentle roar of the grill.

Then, a knock at the front door, followed by Slug's clear, ringing bark.

Mum looked up from her painting. 'That'll be the Siamese twin.'

I ran to the door.

But it wasn't Jessica. Swaying in the doorway, a face full of congealed blood, was Suki, her mother.

'Look what that *bastid's* done? Look, Cris.' She pointed a shaky finger at the bursts of maroon on her eyebrow and upper lip, the split tomato eye.

My bottom lip dropped. 'Who did that? Was it—'

'Who do you think, Cris. Fucking *Charles*. That fat, ginger *cunt*.' She lurched through the door, hitting Slug in the face with a blue carrier bag filled with cans. Hand came up, palm out, in a gesture of peace. 'Sorry, Slug.' She turned on her heel, made her way to the kitchen. I followed, just catching the shock on Mum's face. 'Look, Ca'. Look at that *twat's* handywork.'

Mum was staring. 'Christ, Suki. Your eye…'

'I know!'

'Have you been to the police?'

Suki found her way to the table, slumped into the seat and pulled a can of Stonehouse from her bag. 'No, Catherine. I haven't. But I will.' She clutched my mum's arm and dropped her head close like this was her last speech ever. 'This time I fucking well will, Ca'. I'll have that ugly *bastid* put in jail.'

Half an hour later, Suki was sat in the garden on the concrete step, a fresh can in hand. Mum was stood in front of her holding a faithful old 35 mm Kodak. She squinted through the lens.

'Look at me, Suki.'

Suki looked up, grave and swollen.

Mum clicked away. 'These'll come out in black and white I'm afraid. Film's for an art project.'

Suki smirked, pouting her crumpled mouth bitterly. 'Well, put this in your folder,' she said. 'Very bloody arty.'

I laughed. Suki looked at me, eyes empty of humour and I quickly stifled it. Mum carried on taking pictures from different angles, making sure to catch every detail, down to the streak of blood on the collar of the denim jacket.

'Lift your hair by the – yeah.'

Sticky blood like jam clung to her ear, to the hair around it. Charles had really gone to town on her this time.

Suki hadn't been home the last three days. She'd gone off to the shop for some 'bread' and maybe a can or two early Thursday evening, and simply hadn't returned. This wasn't the first time either. Suki liked to go on benders. She loved nothing more than a free festival, somewhere she could wander around in a drunken stumble, sloshing her can all over the place, her slow blinking eyes on the lookout for other hippies. This wouldn't be so bad if it wasn't for the husband and family.

But Charles was still a *bastid*.

'Listen, Cris, listen.' She grabbed my wrist, leaned in close so her sour, boozy breath pumped into my face with every word. 'I've put up with that miserable bastid for twenty-five years. Twenty-five years. I don't deserve it.' She shook her head slowly. 'I don't deserve it.' Lids lowered, she looked at the setting sun, the chalky smear of pink rising out of a fluorescent orange horizon.

'You need to leave him, Sook. He'll end up killin' you one of these days. We'll get the photos developed, innit? You can go to the police.'

She blinked slowly, brought the floppy rollie that she'd been smoking for the past forty minutes to her shapeless, colourless mouth and sucked. Nothing. She raised a purple lighter to her face and relit.

'Are you listening, Sook?'

Her head swung round to face me, her lank blonde hair swishing like a horse's tail. 'For Christ's sake, Cris, you're only thirteen. You don't understand.'

'Yes, I do.' I'd read enough of my mum's *Take-a-break*s and *Bella*s. I knew about wife beating.

'No.' Another slow shake of the head. 'You don't.'

I craned my neck to look through the back door. Mum was in the kitchen preparing dinner. Her back was to me. I quickly picked up Suki's can and took a few mouthfuls of warm, sour cider.

'Well, it's not like you even love him. You told me before.'

'Did I? Hm. I don't know.'

'So you *do* love him?'

She breathed smoke in my face. 'I don't bloody know, do I?'

'You argue all the time. You're never nice to each other. I don't get it.'

'You wouldn't.'

I rolled my eyes in exasperation. 'For fuck's sake, Suki, you're just gonna go back to him. Again. I can't believe you.'

'Listen to me,' She renewed her hold on my wrist. 'Listen. I'll tell you why I've stayed with that tubby, ginger bastid for twenty-five years. I'll tell you.' She fixed me with a serious look, her lumpy red face swaying back and forth like a pendulum. 'His dick comes up to his belly button.'

I meet Sidney in the crematorium car park. He's wearing black pinstripe trousers, Cons, a nice T-shirt with a horse on it, a black waistcoat and the usual excess of rosaries, crucifixes and bangles. Casual, youthful – that is the dress code. It's what she would have wanted.

'Hey,' he says, and we hug, awkwardly as usual.

'Which way?'

'I dunno.' He points to some smudged figures at the end of the car park. 'Isn't that your mum and sister?'

'I dunno. You're the one with the twenty-twenty vision.' I loop my arm through his, but he shrugs it off. 'No, hold my hand.' So I do.

'So how do you feel?'

He scrunches up his face. 'Just sort of shocked. Like I couldn't believe it at first.' His voice is a dreamy, girly-boy singsong.

'Yeah, me too. But actually it's a surprise she lasted as long as she did.'

'Yeah. God, she was *always* drunk. Remember when I told you how she used to come on to me? Whenever Jessica and Bianca were out of the room – and Charles, obviously – she'd be all' – softly he takes a section of my hair with his spare hand – '"Oh your hair is so beautiful." And she'd, like, stroke my face, tell me how beautiful I was.'

'Were you ever tempted?' I say, and we laugh.

'I always felt sorry for her,' Sidney says. 'I thought she was lonely. Stuck in the house, and Jess was always telling her to fuck off out of her room. She was sad, ya know? Sort of tragic.'

The two figures ahead are starting to become people. Big round woman topped with a brown smear – Mum; short woman, massive arse, topped by white-blonde smear – Veronica. They're waiting for us. I wave, they wave back.

'Didn't she shag one of your mum's boyfriends?' says Sidney.

'Yeah. But he wasn't a proper boyfriend, just some Scottish nutcase who stayed with us for a week.'

'Still.'

'Yeah, I know.'

We reach my mum and sister.

Mum came home from work at the Dog and Bone around half-eleven. I ran to the door as soon as I heard the scratch of the key in the lock.

'Guess what?' I said as she dumped her rucksack on the floor.

'What?'

'Mum, Mum!' Veronica ran into the hall. 'I've been trying to get rid of her. She won't go.'

'What? Who?' Mum hung up her leather jacket, 11 up.

'Who ju think?' I said, hands on hips.

Mum shook her head. 'For God's sake.'

Veronica placed a sycophantic hand on her shoulder. 'I've been trying to get rid of her all night, Mum. She's been here since six.'

Mum looked at me. *What about you?* That's what the look said. Suki was my best friend's mother. Why hadn't I sorted it out? I was comfortable with the woman, on screaming terms with her half the time. Why hadn't I applied my usual bluntness to the situation, told the women to get her fucking arse off our sofa and get home?

'What? Don't look at me. I was upstairs all night. I didn't even know she was here!'

I shot Veronica a look. *Shut yer face.* I'd spent all night playing football in the square with Nadeem.

'What about Jessica?'

'She's staying at her gran's tonight.'

'Christ.'

'I phoned Charles,' said Veronica, 'but he just said, "Tell her to get home," and put the phone down.'

Mum did something with her mouth that was halfway between tutting and teeth-kissing. 'That miserable wanker. Did you ring back?'

'Nuh.'

We were scared of Charles, who never smiled, who only had two facial expressions: pissed off and hard-done-by.

'She's drunk, is she?'

Veronica nodded. 'And I think she's been taking *speed*.' This last word came out whispered.

'How would you know?'

'She told me.'

'Christ!' Mum started marching toward the living room door.

Veronica grabbed her arm. 'Wait. She hasn't taken any here. I think she took it before she got here and it's mostly worn off now. And also – *Mum*' – in a hushed voice – '*I think she's been raped or something.*'

Mum turned round. 'What?'

'She's been at some biker festival. And she was hanging round with Hell's Angels. And she woke up with no clothes on or something. That's what Sharon said.'

'Sharon?' Sharon was Suki's closest friend. Also a fan of the cider.

'Yeah. It was Sharon who brought her round. She brought her round and left her here. And *I've* been stuck with her!' Veronica looked over at me, eyes narrowed.

Mum didn't see this. She was having a think. Everything had changed. Because of that word. *Raped.*

An hour later. I was downstairs with Mum and Suki. Veronica was in bed – my turn to take some of the load. It was a school night, but tough. That was Mum's favourite word. Tough. I was going to help her with the drunk rape victim whether I liked it or not. Tough.

Suki was perched on the armchair by the window, elbows on her knees. Sometimes one of her elbows would slip and her body would lurch forward. A couple of times this happened while there was a can in her hand, and Mum would wince as warm cider sloshed onto the carpet. I sat next to Suki, and Mum next to me. Slug was curled up by the fire with the cat. The TV was on, volume low. *Married with Children.*

'That fucking Sharon doesn't know what she's talking about,' Suki slurred, looking at my mum through swollen lids.

'But you woke up with no clothes on.'

'That's rubbish, Ca'. Rubbish.' She put her can down on the floor and called Slug, who stood up, stretched, and came over, wagging. She took the dog's face in her hands and landed a loud, wet kiss on her head. In return Slug wrapped her tongue around Suki's chin and mouth.

'She licks her fanny with that tongue, you know,' I said.

'Oh, fuck off, Cris.' She stroked the dog's head. 'Ca', she's beautiful.' Her mottled face crumpled and her eyes moistened. 'I don't care what anyone says about these dogs. Dangerous my arse. Fuck them, Ca'. Fuck them. Listen to me, my friend: this dog has a beautiful soul. And I'll tell you what' – she let go of the dog's head and raised a heavy finger in the air – 'I'll tell you what, Ca'.' She closed her eyes, head nodding.

Mum waited. Nothing. Suki's clockwork had run down.

I nudged her with my elbow. 'Oi. Suki.'

Eyes sprang open.

'It's late, Suki. Go home.'

'Oh, shut up, Cris.' She picked her can back off the floor and took a swig.

Two o'clock in the morning.

'And so he says to me, he says, "If you come and visit me tomorrow in my shop, we'll have a talk." And I say, "My friend, the first time I saw you, I knew you were one of the good ones," cuz he's a hippy, Ca', like me, a proper old school hippy with a beautiful heart, Ca'. And he says to me, he says –'

185

Suki was telling one of her legendary stories. The sort that went nowhere and had no point. This one had been going on for twenty-five minutes and so far, nothing. But if you didn't know Suki you'd be forgiven for thinking that something *was* going to happen, because of the disbelieving bemusement in her eyes and voice.

Mum sat forward in her chair trying to look rapt. Sometimes her eyes met mine and we exchanged the same wide-eyed message – *fuck's sake*. We were tired. The woman had no intention of leaving. And our sympathy had run out: she probably hadn't been raped, we'd concluded in raspy whispers whenever her attention was absorbed with lighting the wrong end of her fag, it was just that Sharon stirring shit in with the cider.

'He says, "Suki, dear," – he calls me Suki dear – "Suki, dear, my friend, if ever you need someone to just be yourself around, you come to me." And he buys me another drink, Ca', just like that. And his mates are just playing cards. Playing Rummy in the corner and passing around spliffs. And listen; you'll piss yourself when you hear this.' Her eyes close, she smiles, shakes her head. 'This fella comes in, right? Long red hair. Beautiful red hair, like Charles's when he was young. He comes in, right, and he—'

'Suki! Your fag!'

Suki's heavy lids reluctantly lifted. 'What?'

A corner of the curtain was on fire.

'Oh shit.' Suki slapped at the small flame.

Mum jumped up and joined in, her hands slapping at the curtain and Suki's fingers. 'Christ's sake, Suki!' She stopped, examined the charred fabric. Shook her head. There was a smoky patch of black the size of a fifty pence piece.

Suki stood up, steadied herself, gripped Mum's wrist. 'I'm sorry, Ca'. Really, I am.'

'Just be careful. I don't like people smoking in the house at all really.'

'It's time to go home, Sook,' I said, placing a hand on the back of her shoulder and applying pressure, like a bouncer.

'Shut up—'

'No! Stop telling me to shut up! Go home! You're pissed as a fart and it's gone two in the morning. Mum's got college tomorrow and I've got school.' I shoved her, just a bit. 'Go home!'

She turned to look at me, nose in the air, trying her best to look like someone with power.

'She's right, Suki,' said Mum. 'We do need to get to bed.'

Her head swung back to my mum, led by the nose. She examined her face for a while. Then nodded. 'All right, Ca'. All right. I'll go.'

It took another twenty minutes to get Suki from the living room to the front door, another ten minutes to get her off the doorstep. We watched her stumble down the driveway, carrier bag hooked over her arm. She turned back, waved like the queen. Fell into the privet hedge.

Mum shook her head like a disappointed teacher. 'We're going to have to help her home.'

We shuffled down the road, Suki's skinny arms wrapped around our necks. Even though we lived on the same street it took quarter of an hour to get to her front door.

'Where's your key, Sook?'

'Wha'?'

'Your key.'

'I dunno.'

Mum searched through her pockets. Nothing. 'Shit.'

I knocked the door. 'It's not our fault,' I said to Mum.

But it felt like our fault.

We heard the sound of someone coming down the stairs. The landing light came on and the door opened. Sheena. Small white nightdress. Angry. 'What the fuck time is this?'

Me and Mum stood there on either side of Suki, tall and silent as pillars.

'Where have you been, you stupid fucking cow?'

Suki batted the air as if there were gnats in her face. 'Oh leave me alone, Sheen.'

Hands landed on hips. 'No, I will *not* leave you alone, you fucking pisshead! Get in!'

'Don't you talk to me like that.'

Sheena's eyes flashed. 'Now!'

Me and Mum stepped away. 'Sorry it's so late,' said Mum. 'Took ages to get rid of her.' She laughed nervously.

Sheena tipped a stern nod her way. 'Thanks, mate.' She reached out, grabbed her mum by the lapel of her denim jacket, yanked her in.

After the car park there's a small expanse of slick, healthy grass, then the crematorium lodge, where the service will be held. A modest building. Discreet, dignified, clean. Everything Suki wasn't. Me and Sidney arrive, still holding hands. Mum and Veronica trail behind.

There's a smattering of people outside the building. I scan the faces, and there she is – Jessica. It's been a few years. Me and Sidney go up. She's got her gracious hostess face on. It looks practised, but you can just about see the pain it's meant to be hiding. Her old acne scars are hidden under thick layers of ivory foundation and powder. Her glossy, red hair looks like it's been styled in a salon. She's just as skinny as she always was.

Smiling sadly, I hug her. I can feel the A to D boob job. 'Sorry about your loss,' I say.

We air kiss. The last time I saw Jessica we'd been seventeen. Sidney was still friends with her and Bianca so I'd spent an evening in their company, watching *The Craft* in Sidney's pink bedroom. They'd apologised for being teenage bitches ('Oh my God, we were fucking dreadful!') and the night had culminated in me sneaking upstairs to spray some of Sidney's mother's perfume on my crotch because I'd pissed myself laughing.

'Thanks, Cris. Thanks for coming.'

She hugs and kisses Sidney. 'Hey, hun.'

Now Veronica and Mum catch up and there's more hugs and kisses and 'sorry about your losses' to go round. Then we're all standing.

'How did it happen?' says Mum.

'Oh, she went into a coma in her sleep.'

'Shit,' I say.

We all shake our sombre heads.

'Yeah. We don't know yet if it was drugs or booze. Or both. You know what she was like.' She raises a pencilled-on brow and smiles sardonically.

We nod, our eyes on the floor.

There's a moment of silence. And then Bianca's here. Black hair with blue tips swirling about her shoulders, cocoa skin, big round tits straining against her low-cut top.

'You look nice,' Sidney says.

She lays a pink taloned hand on his arm. 'Aw, thanks.'

'How's things?' I ask her.

She laughs nervously. 'Fine, babe.' Quickly looks me up and down. Smiles with her eyes going like centipedes.

The funeral is being conducted by the Reverend Lionel Fanthorpe, an oldish man with a shaved head, clean white beard and a warm, down-to-earth manner. A few years ago he enjoyed some modest TV fame due to an interest in the paranormal and a love of motorbikes. This is a good start.

The chapel is only a quarter full. I sit with Sidney on one side, my sister and mother on the other. Jessica is with her family up front. I want to go and look at them, see how they've grown, especially Ali, Jessica's little sister.

At the front of the chapel, blown up to the size of a poster, is a black and white photo of Suki when she was young. Twenty or so. She's beautiful. Smooth, young skin, long, blonde hair spread over her shoulders, sunlight filtering through the wispy gaps. This was before the drinking turned the capillaries on her cheeks to saffron, her skin to leather.

'Didn't she look lovely?' whispers Mum.

I nod.

'What a shame,' she says, shaking her head. 'She kind of looked like Iggy Pop last time I saw her.'

'That's exactly what I thought.'

The Reverend starts to speak. I wonder how he'll approach this service? What angle will he go for? I've been wondering about this all day.

Fanthorpe knows what he's doing. He decides to turn Suki's hedonism into a good thing. He reminds us of what a fun-loving hippy she was. Full of spirit. Full of love. What a character. How she loved to dance, to convene with nature, how she enjoyed conversing with her fellow man. And, you know, he's right. She was all of these things. Let's just remember these things. We are all smiling fondly. Good old Suki.

A latecomer dressed in black shows up sobbing loudly. She sits in the back. No one I know. I turn back to the good Reverend, who has started reading a poem out of a book. 'Footprints in the Sand.'

'One night I dreamed I was walking along the beach with the Lord…'

I think about the time Suki took us all to the beach in Barry Island, and by the end of the day she was so drunk she fell out of the train.

'So I said to the Lord, "You promised me, Lord, that if I followed you, you would walk with me always… "'

I think about the time I walked in on her shaving her bikini line, one shapely leg hitched up on the bath lip, her muff staring out at me like a monstrous spider.

'The Lord replied, "The times when you have seen only one set of footprints in the sand, is when I carried you."'

I think about all the fucking times I had to help carry her.

The wake is in Suki's local. A quiet pub in Roath. Six years ago Suki moved to Roath to be with her toyboy, leaving Charles and Ali to enjoy Paradise alone together (Jessica had moved to Birmingham, Sheena was living on the other side of Cardiff with her partner). I stopped seeing her stumbling through the streets in Jessica's jeans, and after that time by Roath Park, I didn't see her at all. I guess she was spending her time in this place, bumming drinks and rattling her bracelets to whatever came out of the jukebox.

I see Sheena. Suki's firstborn. I notice her small black dress and realise that she had been the sobbing latecomer at the funeral. She looks a little bloated and old but still gorgeous. I nod her a hello and she stares at me blankly. I quickly pass on by, my cheeks heating up.

Next it's Charles, holding a pint, nibbling his bottom lip, fat as ever.

I came out of the bathroom. Over the sound of the flush system roaring I heard Charles's raised voice.

'Fuck off, Sook!'

'You can fuck right off yourself, you fat bastid!'

An argument. I tiptoed to the top of the stairs and peered over the banister. There they were. I could see the top of Charles's orange head. I became still and watched. I could smell lentil soup.

'Go and run to your fucking mother, slag!' said Charles, stabbing a finger in his wife's direction.

I smiled. He was bringing the mothers into it already.

'Suki, Suki, Suki,' he said in a high-pitched woman's voice, both his hands imitating birds, the thumb and four fingers snapping together like beaks. 'Suki, Suki, Suki!'

Suki spun round to face him. 'Well what about your fucking mother? Charleh, Charleh,' she boomed in a deep northern baritone, her head whipping round theatrically with every utterance.

'Suki, Suki, Suki, Suki, Suki,' he squawked, hands still snapping open and shut.

'Chaar*leh*, Chaar*leh*, fookin' *Chaarleh*!' she roared.

I muffled my laughter with my hand.

'Why don't you go and ask your mum for some money, Suki, you drunk cunt!'

She waved a pair of Vs in his red angry, face. 'Fuck off, Char*leh*, you mummy's boy, fuck right off!'

He flapped an angry hand in her direction and went into the living room. She followed. I sat on the step and listened. The rest of their argument came to me in muffled curses. Cunt. Bitch. Tramp. Bastid. Wanker. Twat. The mothers came back into it after a while, but it wasn't so funny without the actions. After a while their voices grew quieter, their tones less hateful. Then there was silence.

Then there was this:

'Charles. Make love to me, Charles.'

Show over. I stood up and went back to Jessica's room.

Charles smiles a warm smile. 'All right, love?' he says, tipping his head. 'How ya doin'?'

'Good thanks. You?'

'Yeah. Can't complain.' He looks relaxed, at peace. His orange and grey beard is neatly trimmed.

'Were you still friends with Suki then, before she, ya know…'

He draws his mouth down at the sides and tilts his head side to side as if to say, *comme çi, comme ça*. 'I saw her around now and again.'

I nod. 'Well. Sorry for your loss. I mean, I'm not sure if it's your loss exactly, but you know what I mean.'

He grunts a laugh. 'Complicated. But yeah. Cheers.'

'See you later,' I say.

Again a warm smile. 'Yeah, cheers for coming, love. Good to see you.'

I go off to the toilet. While I piss I think of Charles. I remember the time Suki had come home from a piss-up at a biker's festival with her nose broken and bloodied and her eyebrow burst open. Except this time it wasn't Charles, it was some woman she'd got into an argument with, some 'cokehead bitch'. Charles had opened the door to her, seen the blood and despair and immediately dragged her through to the kitchen. He sat her down and started to tenderly dab away the blood with a wet tea towel, saying, 'Baby, baby, what've they done to you?' and crying a bit. And Suki had crumpled her face miserably, spluttered out a sob and sunk her head into his chest. He'd held her, his grubby beard obscuring her face, and she'd said, 'So it's OK when you do it, Charley?' and he'd let loose a snotty cry, his own face crumpling, and said, 'No, baby, no, it's not. It's not.' And they'd held each other a long time. Afterwards Jessica, in a gloomy, solemn mood, had said, with a half-shrug, 'You know, I reckon he'd probably be a different husband to a different wife. Know what I mean?' and I'd nodded. But I hadn't known. I hadn't known anything. I leave the cubicle and there's Sheena. She's rummaging in her bag, a purple lighter wedged between her lips. I smile weakly.

Again the blank look. She takes the lighter out of her mouth. 'Uh, I'm not being funny,' she says, 'but who are you?"

'It's Christina?'

She raises a pale hand to her mouth. 'Shiiit, yeah. Jessica's little friend.'

I laugh. 'Yeah. Jessica's little friend.'

'No offence, mate. What you up to these days?'

'Uh, work, writing. Uh, yeah. Plenty.'

'Writing? Nice one.'

And she smiles.

And what she doesn't know, and what I don't know, is that in a few week's time I'll pass her in the lane that runs behind Whitchurch Road and she will have her whole leg in plaster and she'll be hobble-marching with the serious grim look belonging to her mother's sober mornings, and she will not recognise me *again* and I will keep my eyes fixed ahead as we pass because I'm embarrassed by my insignificance. And in two years I will attend her funeral because she didn't wake up one morning, like her mother; she just didn't wake up, but unlike her mother, there will be no drugs in her system and no identifiable cause of death, and I will meet Jessica and Bianca again. We will all gather in the pub, a different one to this, and me and Sidney will look at the photos of Sheena her weeping friends have stuck to the pub walls and drool over her beauty and say the usual things, and I will piss in the toilets listening to Sheena's friends swap fond stories about going on ketamine benders with her, *horse tranquiliser* benders, and afterwards, me and Bianca will drink wine and talk about sex in wonderful giggling detail while my Dad eats quiche and sneaks glances at Bianca's perfectly round tits and I will go home wondering who's next.

Sheena touches my arm, lightly. 'Well, see you in a bit, mate.' And she's gone.

'You should both come up to Birmingham for my birthday,' Jessica says to me and Sidney. 'It'll be amazing.'

'That'd be so fun,' says Sidney, sipping his vodka and lemonade.

'Yeah, let's do it,' I say, knowing it'll never happen. 'Twenty-fourth of October. Carved into my memory forever.'

'And May the fifteenth for you,' Jessica says to me smiling. She turns to Bianca. 'You're coming up anyway, aren't you, Byank?'

'Yeah, course, babe.'

'No invite for me then?' says Mum, feigning hurt, and Jessica giggles. 'You're welcome anytime, Cath,' she says. 'I mean, I did spend half my childhood eating your food and sleeping over your house.'

Mum flaps a hand. 'Oh, Christina was over yours just as much. You were like Siamese bloody twins.'

At the other end of the room the toilet door slams open and Sheena almost falls out. Jessica rolls her eyes.

'That was a lovely picture at the funeral,' says my mum. 'She was gorgeous.'

Jessica nods sadly. 'Yeah, she was.' She is looking down at her gin and tonic and playing with the straw.

'Such a shame,' says Mum.

Jessica nods again. Tinkles her ice cubes.

'No mother is perfect,' says Mum.

'Indeed,' I say. 'Freddy Krueger?'

Mum looks down into her Diet Coke, mortified. 'I know. I was too young to have kids. I was twisted.'

'Mothers are shit, daughters are shit, we're all shit, so let's just roll in our shit and get drunk,' I say.

'Hear hear!' says Sidney, giggling.

'I guess Suki would approve,' says Mum, and Jessica nods.

Mum sips her drink. 'What was your relationship like with her towards the end?' she asks Jessica.

She looks up. 'It was good actually. A lot better. We got close, you know?'

'That's good. I remember how you used to be with each other.'

She raises a hand, palm out. 'I know! I was fucking horrible to her.'

'Well. She *was* a massive alcoholic. You put up with a lot, and you were so young. It wasn't fair on you.'

'Yeah, but she wasn't always bad, you know?' Her eyes meet my mum's, just for a second. She smiles. 'When she was sober she was kind of like a normal mother.'

'Oh for God's sake, Ali, it's not going to hurt you. Just hold it there. That's right, just – Ali, for God's sake!'

The strands of grass drifted to the ground as Ali's little upturned hand shot back. The horse looked down at the girl through large brown glassy eyes.

'It's gonna bite me, Mum.'

'Don't be stupid. Look at Jessica and Christina. Do you see their fingers being chewed off?'

I ripped some grass out of the ground. 'Watch me, Ali,' I said. I stretched my arm over the small wire fence and offered the grass to a russet stallion with a white diamond between its eyes. 'Look at my hand when he – look.' The horse approached, leaned down and slurped up the grass, his bristley chin tickling my palm. 'See? He won't hurt.'

Ali looked up at me through her lashes and shook her head slightly. 'I don't want to.'

'No one's forcing you,' said Suki, rolling a cigarette.

Jessica tapped me on the arm and pointed at a restless horse with sticky-out ribs. 'Look at him. Pure skinny. We should feed him up.'

'Whoa,' I said. 'Look at his ribs. Sook – look at his ribs.'

Suki squinted through the sunlight. 'Why don't you feed him up?'

'I've already said that, you mong,' said Jessica, ripping up more grass.

'I reckon we should come after school every day to feed him,' I said.

'Ali – fuck off a minute.'

Ali was hanging off Suki's arm, trying to get into the carrier bag hanging off her wrist. She was trying to lick her Rizla. 'Hang on, love.'

'Mum, gimme my ball.'

'Wait. Hold your horses.' She realised what she'd said, laughed softly to herself. 'Didju hear that?' Shaking her head, she pulled the ball out of the bag and passed it to her. 'You want some sweets too?'

She dropped the ball, her small pale face going like a toy commercial. 'You got sweets?'

She smiled and nodded, the sunlight forming a platinum aura around her head and shoulders. Suki didn't usually buy sweets. Suki usually bought cider. But today was one of those rare days where she drank nothing but coffee. I even saw her eat breakfast this morning – a small bowl of Special K.

'You best 'ave some for me, woman,' said Jessica, running her hand up the skinny horse's long nose.

'I might have.'

'What type?' she said with an air of suspicion.

'Ur.' She looked in the bag. 'Whatcha-call-em. Opal Fruits. And Skittles.'

'I want the Skittles,' said Jessica, shoving me out the way and holding out a hand.

Suki looked at me. 'What about you, Cris?'

'She'll 'ave what she's given,' said Jessica, smiling.

'Don't be rude, Jess,' said Suki.

'Nah, it's OK,' I said, smiling back. 'I'll have whatever.'

'Greedy bitch,' said Jessica.

'Smelly whore,' I said.

Suki threw me a packet of Opal Fruits. 'Thanks.'

We sat down on the grass. Ali lay on her stomach, crammed a handful of sweets into her mouth and spent a couple of minutes chewing them into an off-pink mush. Jessica got up and fed the skinny horse a palmful of Skittles. It chewed slowly, like a cow. We all laughed. Jessica got back down on the floor and lay back, resting her head on her mum's lap. Suki stroked her hair with one hand and lit her fag with the other. Smiling serenely she blew smoke into the hot, still air.

Nan's Dogs

My dad, thirteen. Waiting in the doorway for his mother, the dog sat behind him. Eileen's been away for a week, on a cruise around the Norwegian Fjords. He's looked after the dog for her while his dad works. A taxi pulls up. Eileen opens the passenger door and climbs out, stilettos first. The taxi driver gets out the other side and goes round to the boot. Eileen totters up the garden path like Barbara Windsor, in a robin egg blue two-piece. She approaches her son with open arms.

'Oh, I've missed you!'

My dad's face goes slack and gawping. His own arms open robotically, awkwardly. He does a hesitant smile.

Eileen slides past him and wraps her arms around the mongrel wagging in the hallway.

'Oh, I've missed you, my lully boy!'

The thing about Nan is she prefers animals to people. That's what she told me once. After dad got busted for growing weed for a third time and it was printed in the *South Wales Echo* for all the Catholics and neighbours to see.

'Animals'll never let you down, Christina. Dey'll never hurt you.'

She briskly rubbed Rutger's head and sipped her tea. She was sitting in her forest-green leather armchair, pink rollers in her grey hair. She had the splendidly fat Rutger draped over one half of her lap and Ben the small collie-cross on the other. Bazzle, the ginger tom, was curled up on top of the chair's headrest, next to her head. She sipped her tea and watched *Countdown*. Sometimes she'd offer a five-letter word to the TV. Then she'd pat Rutger's head and start on again about how animals love you uncon*dish*unally.

The thing about Nan's dogs is most of them used to belong to Mum. It's a family joke, how Eileen gets all the cast-offs. She even got me.

The first dog was Yoni, a sand-coloured collie-cross bitch. I can't remember why Mum got rid of Yoni. I only remember Nan taking Yoni off her hands, looking after her for thirteen years. Then me and Dad burying her in the garden, near the ornamental well, after cancer had reduced her to bones and lumpy fur.

Then there was Ben, a small black mongrel who once belonged to Jeremy. When Jeremy moved in, Ben came with him. He had a nice enough temperament and Slug didn't mind him, unusually, but he was terrible for running off. He liked to wander round Cardiff sniffing out bitches. He'd return to the house hours or even days later looking happy and tired. So Mum and Jeremy decided he was a sly, ungrateful weasel of a dog. And Nan had him.

Bazzle started out at Paradise Place too. He would sneak into next door's house and shit on their bed.

She even had Rutger. She looked after him when Dad was in prison and ended up keeping him. Nan adored Rutger. He was still as handsome and charming as ever, despite all the fat. Like John Travolta. She couldn't walk him. To make up for this she would give him treats – whole sandwiches, pork pies, biscuits – and his rolls of fat multiplied.

So there was teeny tiny old Eileen, a flatulent, walrus-sized pit bull on her lap, as well as Ben and the cat – all of them squeezed on to that green leather armchair in a furry mass. A pair of clinking knitting needles sticking out. Like something from a cartoon.

One day Ben ran off and didn't come back. He was old, almost fourteen. Nan rang up the vets and the RSPCA animal shelter. Put up posters. Nothing. He'd probably been run over. Nan spent a week in bed, not sleeping, just lying there grieving.

A month later. The day of Veronica's wedding to David. Nan left the front door open and Rutger got out. He was half-blind now, and fat as a hog. A week before he'd been attacked by a Rottweiler while out walking with Dad, and this had triggered something in his old canine mind. He galloped the streets, crossing roads, stopping traffic, before killing a small dog in front of its terrified owner. He had to be put down. I was at Mum's putting on my wedding make-up. I was nineteen. I was Maid of Honour and I was dressed all in black with slutty knee boots, because I hated lilac, and this is why I'm edged out of all the wedding photos, which is fair enough, except David, the groom, wore a Muppet tie and he's in *all* the photos. Dad brought Rutger to the house in Paradise Place for a final goodbye. Mum and Rutger hadn't seen each other in years. He greeted her like an old friend, wagging and smiling with half his muzzle. She stroked his bum-shaped head, her blue-black mascara running. The Last Pit Bull. We all hugged him tearily, Veronica in her lilac wedding dress, one eyelid smeared with glittery lavender, me with a face blanked out with ivory foundation, a sad clown. Dad standing in the street, alone, still banned from the house.

Nan didn't make Veronica's wedding reception. She stayed in bed crying. Dad just sat at a table staring silently at his undrunk pint and unwrapped cigar while Veronica danced slowly under the swirling spotlight with her new husband. 'Eternal Flame.'

I was moving to a Halls of Residence in Bristol. I was in the kitchen with Nan, picking out some cutlery from the drawer to take with me. Bazzle was sitting on the small oval table licking the soft pink pad of his paw. Nan was stirring the milk into her tea.

Suddenly she dropped the spoon and it clattered on the worktop. She turned to me, her face extra-wrinkled. She was crying.

'You're leavin' me! First I lost Ben and den I lost Rucker, and now I'm losin' you!'

She put her rigid arms around me like a factory robot, did a big gasping sob, then moved away. The tears stopped as suddenly as they came and she stood there looking sad and ashamed.

I was stunned. I didn't think she liked having me around.

'It's OK, Nan. I'll come and visit every month. And look –' I pointed at the cat – 'you've still got Bazzle.'

She nodded and picked up her tea. Walked away sniffing.

She doesn't really prefer animals to people. She just thinks she does.

She got a new dog, Jack, a small mongrel from the pound. He would sit up on his haunches with his paws dangling, looking at me with large pathetic eyes. He smelled bad – he had a blocked urinary tract and the vet had made a makeshift never-to-heal hole at the base of his penis, where all his piss sprayed out in a yellow fountain, soaking his belly and legs. But it didn't matter that he made her bed stink of urine and dank old fur – she loved him like a son.

One summer afternoon I was woken from a nap by a knock on the window. I got up, moved the curtain. A man in a leather jacket. He hurriedly beckoned me with his hand. I went to the front door and opened it a gap

'Are you Christina?'

I nodded.

'Your grandmother's hurt. She's in the lane. Near the gospel church.'

I got dressed and ran to the lane. Nan was lying on a stretcher on the lumpy concrete floor. The man in the leather jacket was there. A few other people, concerned or nosy. One of them, a plump woman, had Jack on a leash. Paramedics moved around in a calm hurry.

I ran up to Nan.

'What happened?'

She looked up at me. 'Oh, it's you. I got knocked over by a dog. I've broken my 'ip.'

Her tone was totally normal. As if she was talking about the weather.

'Wha' happened was, I was walkin' Jacky an' dis big dog ran up and attacked him. An' I got in da way, see, an' it sort of jumped up an' pushed me over.'

'Are you OK? Are you in pain?'

She smacked her lips. 'Nope.'

One of the nurses at Heath Hospital found a lump in Nan's breast. Cancer. Nan had the hip operation and afterwards underwent radiotherapy and was put on a long course of Tamoxifen. She recovered quickly from the hip injury, and was soon given the all clear from the cancer.

'Dey never woulda found it if dat dog hadn't attacked us,' she told me. She looked at the dog on her lap. 'Would dey, my lully boy? Dat 'orrible dog saved my life!'

Here's some things about my nan:

She is one of six. She had two sisters and three brothers; now there is only one brother left, Patrick, who looks like Hoggle from *Labyrinth* and goes around hitting people with his walking stick. Nan was the youngest and the most doted on. Little Eileen.

Her favourite meal is fried egg and chips.

Her father fought in the First World War and he was there in the trenches that time that both sides put their weapons down to sing Christmas songs. He was a lovely man by her account, but her mother was mean. Her nickname was Floorboards because

202

you could always hear her sneaking about to listen through doors.

After my dad she had a spate of miscarriages and stopped trying for more children, which is why he is an only child and therefore 'spoilt rotten'.

She is shrewd with her finances but generous with family.

One night my nan got tipsy and told me about all the ideas she has for novels. Over eighty years she has stored up the barebones narratives for several historical epic family sagas. This rich inner life astounded me because talking to her, you wouldn't think she had it in her.

When she was younger she had men fighting over her. She chose my grandad in the end because he wouldn't stop hounding her, but previous to this she'd been engaged to another man for six years. That went sour when he told her that though he'd marry in a Catholic church, he wouldn't want his children being brought up Catholic. The day before Nan and Grandad's wedding, this man left a record on her doorstep. An Eddie Fisher song with the lyrics, 'I am walking behind you/on your wedding day/and I'll hear you promise to love and obey/Though you may forget me/you're still on my mind/look over your shoulder/I'm walking behind.'

She has always been very proud of her tiny waist and mortified by her thick ankles.

She was a secretary for fifty years.

In all their years of marriage, my nan and grandad never saw each other naked.

She was rehearsing for a small concert at a Catholic social club in Penarth, her and her friends – 'the girls' – from the Union of Catholic Mothers. A little routine. They were dressing up as nuns and doing two songs out of *Sister Act*. Maureen, the fattest out of them, was playing Whoopi. I tried to tell Nan that it wasn't cool for Maureen to black up, but Nan just waved away my words with her tiny old hand and pressed play on her DVD player. 'Hail girls.' 'Hail Mary. What's up?' 'Well, Jerusalem's become a real drag.' And Nan got into position with her walking stick and started rehearsing the moves while Jack watched from the armchair and Dad lounged on the settee, stoned, with his fourth bowl of Coco Pops.

The night of the performance she came home brandied up with her nun headpiece still on, and she hobbled up to Jack and said, 'Oh my lully boy, you should have seen me!' She turned to me. Her green eyeshadow was all over her fat nose. 'I wish dey let dogs in, Christina. I woulda brought Jacky.' She banged the floor with her walking stick. 'Kettle on! Kettle on!'

I went to the kitchen to put the kettle on, imagining Eileen in a dark church doing a private concert for Jack and the ghosts of Rutger and Ben and all her other dead dogs.

There's not a man today who could take me away from my dog…
myyy dog…

Jack'd had lots of small strokes and his head hung all wibbly wobbly to one side. He'd become incontinent and had trouble eating. He was deaf and almost blind. He couldn't go up and down stairs any more and he was on delicious liquid codeine to suppress a relentless cough. It was time. The day before he was due in, Nan lay in bed with him, holding her old face next to his old face and stroking his muzzle.

'I'll see you again some day,' she whispered to him. 'Dey let dogs in, dey *must* let dogs in.'

I heard a small, tentative knock on my bedroom door – Nan's knock. As usual I yelled 'Come in!' three times before the door opened and she came in. It'd been two weeks since Jack died and she looked grey-faced and smaller than ever. She was wearing brown slacks and a light-pink wool jumper covered in burn marks and tea stains. Odd socks with holes in. She hobbled into my room. Sat on my bed. 'I still can't eat.'

'What have you eaten so far today?'

She pulled a face. 'Only a bit o' dry toast. I can't manage nothin' else.'

'You need to force yourself, Nan. The less you eat, the lower your energy, the worse you'll feel.'

'I don' feel like nothin'.' She looked around my room, eyes lingering on the poster of Madonna hitchhiking with her tits out. 'I moight try a bit of fish later.'

I nodded. 'Take your vitamins.'

She stared at her lap. 'I can't stop thinkin' of Jacky. I keep goin' to smoov him an' he's not dere. I go out the garden to talk to him three times a day. I walk up an' down da patio for some exercise an' then go by where your dad buried 'im an' I talk to him. But I can't smoov 'im.'

'Smooth the cat,' I said.

She shook her head. 'I miss my Jacky.' Her face crumpled and she made a sad wailing sound. Chest hitched. And then she quickly stopped the tears dead and looked at me. Smacked her lips. 'I gotta phone dat man about doin' da kitchenette. He's gonna fix the lights an' paint da ceilin'...'

She went on, talking about the kitchen that needed doing. I remembered The Time That Stupid, Thoughtless, Bloody Woman Started Talking About Her Fucking Curtains Five Minutes After The Funeral. And I finally understood.

Dad's Drugs

We climb the steep hill, grabbing on to rough, woody bushes and clumps of weed. The empty carrier bags attached to our belts flap and rustle. Sal finds a mushroom and calls my dad over.

'This one?' she says.

He looks at it. 'Yeah. See how it's like a nipple on the top?'

She is my girlfriend, by the way, Sal. We only last three and a half years so I won't do a list. But she's very good-looking.

We're heading for a flat-topped tree in the distance, Dad's old marker. 'I used to come here every day,' he tells us. 'Every mornin' I'd climb up and I'd fill black bags full of 'em. Bags and bags of 'em, like.'

'What ju do with them?' I ask.

'Well. I used to eat a lot of 'em. But also I'd take them to Amsterdam to sell.'

We're in Senghennydd. It's November, the end of the picking season. The ground is spongy with recent rains. Up ahead are vast hills of greeny-brown fields dotted with dirty white sheep and trees.

Dad's up ahead stooping down to inspect the ground. He's wearing cut-off jeans, cut-off wellies and a black woollen jacket/cardigan thing with a hood.

We reach the tree. In the distance, under grey clouds, are black slag pits. We climb a gate. Find a few mushrooms, then some more. Soon we're stooping every five seconds. 'Bingo,' says Dad. The mushrooms are clustered around bunches of reed grass.

We fill up our carrier bags. It's a territorial business, and every time I find a large cluster, Dad sneaks over and starts trying to cash in on my find. I shoo him away.

'You don't get so much these days,' Dad says. 'Big black bags I used to fill when I was young.'

'I'm not complaining,' says Sal, letting a handful of slimy-wet fungi spill through her fingers.

We go over another hill and suddenly there's a herd of cows and bulls looking at us.

'Fuck,' I say, clutching Sal's arm. 'Will they charge?'

Dad strides toward the animals, slapping his huge hands together and shouting. 'Move it! Oi! Move along!'

The cows give him dirty looks and start dispersing. Me and Sal watch in awe as Dad herds them away from our path.

'Wow,' I say. 'I didn't know you could do that.'

He does the facial equivalent of a shrug and walks on.

Dad is a nature boy. I've been out walking my dog with him down Blackweir and he's recognised the sound of a particular breed of woodpecker. He knows the names of flowers and trees and weeds. Like me he spent long hours of his childhood playing in woods and parks and fields, but unlike me, he was more attentive to detail. I was mostly thinking about where my next game of Spin the Bottle was coming from. He was exploring.

'Your mother got tossed by a bull once,' he tells me now. 'It was at Stonehenge.' His eyes are sparkling. 'Your mother wanted a wee so she went into this field. I was there with Veronica. I had her in one of those baby carrier things, ya know, the ones you strap to your chest. I saw your mum disappear behind this bush, and the next thing you know, she's flyin' through the air with her knickers round her ankles.'

Me and Sal laugh and the sparkles in his eyes seem to multiply.

We walk on. Soon we find a small idyllic spot and decide to have our packed lunches. The sun has broken through the clouds. We sit on a small stone wall. There are gorgeous oak trees and an old fence and a grazing horse. Like something out of a Constable painting. We eat our sandwiches and drink our tea out of a flask and Dad tells us about Operation Julie and I tell him to stop talking with his mouth full.

'Your uncle Henry always said that everyone should try acid at least once,' said Mum. We were in a bar in Times Square, eating ribs and drinking Budweiser. I hadn't yet compared her to John Candy so we were having a good time. Mum didn't often drink alcohol. Her chest and neck was blotched red and her eyes were gleaming.

'Well, he's right,' I said.

'Maybe. But look at your dad.' She let her jaw go slack and made her eyes glaze over. '"Uuuh. Uuuuuh. Duhh."' Her favourite impression. 'You know the reason your dad doesn't blink much? Because of all the acid. That's what he told me.'

'I think Jeremy would benefit.'

'Oh God no, he'd go loopy.' She drank some beer then wiped the corners of her mouth with a napkin. 'Listen. On the subject of drugs. Listen.' And she leaned in closer.

'When we were living in Flora Street, me and your father, he had all these scroungy friends over most nights. It was like a squat. One night, we had company as usual. I was pregnant with Veronica, quite far along. I remember one of the friends was Spike, this bald guy from London who was staying with us. We were helping him hide out from the police *and* the Hell's Angels. He was quite nice actually. I don't remember who the others were.' She waved her hand. Clearly the others were men like my father. 'They were all taking acid this night. As usual. And I decided – I know it's bad – I decided to take some mushrooms.'

'And you were pregnant with Veronica?'

'I know, I know. I was stupid. I was sixteen. And there was all your father's friends and I – I guess I wanted to – I dunno – I didn't want to be the odd one out. And this was the late seventies,

208

remember, or was it nineteen eighty? Anyway, we didn't know about things back then.'

'I'm not judging,' I said.

'It was only a few mushrooms,' she said, 'but they must have been strong, cuz an hour or so later I was, ya know' – she fluttered her fingers –'tra-la-la, everything's funny, tra-la-la. You know.' She scratched the bridge of her nose with the nail on her little finger. 'So everything's fine, and then suddenly I'm soaking wet.'

'Soaking wet?'

'Yes. My waters have broken.'

'Shit.'

'Yes. Shit. And I was only about seven months along, so – you can imagine. Not only am I tripping, but I'm about to come into premature labour. And there's your father and his friends off their faces. Microdots I think.' Mum's head turned. A waiter in a checked shirt was suddenly standing next to our table.

'Can I get you laydeez another drink?'

I shook my bottle. 'Same again.'

'Can I get a Diet Coke?' said Mum.

'Sure.' He grabbed my empty bottle with a small hairy hand and walked away.

'Where was I?'

'Waters broke.'

'Yes. So my waters have broken and I'm terrified. I tell your dad. He and his friends start panicking; they don't know what to do. And they have all these drugs about the place so they don't want to call an ambulance. And I'm there freaking out.' She waved her arms about like someone drowning to illustrate this. 'I'm only sixteen remember. No mother, no father, just an idiot druggy husband, and I'm about to give birth. And I'm on mushrooms.'

'What did Dad do?'

She smiled and shook her head, remembering. 'He starts trying to climb out the window.'

'What? Why the window?'

'Cuz his friends won't let him go out the door. He climbs out the window and he's hanging out, holding onto the ledge, about to drop. This is a two storey flat, remember.'

'So he's trying to escape?'

'No, funnily enough. He's trying to get help. And he's about to drop out this window but then he changes his mind. He remembers that knees have this habit of shattering. The moron.'

Our drinks arrived. Mum took a slow swallow of her Coke.

'What happened?'

Mum looked at me in this sly way and I could tell that she was saving the best till last. 'That friend of your dad's, Spike, he comes over and he puts his hand in the damp patch on the carpet.' Here Mum started acting it out. Her hand went down onto the table then flicked up to her mouth. She licked her palm. Shook her head. 'Nah,' she said in a London accent. 'Nah.' She repeated this, lightly slapping the table and licking her palm, shaking her head and saying 'nah' in a London man's voice. 'Nah,' she said.

'It's piss.'

She became still, looked at me with her light blue musical eyes.

I blinked slowly. 'So basically you took some mushrooms and pissed yourself?'

Smiling, half-proud, half-embarrassed, she nodded.

Here are some things about my dad:

He has three tattoos, a faded swallow on one hairy forearm and a scroll saying 'Neil' wrapped around a love heart on the other. A yin-yang sign on the top of his back that he got when we were holidaying in Kos.

He supports Liverpool FC and Cardiff City FC.

He's afraid of snakes and sharks. He didn't go anywhere near the sea for twenty years after watching *Jaws*. He's also afraid of funfair pirate ships, and once my mum made him cry by gleefully shaking the carriage when they were almost vertical.

He's not much of a reader, but when he was fifteen he stayed in his bedroom for three feverish days and read *The Lord of the Rings,* stopping only to eat, pee and sleep.

He talks with his mouth full, sucks the mushy food out of his false teeth and picks his nose in public.

He favours slapstick humour.

He is patriotic and loves coming up with factoids about Welsh people or Welsh inventions. That end song, 'Baby Blue', on the last episode of *Breaking Bad* is by a Welsh band, did you know?

The reason he has false teeth is because he didn't start brushing his teeth until he was thirty-five.

He fancies Alexandra Burke and Trisha Goddard and Stevie Nicks and Kate Bush.

He once had psoriasis on his eyeball.

When I was eighteen and living on Nan's settee, and Dad was dossing on a blow-up mattress in her conservatory, we had this routine. I'd come home after college, do my homework, eat some noodles, watch *The Simpsons*. In the night, Dad would come home from wherever. He'd be stoned, eyes like small dopey burger baps, the whites frazzled pink.

Straight away I'd say, 'Got any weed, Dad?' and he would shake his head.

'I bet you have,' I'd say.

'Nope. We ran out. Where's your nan?'

'In bed.'

He'd flop himself onto an armchair and grab Rutger onto his lap. We'd watch TV in silence. Then I'd say, 'You *have* got weed, I know you have,' and he'd shake his head.

'Daad! You *have!*'

I'd get off the sofa. Lean in for a sniff. 'Ah! I can smell it.'

'That's just cuz I been smokin' it,' he'd say, avoiding my eyes.

'No. I can smell *fresh* weed.'

I'd stand there looking over him and Rutger, hands on hips. He'd sigh. 'All right then. Go and make me a cup of tea.'

And that was it. I'd run out the kitchen and make him tea. Two teabags, three sugars, full fat milk. I'd make a nice cup – slowly dragging the teabags through the water to get all the strength out. I'd come back to the living room to find a small chunk of hash or bud on the settee's armrest. I'd skin up and we'd smoke the spliff, watching American sitcoms on Paramount Comedy.

Almost every weeknight, the same routine, with some variation. Like maybe some nights he'd also make a massive omelette filled with red peppers and ham and cheese, or greasy, chunky bacon sandwiches or experimental toad in the hole, and I'd always decline at first because I was trying to starve myself, but eventually I'd give in and have a bit. And it would taste wonderful.

Dad's drugs:

LSD – His first and favourite. As a teenager he'd been a football hooligan. Destructive, anarchic, hard – the kind of boy you cross the road to avoid. Then, at eighteen, he took his first acid tab. The next day he decided to grow his hair long and has been a pacifist and a scaredy-cat ever since.

Cannabis – He only got into cannabis because of the shortage of acid caused by Operation Julie, which was a police raid that wiped out the biggest LSD manufacturer in the world (based in Wales – my dad's favourite bit). He still smokes cannabis and has never suffered from paranoia, though sometimes it makes him think 'deep thoughts' about dying and nothingness.

Heroin – Addicted for a year. Used to inject. I once asked him what cold turkey felt like, and he said it wasn't as bad as *Trainspotting* made out, but it gave you this horrible feeling in your legs, like you wanted to kick the walls, which is where the phrase, 'kicking the habit' comes from.

Morphine – Him and his friends used to sneak onto boats anchored at Cardiff Bay and steal their emergency morphine supplies. One New Year's Eve, they waited till everyone at the

212

dock was drunk and proceeded to swim from boat to boat, stealing every last bit of morphine from the small white trunks roped to the deck. They came away with thousands of pounds worth of the stuff.

Amphetamines – Addicted between the age of twenty and twenty-three. Used to inject it. Used to inject everything. Back when him and Mum were living in Senghenydd he was a guinea pig for local drug dealers – he would inject their speed and tell them immediately if it was any good or not.

Prescription opiates – Took them for his back pain, got addicted, stopped taking them.

Cocaine – Dabbled.

Magic mushrooms – In his mid-twenties, before Jehovah, he would take the dogs for a walk down the castle grounds and pick thirty or so, eating them as he went. He would go home lightly tripping and Mum never knew.

Prozac – For after the divorce.

Crack – He first tried crack cocaine when he was in his forties. He liked it but never made a habit of it.

MDMA/ecstasy – See Crack, above.

Dad is looking old now – white-striped sideburns, eye wrinkles like clay-cracks, grizzly chest hair, a Steptoe mouth. But the same light blue irises blazing out of those never-blinking eyes. He dresses in Jimi Hendrix T-shirts and cut-off jeans and Converse trainers. He has the air of a manchild. He'll sit around my nan's living room, smoking bongs, watching rugby and eating biscuits with his friends, and then he'll hear my nan padding in from the kitchen and quickly hide the bong behind the chair, and him and his middle-aged friends try and stretch their stoned eyes open to the normal, sober size and Dad's friend will say, 'Good evening, Mrs Jones,' with Hobnob crumbs on his jumper, and Nan will eye them suspiciously and return to her bedroom with her bum hanging out of her pyjamas.

Dad's been single for a long time now. There had been Janice; early forties, built like a refrigerator, looked like she belonged in a women's prison drama. She was tough and rough and loud and fun. She had bright blue eyes that glittered more than most, and a voice like burnt toast. She had huge tits and vertical scars on the inside of both wrists. She introduced Dad to vodka and wild sex and dancing. They were nuts for each other. 'Oh, I loves ya favver, I loves im to bits,' Janice would say, stroking his hairy arm while he grinned like a happy chimp into her glittering alco-pop eyes.

She was too wild in the end.

Forty-five. That's when Dad's heart broke for the first time.

Then there was Tracey. She was as fat as Mum. She had black hair, creamy skin, very lovely brown eyes like half-melted truffles and long, saggy ears; naked and bald she'd be Buddha. She was a care worker. She had OCD and scrubbed her house with bleach and her hands were raspy-rough as cats' tongues. She was placid and nice, and she spoke in a slow, velvety Cardiff hum. 'Aw, Nee, pass me my fags, will you, Nee? Aw, thanks, babe. Now, Cris, I'm not bein funny or nothin, but when I was workin in Fairbrook back when I was thirty – pass me my lighter, Nee? Aww, thanks, babe. Like I was sayin, Cris....'

Dad wasn't *in* love with her. It was like Mum all over again. He only drew it out for three years this time.

Him and drugs, though: for better or worse, for richer or poorer, in sickness and in health.

Oxwich Bay, the Gower. Me, Sal and Dad trek across miles of sand. There is no sun in the sky – it's hidden behind thick white cloud. But we're not here for the sun.

We walk until we reach Three Cliffs Bay. Beautiful clean sand and a curved, craggy cliff face wrapped around the beach like a lover's protective arm. We sit on a large rock and get out our flasks and cups. We have sugary mushroom tea.

214

'I'm a bit nervous,' says █

pressed together. It's his firs█

'When I was younger it was █

or whatever. I wouldn't even th█

up, like. Now though, I've real█

you know?'

Sal sips her tea, twitchy eyes █

you ever had a bad trip?'

'Yeah, a couple.' We sit on our █

to feel something. There's a chu█

bathing costume picking up shells a█ █ping them in a bucket.

'Do you think she's retarded?' I say.

Sal shakes her head. 'I think she takes the shells home and makes jewellery out of them. She sells them to her friends. And they only buy them because they feel sorry for her.'

'*I* feel sorry for her,' I say.

'I fucking hate her,' says Sal, and we explode laughter, shaking our heads incredulously like we don't know what's so funny.

We decide her name is Shelly. Dad loves this and cannot stop bringing it up. 'I wonder how Shelly's doin'?' he says every two minutes, smiling.

My face is getting tighter and my grin feels wide and stretched, as if the edges are being pulled by gentle but insistent hooks. My laughter feels like a handful of petals.

We get up and head back to Oxwich Bay. It's almost twilight. A man rides a black horse past us and we all stop and stare, mouths open.

The world starts looking strange. Wavy. Fragile. Lovely. We walk. Dad wraps his arms around himself, says he's getting nippy. I lend him my black hoodie, which is far too small for him. He sucks his belly in and zips up. He's wearing black wraparound shades.

Sal starts giggling. 'You know what he looks like?' she whispers.
'What?'

...ars.'

...h my God, he *does*! He has the *essence* of one,

... says Dad.

...ook like a biker mice from Mars,' I say.

...Do I?' He thinks for a while. 'Well you two are Beavis and Butthead.'

We grip our stomachs and hunch over laughing. 'Oh my God, we *are*!' I say.

Sal gets down on her knees and starts examining a dead starfish. 'Wow,' she says. I get down and look. It's throbbing and mega-colourful. 'It's, like, it's like, alive at the same time as being dead,' she says. She puts it in her pocket. Stares at my face, hypnotised. Laughs.

It's dark now. Up ahead we can see the yellow lights of the Oxwich hotel. We can hear voices on the air. I feel like Rip Van Winkle. We get there in twenty. The guy at the bar has a weird face. We can't tell if he's beautiful in an otherworldly way or if there's something wrong with him. We stand and stare, mouths clenched to stop words and laughter streaming out, like naughty children. We order tea and prawn mayonnaise sandwiches. We take them outside and sit at a table overlooking the night-blackened beach.

'I'm not sure what to make of this,' I say, mouth trying to eat and smile at the same time.

'What? The trip?' says Dad.

'No. The sandwich.'

'I like both,' says Sal, chewing, and managing to look both vacant and alert.

'It's nowhere near as strong as the trips I used to take,' says Dad. 'But it's nice.'

'Don't talk with your mouth full. Biker Mouse.'

Afterwards, we lie on the beach and look at the stars. We're silent for half an hour. I think about how small I am in the universe, insignificant, inconsequential – because that's the kind of thing you're supposed to think – but I'm not convinced. Even psilocybin and a vast starry sky cannot shrink me.

Either way, it's beautiful and that's all that matters.

Dad gets up on his elbows. 'Mine's starting to wear off.'

'Mine too,' says Sal. 'But it's still nice.'

'I feel cosy,' I say. 'Like, emotionally cosy.'

'I'd be even more cosy if we were back in the van,' says Dad, smacking his lips.

We go find his white van in the Oxwich Bay car park. We sit in the back listening to a local radio station. Welsh-speaking alt-rock. The window is open and the music combines with the breeze and sounds extra special. Dad is curled up in the middle of the van, knees touching my knees. He skins up. I find a banana and slowly peel it. I have a moment with the banana. For a while I feel like it's my friend, like it has a personality. But I still eat it.

Dad lights his spliff, smokes it and passes it to Sal. 'I'm snug as a bug in a rug,' he says.

'You're like an Egyptian princess,' I say.

Sal smirks out a mouthful of smoke. 'Want us to fan you and feed you grapes, Neil?'

'Hmm,' says Dad. He's silent for a while. And then: 'I wonder what Shelly's up to?'

Little Bastards

We're at Wetherspoons for Veronica's thirtieth birthday. It is also two days since she filed for divorce. A double celebration.

'Wha' we 'avin'? White or red?' Dad says to me, gripping a handful of notes.

'Let's stick to white. Get the house one, the – whassit called? – Pinot something – I can never say it. Greesho? Gree – I don't fuckin' know. That one.'

'Origh',' says Dad. 'And a Coke for Chantelle and – Veronica? Wha' you 'avin'?'

'Just a lemonade.'

I slap the table. 'Have a fuckin' drink, Vron – it's yer birthday!'

Veronica pulls a face. 'I got a headache.'

'Well that's what happens when you let yourself get so stressed.'

Veronica's brows come down. 'How can I fuckin' relax with *her* around?' She points at Chantelle, who is sticking her bottom lip out so far she looks like a parody of sulking. 'She's stressin' me out.'

'It's not *my* fault,' says Chantelle – scowl, huff – before hunching over her new mobile phone, which she will get bored of in one week.

Veronica flaps a stroppy hand. 'I'll just 'ave a lemonade.' She rubs her temples. 'I might 'ave a vodka later.'

'OK,'says Dad. 'So. Bottle of pinot gree – wha'ever it is – Coke, lemonade. Mum – yer 'avin' wine again, yeah?'

'Wha'?'

'You're having wine, yeah?'

My nan squints. 'Pa'don?'

'Oh, for fuck's sake, Nan, put yer hearin' aid in!' says Veronica. 'ARE YOU HAVING WINE?'

Nan's mouth turns into a small puckered circle. 'Oooh. No. Gemme a ginger ale.' She smacks her lips.

Dad goes to the bar to get the drinks and comes back, giving Nan the change.

'Neil.' Nan taps the edge of Dad's plate. 'You know who used to like white wine?'

'Who?'

'Yer father.'

'Did he?'

She nods, eyes closed, like a wise old sage.

'Oh. OK.' Dad turns to me. 'Why's she tellin' me that?'

'Be nice,' I say. I look at Nan and smile. She acknowledges it with a queenly dip of her head.

'Got anythin' publisht yet?' she asks.

I roll my eyes. 'Will you stop askin' me that? No, I haven't.'

One small wizened hand comes up. 'Oooh kay. Just askin'.' She drinks the last of her wine.

'Nan.' I stand up and lean across the round table. 'Come 'ere.'

Nan tilts forward. I thumb away a smudge of green eyeshadow from the bridge of her nose.

'You look like you've been shot in the face with a make-up gun.'

'Do I?'

'She looks like Bobo the clown,' says Dad.

Chantelle smirks – some Coke sprays out of her mouth, spattering the leftover roasties on the plate in front of her.

'When uh you gonna do my eyebrows?' Nan says to Veronica. 'Cuz I'm goin' ta Penrhys wiv da mothers next Tuesdee.'

'Tomorrow,' says Veronica. 'You wanna get yer lips waxed un all.'

'She wants to get 'er lips sewn together,' whispers Dad, loudly.

Nan runs a finger across her wiry upper lip. 'I use da cream.'

Dad leans in, taps me with his elbow. 'She could make a welcome mat out of 'er tache.' He sniggers. 'She could – huh – she could finally knit that jumper she's been sayin' she's gonna knit me wiv 'er chin hairs.' He looks at me expectantly.

Nan leans forward, small arms crossed, eyeing her son suspiciously. 'Wassat?'

'He said, where's that jumper you said you'd knit him?'

Dad nods. 'Over twenty years you've been sayin' yuh gonna knit me a jumper.'

She blinks slowly. 'Well I'm makin' Gizmo a little coat at da moment. So.' She smacks her lips. Gizmo is her latest dog. A small, middle-aged mutt who she will undoubtedly out-live.

Nan grabs her ginger ale and glass. She picks up her handbag from the floor, puts it on her lap, rummages. She brings her glass close and, furtively glancing around the busy bar, empties a miniature bottle of brandy into it. She takes a sip of her drink, smacks her lips, and grins, her eyes squinting to the size of toe nail clippings.

Somehow we've gotten on to the subject of teeth. Dad is poking out his ratty false teeth then slurping them back in. Chantelle is watching, one cheek resting on her fist, lip curled up.

'Still got all mine,' announces Nan. She shows her set with a taut, lipless smile. Each wrinkle on her kidskin face shifts like sand around her mouth. Her teeth are big and yellowish and strong-looking. 'All my own. Eighty. Eighty years old. All my own.' She places her forefingers at the sides of her teeth like a kid make-believing fangs, and goes on grinning. Me and Veronica snort out laughter. Hard old Eileen has turned, with age, into a strange, adorable little creature.

Dad is picking the scabs off his elbows. I slap his hands away. 'Don't be gross.'

'Guess who I saw down Tesco's the other day?' he asks me, and I shrug.

'Yer muvver.'

'Oh.'

'She looked miserable.'

'She is miserable.'

Me and Mum aren't speaking. Again. It was the usual – two sumo wrestlers on the mat, poised, ready. Throw the rice, commence the stamping ritual. It was petty, the argument, as they always are. Mum and Jeremy have got really negative and paranoid. Paranoid in Paradise. They're having a shared mid-life crisis. Jeremy has already done every hobby and Mum is only interested in housework and getting past forty-five – the age Moira died. She's morbid about it. Morbid in Mynachdy.

'I didn't see Wormtongue,' says Dad.

'Who's Wormtongue?' says Veronica.

'Jeremy.'

'Like in *Lord of the Rings*,' I say.

She shakes her head. 'I 'aven't seen it.'

'Whassat?' says Nan.

'Put yer fucking hearing aid in, Nan!' says Veronica, rubbing her temples.

'*Lord of the Rings*, Nan,' I say. 'A film.'

'Oh.' She glances at Veronica peevish. 'Is it good?'

'Yes,' I say.

She rubs her chubby nose with her palm. 'OK den.'

We don't talk about Mum with Nan. The last time they were in the same room together, for one of Chantelle's birthdays, Nan had gone up to Mum's table, put her hands around her tiny waist, wagged her hips and said, 'Look, Catherine, I've still got my figure, still got my lovely figure,' and Mum had stuck out her large leg and gracefully pointed her toes and said, 'Look, Eileen, look at my lovely ankles, my lovely shapely ankles. See? I have ankles. Look at my fucking ankles.'

Veronica's on the vodka now. She's only had a few swallows and already her eyes have become glazed and dopey. She's stroking her daughter's arm and smiling boozily. She is a sloppy, tactile drunk like Stonehouse Suki.

Here are some other things about her:

She was a very withdrawn, cold child who didn't like to be hugged, but when she was sixteen she had a dramatic personality change and is now the soppiest, most open and affectionate person in the family. We think it might have something to do with hormones.

She is gluten intolerant and has OCD.

She enjoys chart music mostly, but also likes Hole, Garbage and Skunk Anansie.

She divorced David after twelve years of marriage because the love had gone.

After David she will go on to have a three-year relationship with a woman.

One New Year's Eve, in her twenties, she was invited to a party at my mum's. A gentle dips and crisps party. She got hammered, put some trance music on and danced on her own like she was at a rave. She ended up passed out on the kitchen floor by ten o'clock while the rest of the family ate breadsticks and hummus in front of the TV.

Her favourite film is *Lost Boys*.

Anyway. Dad points a massive finger at Nan, his eyes wet and glassy. 'You owe me a crossbow,' he says. 'A jumper *and* a crossbow.'

Nan frowns and folds her arms across her little woollen waistcoat. 'Wha' you talkin' 'bou'?'

''Member? When you promised me a crossbow if I done good in my exams?'

Nan shakes her head. She doesn't mean no. She is shaking away her fool son's words like a dog shaking off mud.

Dad turns to us. 'When I wuz in school, righ', Nan promised

me a crossbow if I come wivin seventh place in exams. Cuz I was in bottom set for everythin', like. Cuz I din give a shit, like. So I started tryin'. Like, akshully *doin'* the work. And I ended up comin' seventh place. In the whole class. And did she buy me a crossbow? Did she, my arse.'

'That's naughty,' I say. 'Nan – where's his crossbow?'

Nan rolls her small, melty eyes to heaven.

Dad grins. 'I ended up buyin' myself one in the end. Well, nickin' one. You know that hole in the kitchen door upstairs? Just above the handle? That was me, that was. Shootin' at my friend, Tony Crean.'

'You tried to shoot your friend with a crossbow?' I ask.

Dad nods, face creased up, chin sticking out like the point of a brogue.

'Why ju do that, Grandad?' asks Chantelle.

'Jus for a laugh, like.'

'Don't you be gettin' any ideas,' I tell Chantelle, who is gaping at my dad incredulously.

'What about that time you set off fireworks in the house?' asks Veronica.

'Yeah. Had a little indoor display.' He's stroking the pubey arm hair that curls around his watch strap.

'Wassat?' says Nan.

I tilt my head in Dad's direction. 'Him, setting off fireworks inside the house that time.'

Nan shakes her head briskly – almost a shudder. 'Oh, he was a bugger.'

'You set off fireworks inside the house?' says Chantelle.

Dad nods. 'It was a bunch of us. We put a rocket in a milk bottle an' set it off in the living room. An' we had Roman Candles goin' off on the floor. Catherine wheels nailed to the walls.'

Nan is still shaking her head. Chantelle has forgotten her mobile phone and is listening closely, big blue eyes fixed on Dad's drunk ones.

'He burnt down a house at St Fagans too,' I say.

'*Really?*' asks Chantelle.

Dad nods. He puts his elbows on the table and lifts an arbitrary finger. 'We used to break into St Fagans. Bunch of us. And this one time we finds this Dutch barn. Probably be worth about quarter of a mill now. There wuz a car inside it, like, an old car. Antique or somethin'. And we set fire to it. I wuz the one who lit the match.' He lifts and wriggles his eyebrows. 'The whole barn went up. Woosh!' He spreads his hands apart, flicks the fingers out. His dentures are china-white inside his crescent mouth.

'Oh, I coulda killed 'im,' says Nan.

'It wuz on the front page of the *Echo*,' says Dad. 'There wuz a manhunt.'

'Didju get caught?' asks Chantelle.

'Yeah. My dad had to pay a big fine. Dinee, Mum?'

Nan does a slow, pissed off blink.

'An' that time I blew up the goal posts at Pentrebane Primary. Member that?'

Nan does another long blink. Her tongue darts out of her mouth like a lizard catching a fly. She glances at me, eyes narrowed. Shakes her head.

Dad turns to us. 'Left a massive crater.' He takes a glug of his wine. 'I used to make my own explosives.'

'Wha' for?' asks Chantelle.

'Cuz he was a little bastard,' I say, and Dad nods.

Nan sips her drink. 'I shoulda drowned 'im at birf.'

Outside, Nan gives Dad a tenner for the taxi, but when the taxi comes it's only a four-seater. I volunteer to walk home, and Dad and Chantelle join me. We cross the road.

'Wha' you gonna do wiv that tenner Great-nana gave you, Grandad?' Chantelle asks.

'Keep it.'

'Really?'

'I'm a litt-ul *bast*ard,' says Dad, rubbing his hands together.

I give him a look. 'He's going to give it back when we get home. Aren't you, Walter?'

He nods. He doesn't mind being called Walter since *Breaking Bad*.

'Chant,' I say, 'you don't nick from family. Well, really, you shouldn't nick from anybody, but if you *are* gonna nick, make sure it's not from your family. Cardinal rule. OK?'

Chantelle nods. 'I've already said I aint gonna do it again.'

'She's a little bastard like me,' says Dad.

'The curse is strong in her,' I say.

'What curse?' says Chantelle.

'The curse of Gwendolyn. It's a witch's curse passed down from generation to generation. You're going to have a daughter and she's gonna be awful. Same for me. We're both fucked. Scuse my language.'

'I swear I ain't gonna do it again.'

'Good. And listen: don't nick from small businesses either. Don't nick from *any*where – I've been caught twice and it's really embarrassing. And it's wrong. But especially from small businesses. If you're gonna shoplift, do it in Tesco. Tesco is evil. Innit, Dad?'

Dad nods.

'But obviously, don't shoplift at all. OK?'

Chantelle points at the road. 'Look, Cris – it's them.'

Sure enough, the black taxi carrying our relatives is trundling toward us. I can see Veronica's light-blonde hair in the back, the top of Nan's grey perm. The driver, an overweight Asian guy in a grey beanie, is steering with one lazy hand. The road is busy and traffic is slow. We stop and wait. As the taxi drives past I lift my top over my head and go 'Whooo!' Dad and Chantelle laugh and make Whooo noises of their own. I pull my top back down and the taxi has passed.

'I'm gonna regret that in the morning.'

'You – you showed your bra to the taxi,' says Chantelle, still guffawing.

'I did indeed.'

'And all the other cars seen it un all.'

'Yep.'

'Your Auntie Christina is also a little bastard,' says Dad.

'Your Auntie Christina is an attention-seeking twat.' I smooth down my top. 'Come on – let's see if we can get home before that pair of mongoloids.'

We walk fast, Dad stumbling into me every few steps, his furry arm grazing my own, Chantelle hoisting and re-hoisting up her trousers over her perpetual builder's bum, the insipid October sun setting on our backs.

Hiraeth

Cardiff indoor market, a Wednesday. Smell of raw meat and sawdust and cold-brick air. I stand, shuffling my feet and shouldering, re-shouldering my backpack, reading the signs stuck to the outside wall of the booth. Tarot, crystal ball, reiki, horoscopes, palmistry. Card reading – £20.

Sidney comes out from the booth.

'All right?' I ask.

An unsure smile. 'Yeah.'

'What did he say?'

'Loads of stuff. It was weird. And he got so much right, ya know?' He takes out an asthma pump from the inside of his denim jacket and has a puff. 'Except he said I was gonna start cottaging.'

The door opens and a man smiles at me. He is a small, dark-skinned Romany gypsy with black hair and sticky-out ears. He's good-looking, pixie-ish. 'You are next?' he says in a mystical accent. I go inside. It's dark with purpley-red curtains. We sit at a small round table, opposite each other. An electric heater next to us. He gets out his cards, asks me to shuffle them first, then lays out a bright tarot spread.

'You are very defensive, you don't show your emotions.'

'Hmm,' I say, doing a so-so hand gesture. Partly.

'You don't trust people.'

'Not particularly.'

He deals another row. 'You are going to meet someone.

227

Someone is coming into your life. A relationship. You should trust this person, be open with them. Tell me if I speak too fast.'

'It's fine.'

He looks me in the eye. 'Are you in the caring profession?'

I nod, impressed. I don't look like a caring person.

'What kind?' he asks.

'Residential care. Old people.'

'This job is good for you. This is the job you should be doing. You are very good at one-to-one. I can see you working with young offenders, drug addicts. You should stay in this sort of job.'

I pull a face. A 'nah' sort of face.

He looks back at his cards. 'You want to walk away from this job.'

No shit, Sherlock.

He looks me in the eye again. 'You are a very creative person.' Yes, signified by my leopard-print coat and dreadlocks. 'What kind of creative work do you do?'

'I write.'

He nods. 'You are going to have success with this. I can see America. Something to do with America. You are going to try to get published in America…? But the care work – it will always be there for you.'

He deals another row. 'Who is the gay person?'

'Um. Most of them.'

He alters the angle of the electric fire. Fuzzy amber warmth lights up his face, leaves the eye sockets in shadow. 'Who is the person with the drink problem or the addiction to drugs?'

'Most of them.'

'He deals another row. 'OK. I can see reconciliations. In the family maybe. I can see London – you're going to London at some point. You're going to be getting a lot of success – you're confident and it's all going to start happening for you.' He sits upright, large globules of shadow shifting around his fire-lit face. 'Do you have any questions?'

'Yes, I do.' I place my elbows on the table. Take them off again.

'You mentioned reconciliations. I haven't spoken to my mum for over two years and I'm thinking about going to see her…?'

He deals his cards. Examines them. 'Yes. You have problems with your mum. You've never been close. You don't get on.'

I imagine the buzzer sound from *Family Fortunes* when Our Survey Says No. 'When we're on speaking terms we get on really well, like friends.'

'But there is a lot of conflict.'

'Yeah. I tried emailing her last Christmas but it all went wrong. She's really defensive. Insecure. Stupidly insecure. I'm thinking of just showing up at her house…?'

He nods. 'You are right to go and see her. You have the right intuition. She is so insecure it eats at her, like a demon, and manifests itself in all this defence attitude. She wants to see you but she's afraid of a bad welcome.'

'That sounds about right.'

'Any more questions?'

'Yes. OK – so this whole 2012 thing – I know it's bollocks but I still – I dunno – What do you know about it?'

It was Veronica's turn. Petty, inane, nothing. Something about a chicken dinner. Chickens, cigars – whatever. Mum shouted, 'Fuck off fuck off fuck off!' down the phone at her, and that was that. 'I'm not speaking to that woman ever again,' said Veronica as we sat drinking tea in the living room. 'From now on it's just us lot.'

'Whassat?' said Nan.

'Put your bloody hearing aid in, Mum,' shouted Dad.

Veronica looked at us all. Nan was in a Minnie Mouse onesie, a dark mug of tea on her thigh. Chantelle bounced up and down in front of the Nintendo Wii, hitting a ball that didn't exist, her pale love handles jiggling over her sunken hipsters while Dad, sat in his underpants, squirmed a fat finger up his nose, letting Gizmo and Bimbo (my dog) nibble the dead psoriasis skin off his knees, one knee each.

'Fuck her,' she said. '*This* is our family now.'

Every week I cycle down Maerdy Road on the way to the care home where I work, same for the journey home. One Friday I see Jeremy walking Frodo, the German Shepherd. It's dark. He's wearing jeans and a coat over his fleece. He's a solid man now. Frodo is walking in neurotic figure eights as she has done since a puppy. Jeremy has her on a short leash.

Bastard, I think. Bastard.

I see him again a week later. He's coming round a corner with Frodo. I have to turn slightly to avoid cycling into him. We lock eyes. His are glinting in the dark.

This is the fantasy:

Jeremy is caught out cheating. Mum flips out. She's been reading *Take-a-Break* and *Bella* all her adult life – she knows what must be done with cheats, it's very black and white for her. She kicks him out and immediately files for divorce. Jeremy tries to fight for his marriage but Mum's foot is down and her eleven is up and her pointy finger is jabbing away at his adulterous chestbone. The betrayal hits her hard. She realises that she's all alone now, that she's driven off her two eldest daughters and all she has left is a teenage daughter who does no housework and answers back all the time (the curse, the curse) and an ageing German Shepherd who walks in neurotic figure-of-eights. On the plus side, she's already lost over a stone in grief. She bravely and humbly comes to me and Veronica to make peace, and we graciously accept her apology before offering our own. Before, not after – this is important. Mum continues to lose weight until her blood sugar levels return to that of a healthy person and her diabetes practically disappears, which can happen, I've googled it, and me and Veronica and April can now look forward to having our mother live beyond her sixties. Just like after her first divorce, she goes through an almighty blossoming, finds a new job that

230

she doesn't hate, joins a salsa class and even makes friends with Dad again. Most importantly, without Jeremy's influence she regains some of her old values and decides that she was wrong to think Jeremy Kyle was doing a good thing for society.

The residents at the care home, those who lose their minds to dementia or UTIs, the senile and lost, they come up to you when you're doing the paperwork, scraping their zimmers along the floor, pale eyes blinking behind glasses, and they say, 'Excuse me, could you tell me how I can get out of here? I need to see my mother.' It's always the mothers. Maybe one in every ten wants to get to their fathers or their husbands.

'I need to see her. She's waiting for me.'

Always the fucking mothers.

'I'm so nervous,' says Veronica. 'I might need you to hold my hand soon.'

'No way, not round these parts,' I say. 'I'll bet the legend of Finger-me-sis lives on.'

'Oh, God…' She laughs uneasily.

'It's gonna be fine, Veronica.' But as we turn into Paradise Place my belly is going like a cement-mixer too.

We get to the house. Jeremy's car isn't in the drive; it's a Monday, he's in work. It's half-term so April will be home, but that's OK. Even though she is now a horrible teenager and has more than once sent me and Veronica pissed off emails, I know she wants her sisters back.

We reach the door. We look at each other. I knock.

We wait.

The front room window swings open. April leans out, stares at us. Her hair is dyed red, a sort of maroon.

I grin. 'Hey, April.'

Her face breaks into a smile. I can see her muscles fighting it.

'We come in peace,' says Veronica, flashing the V's.

231

Still she fights the smile. 'They're out. They've gone to the bank.' She starts giggling. 'This is so weird.'

We walk up to the window. 'Your dad's not at work?'

'He's booked the week off.'

Me and Veronica look at each other. 'Crap,' I say. Jeremy. Fucking Jeremy. 'What should we do?'

'I don't know.' She looks at April. 'We don't really wanna see your dad.'

'Why do you hate him so much?' says April.

'Well. Because we feel like he's alienated us from Mum,' I say.

'He's not like that anymore,' she says. 'He's a lot better. He got really upset when you said those things about him in the emails.'

'Did he?'

'Yeah. He was crying an' everything.'

I look at Veronica again. 'What should we do?'

Veronica thinks about it. 'We could just…speak to Jeremy?'

I hadn't considered this. He's the devil. So he cried. Devils can cry, can't they? Can't they? 'I don't know. I guess we could try.' I look at April, who has her dad's eyes – both deepset and bulgy – and sharp nose. 'Yeah, fuck it. Shall we come in and wait?'

April goes and opens the front door. Almost my height, maybe an inch shorter – around 5ft 5"? She's thin and dressed in pyjamas with a flimsy dressing gown. Last time I saw her she was still half-child. Now there's only a quarter left.

Veronica hugs her, then I do. She's embarrassed – she tries to break out of the hug too soon and I say, 'Oi! Give your sister a proper hug, you fucking teenager,' and her rebellious cheeks bunch up and a laugh tumbles out.

I go from room to room. Feels like trespassing. I look in my old bedroom, which is now a study with a spare bed. There are pictures of Ron Perlman on the wall – Mum's favourite pin-up. I remember spending whole days in this room with Jessica and Bianca. When the walls were lilac and the furniture from MFI, black. Slouched on the bed drawing Shane from Boyzone, his head surrounded by biro-red hearts, eating crisps, forever eating crisps, talking about blowjobs and culottes and mar-i-jew-aarna. I had my first orgasm in this room, had sex with my first girlfriend in this room. I had panic attacks, diarrhoea, drunken vomiting, crying fits, giggle fits, heartburn, whities, come-downs and ice cream headaches in this room. Now it's a non-room. Somewhere for Mum to go when Jeremy is snoring. Somewhere for Jeremy to indulge his hobbies. There's a violin propped up on top of the wardrobe, its strings coated in dust. Jeremy used to have a friend from work give him lessons. He'd come round, this man, Bertie, a sensitive bachelor with gentle eyes and a cashmere tongue, and he'd teach Jeremy basic violin in this room, and one night, after a lesson, Bertie placed his hand on Jeremy's thigh and fixed him with a loaded look, and Jeremy had always proclaimed that if a poofter ever came on to him he'd deck 'im without a second's thought, bang in the chops, but here he was, standing up, coughing politely and offering the poofter another cup of tea, and how many sugars was it again?

Even dust particles have a story to tell.

I go in Mum and Jeremy's room. Gone are the thick dark curtains that gulped up the daylight. There are framed pictures on the walls. April at three months, bald. Moira at graduation, holding a scroll. Moira and Oscar, black and white, each with a fag between index and middle finger. (I'm surprised the fags haven't been edited out.) Mum and Jeremy, holding each other; Mum a size 16, arms still a bit flappy from the fast weight loss, Jeremy topless, tanned back, a dreamy look in his eyes. There's new furniture but the same tall dark chest of drawers, which the small Ferguson TV used to sit on. We had the Super Nintendo hooked up to it and Mum got into playing Super Mario World, the joy-pad laid on her lap in front of her like a keyboard, her long nails making little clicky noises as she pressed the buttons with her forefingers. I remember the time Mum heard a strange

233

buzzing all night, didn't know where it was coming from, thought she was going nuts. Turned out Veronica had found her Black Mambo vibrator while snooping and accidentally set it off. Dropped it back in the drawer and ran away scared.

April's room. Ikea furniture, one wall pink, the others plum. I remember when we shared it, me and Veronica, before I got my own room. Two single beds side-by-side, mottled pink walls, posters of Vanilla Ice and Donnie Wahlberg and Dieter Brummer and Take That. Veronica getting obsessed with 'All That She Wants' by Ace of Base and playing it back-to-back for a week, lying on her bed listening to that fucking song, tapping her skinny blue-white foot. Me rolling my eyes after every rewind. Getting her back a few months later with Dina Carroll.

I go down the stairs. Wooden now, and varnished. African carvings on the neutral-painted walls. I remember running down the steps one morning when I was little, when I was George, and halfway down my foot landing in soft dog shit, it squelching through my toes like mushy peas. Standing there on one leg wailing, waking the house up. The bottom of the stairs: me, thirteen, sitting on the step, chin in hands, listening to Mum speak on the phone to the social worker who wanted to take me away and put me in care because somehow he'd found out about Nadeem and the sex stuff – probably Suki blabbing her mouth off to everyone in the street after a can or two – me sitting there imagining living in another place with different parents, and it was like going to live with Freddy Krueger all over again.

There are personalised Welsh love spoons hanging in the hall, the handles carved into Celtic plaits. Gifts from Jeremy to Mum. Curly-worded inscriptions burnt in: 'To my Miss Piggy, you are the world, love from your Kermit xxx'. Corny as hell, but I remember how happy they made her after fourteen years with Dad, who never held her hand, not even once.

I go out the garden. Frodo runs up and plants her massive bear-paws on my thighs. There's another dog, a new one, a wiry Jack

Russell. April follows me out and tells me her name is Chav. I fuss them, remembering the bundles of pit bull puppies, how they played, a mess of brown and black, chasing the cat, shitting everywhere. I remember talking through the fence to the brother and sister whose garden sat arse-to-arse with ours. Victoria and Adrian Perry, three and five respectively. Victoria would bring me soft pears and Rusks because she was a big girl now and din' wan' 'em and they would ask about the puppies and I would bring one over, let Victoria poke her finger through the chain link fence and stroke its soft wrinkly neck, and I liked them, especially Adrian who was my age and spoke well, but one day Victoria called Mum a fat cow in a quiet voice, and Mum heard, even though she was at the opposite end of the garden, and I wasn't allowed to play with them anymore.

I go inside to the kitchen, open the fridge. I will never stop feeling like I've got rights to this fridge. I notice a white board on the wall for messages. 'Have a grate day, love your Teddybear xxx'. He's still doing that? There's that vaguely farty fridge smell – vegetables, packaged meat, boiled eggs – wafting cooly in my face.

Maybe I need Jeremy to be the arsehole. The King Arsehole. With his arsehole queen.

Because it means that I'm not one.

But I totally am.

I am Princess Arsehole and my realm is Paradise.

I make a weak cup of tea and sit with Veronica in the living room on the nice new leather settee. Veronica looks like she's going to be sick. Already bulbous eyes bulging out so much she looks like a pale, blue-eyed frog. I pat her hand.

The dogs start barking.

A car has chugged up the drive.

'Oh God,' says Veronica.

'Don't worry, it'll be OK,' I say. The gypsy told me so.

The Greenfinch

It'd only been a few hours, I told her. And it's not like he hadn't done this before.

But there was the eleven coming up like rugby posts on a stormy afternoon.

'It's been all night, Christina, and this time it feels different.'

I drank my coffee and looked out the window as if his car was going to pull up the drive any minute now. 'Has he been taking his meds?'

'He told me he was.' She called out to April who was out the kitchen doing the dishes. 'See if your dad's taken his tablets with him.'

We heard a cupboard door swing open. 'No. They're still here.'

'You could count them,' I said. 'Find out if he's stopped taking them.'

Mum shook her head. 'I don't know how many there's supposed to be.' She heaved herself up from the sofa and grabbed her phone off the mantelpiece. Checked it. 'I can just imagine him in his car in some woods, gassing himself.'

April came back in, folding a tea cloth. She was sixteen now and still skinny with sharply contoured eyebrows and perfectly applied eyeliner which made her blue eyes blaze out of her face. Her hair was dyed red. For today. 'Before he left he had a bath, shaved his head and put on aftershave,' she said. 'Why would you put on aftershave if you were going to kill yourself?' She sat down on the floor and pulled a packet of Minstrels out of her dressing gown pocket. She offered one to Mum, saying something about sugar levels.

Mum shook her head. 'I should eat soon. But I don't feel like it.' She checked her phone again. Sighed. 'So either he's in his car gassing himself or he's with another woman. I don't know which is worse to be honest. Isn't that awful?'

Here are some things about Jeremy:

As a teenager he was heavily into skateboarding and could do all the fancy stunt work on the ramps. He even had a skateboard named after him – the Jezzer.

When he swallows food his eyes bulge like a squeezed toad.

He distrusts religion.

His hobbies so far: astronomy, violin, guitar, ferrets, tarantulas, fishing, snakes, lizards, tropical fish, hiking, porn.

He can do a Rubik's Cube in under forty seconds.

He once talked a man down from throwing himself off a bridge.

He hates drugs.

He eats onions like apples because they're great for the immune system.

One time a drunk white man was abusing a *Big Issue* selling immigrant outside a Greggs bakery and lots of white people stood around, concerned but not doing anything, so Jeremy picked up the drunk racist by the armpits as if he was a toddler and threw him across the pavement and told him to keep his evil mouth shut, and all the white cowards cheered.

When he is happy and well, he is the funnest, most joyful and energetic person in the room, and when he is unwell and plagued with the usual demons, he is the most miserable, negative, judgemental bastard in the room.

He loves eating the grossest parts of a dead animal – the liver, tongue, offal, heart.

He shits himself a lot.

Day two. It was serious now. He'd never been gone this long before. Mum floated round the house with her round face all milky-pale and it was like that time Dad cheated on her with Melissa Hall. The police were looking out for Jeremy's car. Mum said to look in the woods – that's where he went at these times. Usually after secretly coming off his meds and going crazy. 'It's like his brain is full of worms when he gets like this,' Mum said. 'All slithering around up there. Nasty, slimy worms.' But he always came back after a day or a night, full of bashful self-loathing. He'd head straight for the medication cupboard.

I made Mum some cheese on toast. She was sat on the sofa wearing black leggings and a baggy black top. Already in mourning.

'Just eat a bit,' I said, passing her the plate. 'Or you'll end up having another hypo.'

She took a bite and chewed sadly. 'I was out the garden this morning,' she said, 'filling up the bird feeder. There was a greenfinch there. They're really rare this time of the year. Green was his favourite colour. It was a sign.' She put the plate on her thigh. 'It was his soul, Christina. He's dead. I know it sounds silly. But it felt like a sign.'

April came into the room wearing a purple onesie. 'I don't think he's dead.' She sat next to Mum.

'Have you put the washing in?' Mum asked her.

'Yes. *And* I've folded the stuff that was there from before.'

Mum gave me a wry look. 'See what it takes for her to actually help me around the house?'

April rolled her eyes. We went quiet for a while. I could hear the washing machine rattling in the other room and the sound of Mum's fingernails scrabbling around on the plate to pick up her toast.

'Mum,' said April, finally. 'I've got something to tell you, but you've got to promise not to freak out.'

'Oh God, what now?' said Mum.

April met my eyes knowingly, her mouth twisted by a guilty

smirk. As if I was in on this. But I had no idea what she was going to say. I remembered April coming downstairs on Christmas Day last year with freshly-dyed pink hair and that same guilty smirk, and Mum yelling, 'You stupid little twat!' And the time she got her tongue pierced and hid it from Mum and Jeremy for two whole months before poking her tongue out at the dinner table (same guilty smirk) and Mum clasping her face in her hands and shaking her head, and April saying, 'I can't believe you haven't even noticed, it's been, like, two months!' But it couldn't be anything like that now. April would have told me about a new piercing or tattoo. What else? I imagined Jeremy suddenly bursting into the room, dressed as a chicken, and him and April creasing over laughing and saying, 'Psyche!'

'I've been smoking for two years,' said April.

'*What?*' said Mum.

'Now?' I said. 'You thought *now* was a good idea to tell her?'

'Well, yes,' she said, with guilty defiance and guilty beligerance and a fuck-ton of guilty hilarity. 'I thought, like, you would take it better now.'

Mum threw her cheese on toast at April's face. 'You little tosser!' She looked at me. 'It's the curse of Gwendolyn. She's worse than you, Christina.'

April picked a triangle of toast from her hair and ate it. 'Well, it's done now.' She stood up, *still* smirking guiltily. 'Sorry, Mother. I'm going outside for a fag.'

She'd wait a couple of months before telling us she was pregnant.

Day three. I was at home, making tea for Nan, who was full of ancient agonies – old shingles pains and diverticulosis and another dead dog; Gizmo had recently been put down. 'Stop getting middle-aged dogs from the pound,' I would tell her. 'Buy a puppy and it just might out-live you.' Veronica was over at Paradise Place with Mum, making her eat and listening to her melancholic monologues.

My phone rang. Jeremy.

What if it was his ghost calling me?

No, that was ridiculous.

'Jeremy.'

'Hey, Cris.' His voice was croaky and faint. He kind of *sounded* like a ghost.

'So you're OK then?'

'Not really.'

'Mum thinks you're dead. What's going on?'

'I feel so awful, Cris, I'm so sorry for everything I've done, for hurtin' your mum, I should be talkin' to her but I 'aven't got the guts. I'm a coward. I had to leave, Cris, I felt empty inside, like I've got no love inside me no more, I just don't love her no more and it's been killin' me, livin' a lie, I'm so sorry about everything, about how I was with your father and the way I've been with you, I do love you and your sister and I'd like to keep on seein' you, and tell your Mum she can have the house, I don't want nothin', just some clothes and the car, for gettin' to work, but I don't want nothin' else, she can have everything, Cris—'

'Jeremy,' I say. 'You're having a mid-life crisis.'

'I'm not, Cris, it's not that. I just feel so dead inside like I've got no love inside me, it's been a fuckin' nightmare these last few months – '

'Have you been taking your meds?'

'It's nothin' to do with that, Cris, I swear, they weren't workin' anyway, they 'aven't worked in ages, it's nothin' to do with that, it's because I don't love your mum no more and it's messed my head up havin' to pretend I do and – '

And on he went, the greenfinch, his beak full of worms.

Her name was Maria and she worked alongside him in the office (he'd recently been promoted to regional manager). She did admin. 'Dirty, home-wrecking whore,' my mum said, and I remembered Melissa Hall, the first, the original home-wrecking trampy-slutwhorebitch, supercunt from cunt hell. 'Men will never leave you unless they've got someone else lined up,' she said, her elevens like pitchforks. I told her he'd be back. A month, two months, three. Guaranteed. He'd come back with his tail feathers between his legs because he still loved her and this was just a classic mid-life crisis. A *med*-less mid-life crisis. 'No,' she said. 'He's told me he doesn't love me anymore.'

'I don't believe him. He'll come back and you'll take him back.'

'I bloody well won't.'

'You will. And it wouldn't be a terrible thing if you did. Lots of husbands and wives forgive each other for it.'

'I didn't forgive your father.'

'You were sleeping in separate beds. There was no marriage to mend.'

'Christina, he won't come back. He doesn't love me anymore.'

It had been smart of Jeremy to ring me first. I was always gobbing off about monogamy being unnatural. He knew I wouldn't hate him for it. And I didn't. But I remembered the fantasy I used to have, and I thought: well, it's terrible that it had to happen like this, and I don't hate him any more, and I'd rather my mum in a secure, loving marriage, et cetera, et cetera, but wouldn't it be nice if she went back on the divorce diet and lost all the weight all over again and had another almighty blossoming and wore Dr Martens, black with rainbow laces, like she used to, and reversed her diabetes and lived beyond her sixties and stopped thinking Jeremy Kyle was doing a good job? Wouldn't that be *nice*?

'That greenfinch,' she said, 'it wasn't a symbol of his death. It was a symbol of the death of his love.'

Day thirty-three. Uncle Henry was over. It'd been a long time. He wasn't often in our lives, which Mum attributed to his innate selfishness and laziness. He'd had two divorces and there was a grown-up daughter from the first marriage who lived in London.

241

Henry worked in admin and in his spare time he did acoustic sets at local pubs, singing old blues songs. His hair was coarse and grey now and it'd lost its curl; he brushed it back like Jerry Springer. He wore tinted aviator glasses and had a soul patch. He had a large round belly and a permanent eleven, like Mum. They looked very alike now.

'I've only got Nescafé, sorry,' Mum was saying. 'Is it still two sugars?'

'Yeah, cheers.' He was building a rollie on the kitchen table, little brown squiggles going everywhere. Mum didn't say anything. The Catherine who pitched a fit over the sight of a lighter in her house was gone. She'd stopped giving a shit about such things. Just the day before she'd told me that she'd like to try magic mushrooms again. It was beginning. She'd already lost two stone since he left and she was wearing Dr Martens again. Cherry red.

'I thought he was all right,' Henry was saying now. 'I never had a problem with the guy.'

Mum placed his coffee on the table. 'I went and had his tattoo covered up the other day.' She rucked her sleeve up and showed Henry. A purple rose now hid the six letters of her husband's name. 'I told the tattooist about him and she said it sounded like he had Narcissistic Personality Disorder. I looked it up when I got home and it was him all over. It was all about control with him.'

Henry licked his Rizla. 'One thing I learned after my second marriage is that you cannot control women.' He flashed an ironic smile. 'For want of trying. I wish I'd learnt it sooner.'

'I wish Jeremy had learnt it. Why do men always have to try and control everything? Why are they so insecure?'

'It's all about their dicks,' I said, and Henry nodded, plucking tobacco out of the end of his rollie.

Mum sat at the table and started sorting out her tablets for the day. Her Metformin had been lowered because her blood sugars were returning to normal. 'Have you heard the latest?' she said to me. 'He's gone and sold the car and bought a new motorbike.'

'See?' I said. 'Mid-life crisis. It is so classic. I'm telling you, he'll be back.'

Henry nodded. 'He will, sis. She's right. And I think you'd be a fool not to at least *think* about forgiving him. It's not easy being alone at this age.' Henry's second wife had left him a few years earlier and he was still devastated. He was living alone, feeding eight stray cats outside his house and shirking the advances of randy old women.

'How could I forgive him?' she said. 'He's hurt me so badly. I begged him to come back and he won't. Off on his motorbike with his new skank. Even if he *did* come back, how could I forgive him?' Her eyes got wet and her expression became both sorrowful and matter-of-fact, like a hardboiled detective remembering his unhappy childhood halfway through an interrogation. 'He's destroyed me. He might as well have killed me. Sometimes I wish he had.'

'How does the earth smell, sis?' said Henry with his sardonic mouth twitching.

Dad had brewed the wine himself. He was always making his own stuff – growing his own weed, learning to make pasta from scratch, building a TV unit out of wood and breeze blocks. This wine was one of his Shiraz kits. It was comparable to a 5.99 bottle from the off-licence, which was all I ever spent on wine.

'It's nice,' said Mum, taking a sip. 'Well done, Neil.'

'Have you got any lemonade, Mum?' said Veronica.

'There might be a bottle out the porch.'

'You should make a rosé for me,' said Veronica to Dad.

'I don't like rosé,' he said.

It was day forty by the way. Mum was counting. April was at her boyfriend's house for the night. Having unprotected sex probably.

Veronica went to find the lemonade. I followed her out, opened the back door and started vaping. Vanilla fudge. Veronica got her own e-cig out. She had strawberry.

When we went back in, Dad had already finished his glass and Mum was halfway through hers. They were talking about the old pit bulls, their elbows on the table. They looked like old, old friends.

It's our bedtime (eight o'clock) but she hasn't told us to go up yet. She's got a bowl of cake mix resting on her belly and a *Watchtower* magazine in one hand. Eleven up. She always has her eleven up when she's reading. As if she's cross with the alphabet. Me and Veronica are watching *Labyrinth*, bums on the floor, legs crossed, knees touching, cups of squash in front of us.

We hear the front door go and Tugger starts barking. It's Dad. He comes in looking tired and happy in a thick grey jumper and jeans with holes in the knees. He's got a small plastic pistol in his hand. It has elastic bands wrapped around springs and a little fuse, like what you find in a plug, for a bullet. Mum gets up and has a look at it, smiling. She tells Dad to kneel on the floor with his mouth open and he does, his yellow false teeth showing. She stands and aims and fires and the little fuse shoots across the room and bounces off his shoulder. They both start laughing in that way that leads to wet knickers, Mum bent over her stomach, the gun shaking at her side and Dad with his face screwed up and his big chin sticking out and big donkey laughs coming out. He chucks the fuse back to Mum and she catches it and re-loads. I ask if I can have a go and she shakes her head, still laughing. Dad opens his mouth again, wider than before and little nose laughs are making him shake. Mum aims and fires. The fuse hits him in the ear and he grabs at it, howling, and then they both start laughing again.

'I swear, they're crazy or somethin',' whispers Veronica.

Dad rolls around on the floor, batting away Tugger who's getting excited and trying to nuzzle his neck. Mum runs across the room to find the fuse, shrieking with laughter. She finds it and re-loads. Veronica is jumping up and down in front of the

TV shouting, 'Stop it, stop it,' but I'm not, I just want a go on the gun and I don't understand what's so funny. Dad clambers back on to his knees and opens his mouth, blinking tears. Mum goes to aim but stops. She's laughing too hard to concentrate, her eyebrows tilting out like opening drawbridges.

I go and pick up her bowl of cake mix and finish it off, watching.

Mum never gets the fuse in his mouth, but she gets his chin once, and his shoulder a few times. Afterwards they let me shoot at a cushion propped up on the sofa. Dad pulls his top off and lies on the carpet on his stomach, and Mum gets down next to him and starts squeezing the blackheads on his back which curl out like little grey strands of toothpaste. Veronica watches each squeeze with her gob hung open.

I aim and fire.

Night time of day forty. Mum's eyes were like dopey burger baps, the whites a sizzled pink. I always forgot how bulgy her eyes were – the same eyes Moira had, as well as Veronica – because she had a fat face and so the bulgyness was lessened by perspective. Jeremy had bulgy eyes too – she had that in common with him. And her eyes were close together – she had that in common with Dad. 'Never trust someone whose eyes are too close together.' Where was that from? Was that a thing? No, I was confusing it with 'Beware men whose eyebrows meet'. That was from *Company of Wolves*, which was the sexiest film without sex in it ever.

Mum and Dad were stoned. Drunk and stoned. He'd brought his little handheld vaporizer along. 'Imagine if Jeremy could see me now? Neil Jones, bringin' evil, evil drugs into his house!' He rubbed his massive hands together. 'Eeeevil.' Mum smacked his arm, saying, 'Oh, shut up, Neil, I already feel like he's watching me.'

Two pairs of little dopey burger baps, frizzy red in the middle, emphasising the shocking blue irises, four little burgers, too close together, beware.

The radio was playing. Dad had changed it over from radio 2 to 6music, to show how young and cool he was to Mum (Dad: 'I can't believe he sold my sound system and bought this pile of crap. That sound system was top of the line, like, it's a travesty.'). Obscure bluegrass music played. Veronica was drunk and snoring with her head on Mum's shoulder. The excitement had been too much for her. Mum kept going on about 'his bloody music', meaning Jeremy's bloody music – Iron Maiden, Cannibal Corpse, Metallica. Though he did, she said, like some good bands. The Doors, Led Zeppelin, The Who, Bowie. 'You know, that kind of stuff.' She waved a lazy arm. 'He liked bloody Abba though. And he said he used to have a crush on Agnetta because of her curly brown hair, and course, when he met me, *I* had curly brown hair. And he used to say he had a crush on Hattie Jacques from the Carry On Films, but he only said that when I started getting fat again, so it was probably bollocks. Just trying to make me feel better. Well, he wasn't thinking about making me feel better when he went off with that scabby *whore*.' She blew a raspberry and waved her Vs to the air. 'Fuck 'em.'

'I always thought he was a feeder,' said Dad. 'Feeding you up to keep other men away.'

'Nah. I got fat all by my fat self.'

They started giggling.

We heard a bang from the kitchen.

'What was that?' said Mum, trying to open her eyes properly.

Dad picked up his wine and took a sip. Like lord of the manor.

'Christina, go an' have a look.'

I got up and staggered toward the door.

'Wait, Christina,' she said. 'I know who it is.' She heaved herself up to a more upright position, straightening her back and jolting Veronica awake. Mum fixed me with a serious look. 'Now, don't go mad, Christina. But I invited Freddy over. I was going to check with you first, but I didn't think you'd mind.' She cleared her throat. 'He must have climbed up through the toilet when we were talking. I don't know why he doesn't use front doors like everyone else.' Her face crumpled up. She brought it down to her eyes and wept with laughter, and there was Dad next to her doing his creasy-eyed donkey laughs.

'Wha'?' said Veronica.

I went out the kitchen and turned the light on. There was a mug on the floor, unbroken. I picked it up. It was white with a print of Jeremy holding April as a baby in his arms. Mum must have got it for him one birthday or father's day. I took the mug out to the living room and showed them.

'This was on the floor. Must have fallen off the table.'

Mum frowned. 'How the hell would that fall off the table?'

'Oh, I dunno. Maybe a greenfinch flew in through the window and knocked it over.'

'Maybe a greenfinch flew out of Freddy's arsehole and knocked it over!' my dad said, roaring.

Mum got up and went out the kitchen, her elevens up. She looked around with slow deliberate movements then went out the sitting room. Then the hallway, the toilet, upstairs. We heard her slow tread above us, moving from room to room. 'I thought he was here,' she said, returning to the living room. 'Jeremy.' She sat down and looked at the mug in her hands. 'I don't even remember this being on the table.' She picked up her wine glass and took a crumple-lipped sip. 'He's left all his demons here.' She looked at Dad. 'I know I sound crazy, but the man carries this…energy with him. I've seen stuff. He makes TVs come off and on when he's angry.'

'Crazy old Jezzer,' Dad smiled.

'I cleanse this house of any impurities, negativity, or anything that does not suit or support the people living here.'

The house was dark save for the lit candles, the fierce orange embers of the burning sage smudge stick and her mobile phone, which had the cleansing prayer on it. She wafted the strong, sweet smoke around every room, from corner to corner. 'I cleanse this house of any impurities, negativity, or anything that does not suit or support the people living here.' The lit phone illuminated her pale white cheeks and glassy eyes, made her nostrils look like pear-shaped caverns. She wafted smoke around the TV, the CD player, the bookcase, the fish tank. She went out the kitchen, did the same there. 'I cleanse this house of any impurities, negativity, or anything that does not suit or support the people living here.' The house was quiet. I could hear the fridge humming and Dad noisily chewing a jumbo pack of cheesy Doritos and slurping his wine and I could hear the walls creaking, as if, after a long day of supporting the house, they were cracking their joints. That might sound good in a poem, I thought, drunkenly, if I condensed it a bit and put in something about spines. Across from me, Veronica hung her head out the living room window, blowing out strawberry vapour into the warm night.

Mum took her sage upstairs, almost tripping over Frodo in the hall. 'Move, you stupid old bitch!' We heard her continue the incantation in the upstairs bathroom. 'I cleanse this house of any impurities, negativity, or anything that does not suit or support the people living here.'

'Be gone, vile demon!' roared Dad.

'You're loving this,' said Veronica, batting at the vapour that had blown back into the room.

Mum came down finally. The sage stick was down to a couple of inches. She dunked it into a mug of cold water and there was a gorgeous sizzle. She switched the living room light back on and we all blinked. I could see that Dad had opened a third bottle of wine. He had his false teeth out and was sucking the orange Dorito mush from it.

'That's better,' she said, sitting down. 'It feels lighter in here already.' She pinched a Dorito from the bag and chewed it thoughtfully. 'Worth a try.'

It was almost midnight when Mum got the text. She stood up fast, re-reading it. 'He's at the end of the street!'

'Who?' said Veronica.

'Jeremy! He wants to talk. Shit, shit, shit.' She paced the room. 'How can I see him now? I'm stoned.' She prised her eyes open with her thumbs and forefingers and stood there like that for a while, her anxious eyeballs staring at nothing.

'Invite him in for a spliff,' said Dad, grinning.

'It's not funny, Walter.' She went out the hallway and I could hear her scrabbling for her lipstick in front of the mirror. 'My eyes look like pissholes,' she gasped.

'You're not going out to him, are you?' said Veronica.

Mum came back in the room with her Heather Shimmer on. She was spraying perfume on her cleavage, April's Beyonce perfume. 'I'm gonna go out and see him. I wanna hear what he has to say.'

'Open the windows,' she said to me. 'Just in case.' She held a hand up, palm out. 'I know. I'm a bloody idiot.'

'Want us to hide Dad under your bed?'

She looked at Dad. 'Sorry, Neil. It's been lovely to see you but I have to hear him out.'

'Make him suffer,' said Dad. 'Don't make it easy for him.'

'Oh, I bloody won't,' she said, pulling a face that signified she meant business, *bollock-stomping* business.

They were outside the Fisks', a fuzzy bundle in the distance. The street was dark except for the intermittent spots of amber street-light. I didn't have my glasses with me.

'What are they doing now?' I asked Veronica.

'Still just talking.'

We were shoulder to shoulder at the upstairs window of my old bedroom, three of us, just our heads peeking out. I could still smell sage in the air. Far away I could just about see the dark smear of Caerphilly mountain. The sky was grey-black with haze.

'If he comes back I reckon he'll ban me all over again,' said Dad.

'Maybe,' I said. 'But who knows? A lot has changed.'

A cloud of strawberry vapour hit me. 'I can't believe she's gonna take him back,' said Veronica.

'We don't even know if she will. We don't even know if that's why he's here,' I said.

'And she's lost so much weight since he's gone,' she said moodily. 'I bet she'll put it all back on again.'

Dad farted. 'That was me,' he said.

'Oh my God,' said Veronica. 'They're kissing.'

I narrowed my eyes but it was all a grainy blur. 'Are you sure?'

She nodded. 'Really, Mum? Fucking hell. She's only been out there two minutes.'

'Well, she was spraying perfume on her tits, so, like, what did you expect?' I said.

Dad sighed and turned away from the window. 'There goes my free pass to this house.' He slid his back down the wall and landed on his arse. He drank wine straight from the bottle and gazed thoughtfully around the room. 'He may be a dickhead, but he knows how to decorate a house. I'll give him that.'

Dad and Jeremy passed on the driveway. Dad gave him a drunken salute. Jeremy's face was gaunt and pale, his eyes like boiled eggs. He tipped a stern nod to Dad.

'Mid-life crisis,' I said to Jeremy. 'Classic.'

'I know,' he said bashfully, his hands in his pockets.

'I'm not happy with you,' Veronica said to him.

'I know. I'm sorry.'

We went down the drive, the three of us and we heard the front door close.

'She's gonna shag him now,' said Veronica. 'After all he put her through. And she's gonna go back to eating crap.'

We passed the Frosts'. All its lights were out. Richard, the scummy Judy-ruining son was in prison now, for burglary and drug dealing, and Linda, the mother, was hooked up to an iron lung in Llandough Hospital. It was a quiet house now. No fag smoke, no chip fat, no fun. I turned back to look at Mum's and it was still the same house, Jeremy or no Jeremy. My dad's furry arm grazed against my own and I thought about Mum and worried. But it would be OK. It would be OK.

Because Mum would take Jeremy back and though he would remain the same old Jeremy, juggling his moods like chainsaws and flitting back and forth between jolly fun stepdad and crouching thundercloud, Mum would go on losing weight, and she wouldn't wear the Dr Martens much because they were so bloody hard to break in, but she would keep losing the weight, stone by stone. She would find a new job as a receptionist in a Catholic care home and fall in love with its chicken gardens and moody shrines and warm priests and funny-weird nuns, looking back at Asda like Lot's wife looking back at Gommorah, and yes, she would keep losing the weight, stone by wonderful stone, reversing the diabetes to the point where she no longer needed insulin, leaving her three daughters with a sense of hope, because if you see a fat diabetic person over the age of 60, take a photo, they're as rare as unicorns. I read that somewhere. Jeremy would buy a Harley, which me and Veronica would smirk at because it was just another extension of his mid-life crisis, *classic*, but Mum and Jeremy would go out on it, riding around South Wales in their leathers and taking pictures of themselves smiling in the midsummer sunshine, light bouncing off their sunglasses, and Dad would never come to Paradise Place again, but Mum would see him about and stop for chats, which is better than the old alternative, and it is true that she would continue to believe in the Reverend Jeremy Kyle's good work, but Rome wasn't built in a day.

'I could really go for some chips, now,' said Dad.

We passed the miserable square-faced bastid's house. I picked a leaf from his privet hedge, folded it, scrunched it, flicked it.

More from Honno

Short stories; Classics; Autobiography; Fiction

Founded in 1986 to publish the best of women's writing, Honno publishes a wide range of titles from Welsh women.

Freshers, *Joanna Davies*

Sex, drugs and rock'n'roll amidst the ivory towers in the early 90s… What it's like to leave home and find a whole new world waiting, one that is frequently unkind to the unwary and inexperienced.

One of Rachel Trezise's top 10 Welsh underground novels, chosen for the Guardian

Girl in Profile, *Zillah Bethell*

Three voices, three loves, three lives, in Paris and Wales – before children, with children, after the children have gone.

"At times as subtle and luminous as a Gwen John painting, at others it is dirty and real, but no less affecting."
Jo Mazelis

Small Scale Tour, *Caroline Ross*

Ham is a resting actor, but his eccentric Afghan employer is proving fertile ground for his latest TV script. Lust, love and death all in one life-changing season for Newcastle's Kicking Theatre Company.

"Ross's novel is a tragi-comic tour de force, expressive, exuberant and poignantly reflective: I found it compulsively readable."
Stevie Davies

Inshallah, *Alys Einion*

With twin boys only months old, Amanda arrives in Saudi Arabia to live with her abusive husband Mohammed. Her new life is strange and confusing – somehow she must escape, but not without her children.

"The compelling story of one woman's extraordinary journey... by turns gripping, provoking and vividly sensory."
Tiffany Atkinson

All Honno titles can be ordered online at
www.honno.co.uk
twitter.com/honno
facebook.com/honnopress

ABOUT HONNO

Honno Welsh Women's Press was set up in 1986 by a group of women who felt strongly that women in Wales needed wider opportunities to see their writing in print and to become involved in the publishing process. Our aim is to develop the writing talents of women in Wales, give them new and exciting opportunities to see their work published and often to give them their first 'break' as a writer. Honno is registered as a community co-operative. Any profit that Honno makes is invested in the publishing programme. Women from Wales and around the world have expressed their support for Honno. Each supporter has a vote at the Annual General Meeting. For more information and to buy our publications, please write to Honno at the address below, or visit our website: www.honno.co.uk

Honno, 14 Creative Units, Aberystwyth Arts Centre
Aberystwyth, Ceredigion SY23 3GL

Honno Friends

We are very grateful for the support of the Honno Friends: Jane Aaron, Annette Ecuyere, Audrey Jones, Gwyneth Tyson Roberts, Beryl Roberts, Jenny Sabine.

For more information on how you can become a Honno Friend, see: http://www.honno.co.uk/friends.php